STARSEER'S RUIN

STARSEER'S RUIN

ADRIAN TCHAIKOVSKY

BLACK LIBRARY

A BLACK LIBRARY PUBLICATION

First published in 2025.
This edition published in Great Britain in 2026 by
Black Library, Games Workshop Ltd., Willow Road,
Nottingham, NG7 2WS, UK.

Represented by: Games Workshop Limited – Irish branch,
Unit 3, Lower Liffey Street, Dublin 1,
D01 K199, Ireland.

10 9 8 7 6 5 4 3 2 1

Produced by Games Workshop in Nottingham.
Cover illustration by Alex Gor.

A CIP record for this book is available from the British Library.

ISBN 13: 978-1-83609-482-1

See Black Library on the internet at

blacklibrary.com

Find out more about Games Workshop
and the worlds of Warhammer at

warhammer.com

Printed and bound in the UK.

To Cayman of the Lambda Zone.

The Mortal Realms have been despoiled. Ravaged by the
followers of the Chaos Gods, they stand on the brink
of utter destruction.

The fortress-cities of Sigmar are islands of light in a sea of
darkness. Constantly besieged, their walls are assailed by
maniacal hordes and monstrous beasts. The bones of good
men are littered thick outside the gates. These bulwarks of
Order are embattled within as well as without, for the lure of
Chaos beguiles the citizens with promises of power.

Still the champions of Order fight on. At the break of dawn,
the Crusader's Bell rings and a new expedition departs. Storm-
forged knights march shoulder to shoulder with resolute
militia, stoic duardin and slender aelves. Bedecked in the
splendour of war, the Dawnbringer Crusades venture out to
found civilisations anew. These grim pioneers take with them
the fires of hope. Yet they go forth into a hellish wasteland.

Out in the wilds, hardy trailblazers restore order to a crumbling
world. Haunted eyes scan the horizon for tyrannical reavers
as they build upon the bones of ancient empires, eking out a
meagre existence from cursed soil and ice-cold seas. By their
valour, the fate of the Mortal Realms will be decided.

The ravening terrors that prey upon these settlers take a
thousand forms. Cannibal barbarians and deranged murderers
crawl from hidden lairs. Martial hosts clad in black steel
march from skull-strewn castles. The savage hordes of
Destruction batter the frontier towns until no stone stands
atop another. In the dead of night come howling throngs of
the undead, hungry to feast upon the living.

Against such foes, courage is the truest defence and the most
effective weapon. It is something that Sigmar's chosen do not
lack. But they are not always strong enough to prevail, and
even in victory, each new battle saps their souls a little more.

This is the time of turmoil. This is the era of war.

This is the Age of Sigmar.

DRAMATIS PERSONAE

Vael Scar-Helm – *Stormcast Eternal, one of the Hammers of Sigmar*

Crosillan – *Stormcast Eternal Knight-Arcanum, former comrade of Vael*

Kenlo Marinta – *human, quartermaster*

Perlo Marinta – *human, mage, his sister*

Stanner – *human, Wildercorps scout*

Lofus – *human, Steelhelm sergeant-at-arms*

Regis – *human, Fusilier*

Groslyn – *human, Steelhelm*

Fenwech – *human, army marshal*

Arnulf – *Stanner's dog*

Sek'atta – *Slann Starmaster*

Irixi – *Skink Starseer*

Gokumet – *Saurus veteran*

Oaxmal – *Chameleon Skink scout, hunter of Huanchi*

Zitzel – *Skink translator*

Ferskine of the Eleventh Bell – *Skaven Plague Priest*

Part 1

RAISED FROM DUST

CHAPTER ONE

VAEL

Lancing down from a clear sky to the plazas of the great temple. Towering friezes of jade and gold and obsidian loomed over him, depicting squatting shapes with eyes like wells. The sound of thunder, first of their arrival, then of the charging of the beasts. Darts rattled off his armour. Beside him, an arcing purplish bolt blew one of his companions apart. Then they were clashing, Vael and his valiant few against a tide of scaled flesh. Great hulking beasts with crested lizard heads battering at him with toothed clubs or ramming with stone-bladed spears that clove through steel like mud.

A voice, his commander – 'Sigmar, show us your purpose!' – as the lines bent, their shields upraised against the brute power of the enemy. Vael's hammer, descending like judgement, smashed fang-filled snouts, battering down on these beasts of...

'These are not things of ruin!' someone was shouting. Crosillan the Knight-Arcanum, the wise. 'Why are we fighting here?'

'Just fight!' The commander's bellow, and indeed the monsters were giving them no quarter, no chance. And the spears of Sigmar's lightning flashed and flashed, deploying more Stormcasts to the tilting

balconies and sacred squares of this place. Shattering stone and statue, punching through to…

Nothing. To nothing. Below was only empty space and the far-distant hunger of the ground…

In riding the lightning he forgot himself.

Searing blue out of a sky choked with green-black cloud. Descending like Sigmar's judgement onto the walls. Seeing, as he passed through that moment of electric transition, flash after flash, his allies manifesting all along the battlements. The searing judgement of Azyr, *Sigmar! Sigmar!* The host of the Stormcasts, the hammer of the Eight Realms, come to… come to…

Beyond the walls was a crawling host of vermin. Vael stared. To the world his face was a golden mask, serene, inhuman, devoid of flaw. Within it, he reeled. He turned, hands clutching about the hilt of his hammer. Sigmar's hammer. The symbol of his… of his…

A city stretched behind him. Not the celestial architecture of Azyr, just… stones. Sticks. He remembered it, the pattern of its streets, but there had been flames, the buildings cast down in ruins as the hosts of–

'Brother!' a metallic voice hailed him. 'They come! Ready yourself.'

He wheeled round, seeing a great tide of rodent flesh surging towards gates that, in his memory, were sundered through already. He had seen a tide of green orruks smashing gleefully through them, their great tusked beasts bellowing and swaying, struck through with arrows of lightning yet still charging… He…

No, that had been…

Vael Scar-Helm dropped his hammer at his feet and clutched at his head. He was being deceived. This was a stratagem of the powers of Chaos. The Bringer of Desires had clouded his eyes, the Lord of Rot had infected his mind. He remembered this place. He had fought here. It had been ruined. It had been new-built. It had–

He gripped the parapet. The metal voices swirled around him, calling his name like mocking ghosts. 'Vael! Vael!' The vermin horde were scaling the wall, just climbing up one another in their chittering desperation to reach the top.

'Where are the warhosts of Nagash?' Vael demanded. 'We come to save these people from the Lord of Death.' He remembered it so clearly. The tide of bone and steel coming at them. The pure certainty that Sigmar's thin line of gold must not buckle, must never yield. And yet they fell, in the end. The city could not be saved. The dead had claimed these streets and the spears of the necrotic troops had pierced him through his mail, and he had died.

The first of the rats crested the wall. His hammer lay at his feet, but his hands reached out and tore the thing apart, without any need for him to direct them.

Did Sigmar not catch us? Are we the slaves of Nagash now, dead forever and defending this place for the dead against the vermin?

The rats fell back. Bolts of searing blue stabbed into the mass of them. Along the wall, men and women discharged thunderous weapons of smoke and noise. He did not know them. He did not know any of them.

'Brother!' A mailed hand on his arm, hauling him round. 'Are you injured? Take up your hammer, they will come again.' A blank gold mask of a face, peering into his own. A voice he did not know.

'No!' Vael roared. It was a trick. It was all a trick. He had seen this city die. He had seen them all die, even as he had died. A hundred times he had died. He grappled with the gold-armoured figure before him, feeling as though he was fighting his own reflection. 'I do not know you!' he shouted. 'You are dead!' Tearing the mask from his mirror image's face, expecting the pallor and corruption of a corpse.

A woman, dark-skinned, dark-haired, staring at him. 'Vael,' she said, and he did not know her. She was not of his company. She had not been crafted with him at the dawn of Sigmar's resurgence. He threw her off. He took up his hammer though his hands shook.

'Where are the hosts of the dead?' he shouted at her. 'Where are the legions of the Everchosen? Where are the defenders of the temple-city?' Images were flashing and searing in his head as if the spears of Sigmar were piercing his skull. He had fought here. He had seen these walls built. He had seen them destroyed. He had died here. And here he was once more.

'Vael, they are coming again!' the woman shouted at him. He saw the crackle of fury about her eyes, her frustration with him.

Beyond her, the gunners leant over the wall to shoot, and past them more of Sigmar's chosen, loosing crackling bolts and javelins.

'What does it matter?' Vael scooped up his hammer. 'You are all transient!' he yelled at the defenders, at the wall, at the world. 'I have won this ground before. I have lost it. I have died here. We win, we lose, it never ends! Who are we?' Lightning was weeping from the corners of his eyes. 'Who even are we?'

A hulking thing hauled its way over the parapet, bulky as an ogor, its head little more than gnawing incisors the size of shields. With a howl of despair Vael whirled and struck it with all the strength Sigmar had beaten into him. Felt its misshapen, stitched-together form collapse under the blow. The blades of the scrabbling things behind it scratched at his mail and he wept sky-fire as he beat at them. He would kill them. They would kill him. It wouldn't matter. Nothing would change. He was caught in a cage of lightning. It would never let him go.

He did not die. Not for want of trying, but the rats and their monstrous creations could not bring him down. He found he hated them for it. That they hadn't been enough. Hated the walls for still standing. The citizens of the city – whose name he could not even recall – for being alive at the end of the day, when the remaining rats crept away into the earth. Vael leant his elbows on the walls and stared out after them, feeling each sundered point in his mail where they had almost been good enough to bring him down.

'Brother.' That same woman, the one he didn't know. The one who had not been there when he was made. When Sigmar had crafted the first of his eternal servants out of the fires of Azyr. 'Brother, we are called.'

Vael looked up. Of course they were called. The lightning would return them to Sigmar's halls, where they would train and study and… He would not call it living.

'I remember.' His voice was a croak.

The woman's face was new enough that he still saw empathy on it. She had not died enough to have that hammered out of her. She still thought it mattered. 'Brother?' Respect, in that voice. A new-made pawn of Sigmar speaking to one of the very oldest. A son of the first forging, who had died in Sigmar's service more often than she had sat down to eat.

'I remember,' Vael said again. He didn't want to. A moment ago, it had been the forgetting that tormented him. Now it was what little remained. *Take this burden from me, Sigmar. Rid me of the last of myself, so that I may better serve you!* But the remorseless descent of the hammer had somehow struck away his certainties and left him with only the memory of when he was weak.

'What do you remember, brother?' The woman leant on the wall beside him, her face staring at his, trying to read him. But Vael's features had been written over too many times, life after life, battle after battle, death after death.

'Sigmar,' he said hoarsely. 'When he chose us. Took us at the point of our first deaths and remade us. His champions.'

'That must have been glorious,' she said, and he felt the prickling fire at the corners of his eyes.

* * *

In riding the lightning he remembered.

The scaled warriors, fighting with cold fury at this intrusion. His hammer descending on them, but there were more and they knew no fear of the lightning. He saw his own determination in them, the rigid righteousness of Sigmar's chosen turned back on him. A spear lanced under his pauldron, a javelin jabbed into his knee. A keening, flying thing swooped down and caught up the warrior beside him, hauling the gold-armoured form into the air and tipping him over the rail into… empty air. They were aloft. A city that was a temple that was a vessel, coasting over twisted, death-clutched ground.

And slanting, the carven tiles beneath Vael's sabatons now at a dangerous angle. He saw cracks in the stones and between the stones. The lightning played about the place, Sigmar sending his finest into this skyborne fray whilst below, the hosts of ruin seethed through the crooked trees of Shyish. The true battle, that they were supposed to be fighting.

The voice of Crosillan, the Knight-Arcanum, 'We are not supposed to be here! Commander–' Cut short by the roaring of a monster that thundered out from between the tilting spires. Man-length jaws closing on gilded mail, thrashing and shaking the warrior-mage into fragments and pieces.

Vael charged it, slammed his hammer into the scales of its leg hard enough to stagger the behemoth, and then a blow slanted off his back-plate, sending him staggering. He whirled to see a great champion of the reptile warriors there, a head above the others, armoured in gold-and-green stone. Its club was of wood and copper and onyx, but crafted in some way that made it harder than steel. It roared into his masked face and he yelled right back.

The ground sloped beneath them. He could see the towers of the place falling. The great frog statues toppling down on the combatants of both sides, wreaking indiscriminate destruction.

Not our battle. Not where we should be. *The lightning of Sigmar, interrupted on its way to the earth. Pointless, pointless, but no way to tell these monstrous beasts.*

He took the descending force of the creature's club on his hammer haft, feeling the appalling strength behind the blow. Feeling his soles scrape two feet backwards, then further as the stone beneath him shifted and dropped. And still the lightning speared down, completing the act of ruin. Below, on the distant ground, Stormcasts and Archaon's followers fought under a rain of broken stone and fragmented statuary.

Vael roared and the beast lunged forwards and caught his golden mask in its jaws, the metal buckling beneath its bite. It tore his gilded, perfect visage aside and exposed the flesh beneath, the truth of him. He felt the fangs go in, gouging his brow, his cheek, his chin, piercing his eye. He felt fierce. He felt alive, even as he died.

Later, he stood before a mirror in the argent halls of the Stormcasts, the flawless complex of white stone where they trained and studied and… waited. Waited on Sigmar's need, for what else was there for them? He stood in a grand chamber and studied his own reflection, not vanity but as though meeting a stranger whom he ought to recall. He saw… his face. Not his face. The features he'd had when he'd lived, and that had been recreated on Grungni's anvil after he'd been denied his first, mortal death. The features he'd carried into the lightning in his first sortie as one of the chosen, the Stormcast Eternals. The script of countless wounds unwritten. Restored, as he was always restored. The marks of every deathblow stolen from him, along with the memories of how he received them. How many times? He only remembered that he couldn't recall.

There had been those who might remind him, once. His first comrades, those whom the lightning had sent into battle alongside him from the start. One by one he had lost them. Some had outlived him in one battle, or died ahead of him, so that their cycles of rebirth and destruction had fallen out of sync with him and they had passed like ships, never meeting again, grown distant through a disjunction of lives. Others had died more, been remade more, until it had overwhelmed them. Grown strange, grown inhuman, losing the last of themselves until they became a threat, physical or existential. *The Ruination chambers,* went the word. The last home Sigmar reserved for his servants who had grown too fierce and maverick for regular deployment. *They will have a place there reserved for me.* But not yet. Of them all, he clung on to the last scraps of himself. He was Vael, and once that had meant something.

He took out his knife, the small one he used for eating. Death and Sigmar had robbed him of so much, but there was one thing he could take back. In this way, Vael exercised what little control he had over his life. He touched the tip to his brow, paused not because of remembered pain but because he wanted to get it right. To write here on his skin the record of his first true death. Not the mortal death he'd been snatched from by Sigmar, but that first time he was slain in Sigmar's service. Lightly, almost briskly, he traced the jagged imprint of the first fang, and blue-white fire hissed from the wound. The pain… the pain was terrible, but it was living. It was *his.* It couldn't just be taken away from him.

He marked and marked, working across the left side of his face neat as embroidery. No blood, just the sizzling crackle of the power within him. He cut until the jagged imprint of the reptile's teeth had been returned to him, the memory written anew. For a moment the tip of the knife paused over his eye, but no, not yet. A few more memories lost in the fire of Reforging and perhaps it would be time for that sacrifice too.

'Vael.'

The voice startled him. He had been staring into the mirror for… He wasn't sure how long.

'Your comrades have expressed concerns, brother.'

'They are right to,' Vael said. He turned to examine the other man's face and saw no concerns. *Concerns* were something the Reforging beat out of you, eventually. It would be the newer of the chosen, those from later forgings, who had spoken up. Those who still remembered who they were, and that they were supposed to care. They would change. Not *learn*, even, but forget.

'I remember,' he said. The words just came out.

The man across from him waited. Vael's comrade, his friend of a hundred lives and a thousand fights and more deaths than anyone should have to endure, but what was his *name*? Vael scrabbled for the memory, but the glare of their surroundings burned it from his eyes. The alabaster white, the gold, pillared architecture stretching out forever, throwing back not the feeble light of suns but that of the very shining sky of Azyr. Beauty and perfection, and sterile. A fit place for the Stormcasts to train and study and wait to be cast like lightning into the other realms.

'I remember when he chose us,' Vael said heavily. *He*, said in that specific way that left no doubt as to who was meant. Vael, the barbarian, the brute, the mortal champion. The warrior who, when his people had pledged themselves to the powers of Chaos, had refused. Who had fought every kinsman and monster sent against him until they had brought him down. Vael the proud, finding himself in the blazing shadow of a god.

The understanding granted him by Sigmar. *I choose you to be my instrument, to reclaim the realms from Chaos. You shall not fall, save that you shall rise again. You shall be my perfect, eternal champion, forged in the lightning.*

'I too, brother,' said the nameless man across from him. 'It was glorious.' A smile; the last remnant, on that blank face, of the man who had once worn it.

Vael's lips moved, but he could not say the words. Could not tell this blithely content shell in front of him, *I said no. I told the*

God-King no, but he remade me anyway. Hammered me and tested me and turned me into his weapon. But I said no.

He wanted to say, *I am not fit for Sigmar's service,* but that was not true. It was all he was fit for. The blazing purpose sealed into him. Even now, the moment his god called his name, Vael's heart would leap with unquestioning obedience.

'We all lose something in the Reforging,' his old comrade told him. 'Hold only to the cause, brother.'

It was true. They lost identity, they lost memory, they lost the names of their families and the faces of their friends. And now Vael found within him just a mangled, melted-together mass of battle after battle, victories, defeats, deaths and rebirths and deaths and deaths and deaths. There was nowhere in the Mortal Realms he had not shed blood, and the recurring hammer of Sigmar's Reforging had finally beat the meaning from it. No triumph that time would not erase, no defeat that would not be lost to the ages.

He had no words, for this man without a name. He turned and walked away.

I have to go back, he told himself. *I have to see it again, before even that is taken from me.*

CHAPTER TWO

KENLO

Marshal Fenwech's second-in-command looked down on Kenlo. Taller, rangier, with that weird, pallid shade some of the Azyrite high command had. A childhood kissed by the radiance of Sigmar, was what they said. A childhood spent not getting their hands dirty, was Kenlo's theory. Not like him, who'd spent his young life trailing the pike at his father's heels, looking after his kid sister while scrounging food and running errands. Surviving, in the cramped, tomb-like poor districts of Lethis. And plenty of fighting, too, from scrapping with other kids within the camp or the city to putting a knife into a hobgrot trying to pillage the baggage train.

'Nails,' said Marshal Fenwech's second, down his nose.

Kenlo affected bafflement, looking around at the others about the fire. 'Nails, sir?'

'For horseshoes. The smiths are out. As quartermaster, it is your responsibility to–'

'Oh, *nails*, sir. Right away, sir. Only last I heard, they took most of 'em for Arch-Knight Geff's lance, sir. So we might be short.'

The second stared at him, expressionless. 'Two crates nails, delivered to the squad smithy,' he pronounced, as though Kenlo hadn't spoken. And then: 'Boots.'

'Boots, sir?'

'Boots, eleven pairs.'

'Eleven boots, sir?'

'Eleven *pairs*,' the second said, as though each word was a cog clicking into place in a mechanism. 'Delivered to command.'

'Sir, on account of we've been marching forty days out of Lethis, there aren't eleven pairs of spare boots in the whole army,' Kenlo said frankly. 'Shyishan earth is tough on the feet, sir. All them bony hands reaching out to snag your ankles.' Not even hyperbole. You didn't need to get far from Lethis before the essential nature of the realm began rearing its head. Roads where the rounded cobbles were already showing the hollows of eye sockets, fields of pale ghost-grass that didn't mark the skin but cut the soul inside, so that you wept memories of the dead you'd left behind. Trees that grew in the shape of gibbets and shook gloom down on those who camped in their shade, so it was evens whether some wretch wouldn't have availed themselves of the branch and the dangling vine by morning. Tough on the mind, tough on the body, was Shyish. And most of all, tough on the feet.

Marshal Fenwech's second wasn't having any of it. His cold, pale eyes scoured across the pack of them, collapsed about the fire. 'If you've failed to properly maintain our stores, then I see plenty of boots here and now that command can make use of. Unless you feel your feet are more vital to the army than my master's.'

Kenlo spat after the man's heels, but only once he had gone. Marshal Fenwech was a disciplinarian who thought morale came from stripes on a man's back. No sense in asking for his particular attention. A fair few of the other reprobates about the fire echoed his defiance, or made comments about the man's parentage. But it was a hollow show. They were all 'Reclaimed', as the slur went. They were the inhabitants of lesser lineages, come late to Sigmar's service. Not those whose ancestors had sat adoringly at the god's feet under his divine protection, while the rest of the realms had writhed under the boot of Chaos.

'What'll you do?' Perlo asked him. His sister, the one who'd made something of her life. Sitting across the fire trying to study, tome open across her knees.

'Find his bloody boots. Find his bloody nails. Someone has them in this army. Someone owes me enough for them.' It was an admission of defeat. Spit all he liked, he had no leverage against high command. It didn't matter how skilled a quartermaster he was, how much he could make out of nothing, there would be neither praise nor recognition from Marshal Fenwech.

Where, then, was he supposed to conjure these boots from, these nails? Around the camped Freeguild force, the landscape of Shyish was light on ready markets and chances to trade. Right now, one horizon was snarled up in dense and knotted woodland that Kenlo had been keeping a particular eye on, while all other points of the compass showed blasted moorland rucked up around great knuckles of rock that pierced through the ragged violet-grey heather like bones through rotting skin. Kenlo didn't like looking at the stones. Timeworn and crawling with lichen, but beneath them the rock had weathered into the suggestion of faces, crowns, robes, as though the land itself was gripped by the memory of dead kings. Grand, awe-inspiring even, but like most of Shyish it was a grandeur that only served to make a mortal feel small and fleeting.

He'd been in the army all his life. Literally. He remembered taking his turn riding on their mother's shoulders, holding a little twig with a rag on it and imagining he was the army's standard bearer. Looking out over great columns of gleaming helms and slung shields, the servants of Sigmar going to war. War in Shyish, no less. And he'd heard that there were forests in Ghyran where the land wanted you dead so its roots could drink your blood. Here in Shyish it wanted you dead because it liked the company, and being dead didn't even bring you peace.

Perlo made some marginal notes in her book, twisting it towards the fire's light to see. And the fire didn't burn cheery orange. All the kindling they'd gathered lit up a ghastly green-white, when you could get it alight at all. The illumination turned them all into walking corpses, the steel of their armour into bone.

Kenlo looked over his sister's shoulder. Not her usual reading, as he knew. No arcane tome she had scavenged, because the high battlemages of Hysh and Azyr jealously guarded the best grimoires for their own use. This was a journal of some soldier from a generation ago. A record of another army that had marched out this way on the road to who knew where.

'It's the same forest,' she confirmed for him. 'Look.' Beside the rough maps, a sketch. The long-dead author's attempt at a weird fan-headed mask with huge round eyes and a great beaming mouth. Almost buffoonish at first, but the more Kenlo stared at it, the colder he felt. Playing host to the creeping sense that human eyes couldn't interpret what it was, even here in this coarse scribble. The way the goggling gaze leered up at him off the page.

'What's that?' Sergeant Lofus asked, looming past Perlo's other shoulder. A big, broad man, unimaginative, cheerfully venal. He and Kenlo had a dozen mutually profitable schemes in their shared past. 'Looks freakish.'

'Something our writer found in the woods ahead,' Perlo told him.

'What, the ones the road doesn't go into,' Lofus said.

'Those woods, yes,' Kenlo agreed levelly.

'The ones they came round and said expressly nobody goes in, on account of how they're haunted.'

'You show me one part of this whole *realm* that isn't haunted,' Kenlo said, rolling his eyes. And honestly, if you lived your life in the army and saw nothing worse than a ghost, well, you'd had a blessed existence.

'Extra haunted,' Lofus decided.

'Those woods, yes,' Perlo confirmed.

'So what do you think?' Kenlo asked.

Lofus blinked at him. 'About the book or the woods or the ghosts or the… boots?'

'This thing.' He jabbed his finger at Perlo's book, at the sketch of the weird face.

'Don't see as I have to think anything of it, save it's freakish.'

'See this word?' Shifted his fingertip to the uneven handwriting beneath. 'See what it says.'

'I do not currently have the wherewithal for that task, no, quartermaster,' Lofus reported dutifully. Reading not being his strong suit.

'Says "gold", Sergeant Lofus.'

'That so, Quartermaster Kenlo?' And it was amazing how nothing specific could change about the slovenly way Lofus held himself, and yet everything was different with him.

'Gold, gems, magic.' Kenlo picked out the words. 'Our diarist here came out of those woods a rich man. Got himself skewered by orruks right after, mind, but there was a lot of that going round at the time.'

Lofus shrugged. 'What's a book know about it?'

Kenlo reached into his shirt and pulled out his lucky charm. A tooth, really. A tooth as long as his index finger, and inlaid with green-and-black stone threaded around with a gleam of precious metal. The inlaid scene spiralling around the tooth showed a procession of weird tailed figures bearing indeterminate gifts towards a bloated, seated form. The style of imagery matched the goggling face in the sketch exactly.

'Our father gave us this,' Kenlo said, nodding at Perlo. 'Just about the only worthwhile thing he left us. Always said he was going back for more, though. Said he and his squad got lost in some woods, came out of it with an armful of this stuff each. Rich men, except he never did know when not to place a bet.'

'May Morrda keep him under her sheltering wings,' Lofus said piously.

'Yeah, well, Morrda *can* keep him. Some of us need to eat, though. Some of us gave our lives to this army and all we get in exchange is fresh orders to march.'

Lofus' gaze flicked from him to the tooth. 'These woods, you sure? The extra-haunted ones.'

'Just means all those ghosts have been keeping the loot safe for us, sergeant. Our dad had crap-all luck his whole life, but it was the living always did worst by him. Here in Shyish the dead are your best neighbours most of the time.'

'He's in,' Kenlo decided, after. He had bedded down. Beside his bedroll, Perlo was trying to wring a little more reading out of the last embers of the fire.

'We want him?'

'We want as many strong arms and backs as we can get,' Kenlo said. 'For the treasure. And Lofus is sound. A good man.'

'Good men wouldn't be considering deserting.'

'It's not desertion. Just a supply detour. On account of how the stocks are so low. Maybe we'll find some ghost with boots to spare.'

'Meaning you'll apply to Fenwech for permission.'

'Meaning I'll beg forgiveness when we're back. Find them some magic trinkets and a bag of gold and it's amazing what people forgive. And that mate of our old man, the one who knew magic, he always said there was *power* out there. What if we bring back something that wins the next battle for us? Enchanted sword, wizard's staff, boots of rat-kicking.'

She snorted. 'Optimist.'

He sat up. 'Perlo, where are we in ten years?'

In the fire's guttering, he saw her blink. 'What?'

'Oh, maybe you're a great mage, assuming they even let you *in* and don't just tell you to grab a shield and join the ranks like your folks before. Me? I'm still doing this or else I'm dead because Fenwech makes a wrong call. I'm dead and I never made it past what our dad was, even though I never made the same mistakes. Give me a pack full of golden masks and fancy neck-rings, though, give me an enchanted blade Fenwech can use to cut the head off the next Chaos lord we meet. That makes me the quartermaster equivalent of a hero. That gets me promoted. It gets *you* noticed by the battlemages, maybe, so you can get the proper books and a few years in some fancy tower to prove yourself to them. And even if not, it gets us rich.'

'If these are even the right woods.'

'Dad marched through here, for sure. It was the time they were heading off that Flesh-eater crusade. Where they had the big battle can't be more than two days away from where we are right now. I'm right, aren't I?'

She was silent too long. He couldn't tell doubt from disapproval.

'Perlo…?'

'I know.' Too dark, now, to see her face, but he heard the resignation in her voice. The knowledge that her saying 'No' wouldn't stop him going. It would just mean she wasn't there when he got into trouble.

'She knows, she says.' A soft voice, from the dark. Stanner's voice, which always made Kenlo shiver a little. The woman talked like she was already dead, and made no sound when she walked. 'What does she know, exactly? Only you're trying to involve me in one of your schemes again, Kenlo, and that always makes my knives itch.'

'What she *knows* is that I'm right, Stanner,' Kenlo told the newcomer. 'She knows this is the place. Or are you about to tell me different? Fenwech didn't have you and yours out in the trees root-ing for a rat ambush?'

A faint gleam, as Stanner whispered up the glint of the realm-stone shard in her lantern, then closed the hood so that a meagre radiance leaked out. Enough to touch their faces.

Kenlo and Perlo didn't look much like siblings. She had their father's russet hair, his long, sharp face. Kenlo was darker, like their mother, with wiry hair and a goat's snarl of beard. The same pointed nose, though. The same sharp, dark eyes.

Stanner's skin was copper-dun, leathered by a life outdoors under the sun of more than one realm, marked pinkish at chin and cheek and over one eye by scars. Her dark, straight hair was tied back in braids on either side, secured with bone beads. She wore a long coat of grey-blue leather, riveted with bronze studs, crossed with bandoliers of crossbow bolts and hatchets. Wildercorps gear.

'They sent us in.' You had to lean close to hear Stanner. She'd spent a lot of time out in what passed for wilds in Shyish. The death had seeped into her bones, they said. She whispered, and it put you in mind of blades hissing from sheaths, of cold winds, of serpents.

'And?' Because another thing Stanner was bad at, along with basic human interaction, was volunteering information. Not the most desirable trait in a scout, surely.

'I went deep,' the woman said. 'It's there, like you reckoned. The ruin. I saw the edge of it.'

'And?' Feeling his breath catch, that they were so close.

'Like nothing I ever saw,' Stanner said. 'Like nothing that belongs here.'

'Well, everything in a hundred miles stinks of death,' Kenlo pointed out. 'So that can only be a good thing, right?'

Stanner just stared at him. She wasn't good with humour either.

'You'll come with us?' Perlo asked her.

'Why would I?' Stanner's cold eyes passed from one to the other.

'You shouldn't go either. Your brother's going to get a lot of people killed someday, with his tricks.'

'Two months ago,' Kenlo said, seemingly apropos of nothing.

Stanner went still. 'You are not holding me to that,' she said.

'Damn, you remember those days, Perlo?' he went on, as though she hadn't spoken. 'Great big tide o' rats chewing up everywhere, everyone under arms and marching. How many scouts we lost, back then! Sent 'em out and they never came back. Until we stopped waiting for them at all, we were so sure the rats were smarter out in the dark.'

He jogged Perlo's elbow. His sister bit her lip, not wanting to get involved.

'Only I said to them, there's no rat-sneak sneakier than our Stanner. Hold on another night, she'll be back with that report we need so badly. Rather than just pulling our whole line back and abandoning her and her people to the plague and the teeth. I said that straight to Marshal Fenwech's face, and – Sigmar's unexpected mercy! – he actually listened to me, on account of how persuasive I was being, and so we were still there when you staggered in with your leg all cut up nine ways. And on account of my fine talk before the marshal you remain alive and with us, Stanner.'

It was, every word of it, true. He had actually come through for her. Oh, surely he'd had a few other reasons to stick around, but *digging up that chest that's supposed to be buried somewhere near here* wasn't going to move the marshal the way *our brave scouts* had. And the chest had been moonshine and rumour, but Stanner really had still been alive and coming back.

'Some might say,' he put in, when it was plain that the scout wasn't going to explode in thanks, 'that means you owe me. Some might say you'd come scout for a little venture of mine, so we can call it quits.'

Stanner remained silent long enough that he'd decided she

wouldn't. Playing truant with a pack of treasure hunters was more than any sense of indebtedness would cover. But Stanner nodded, just once. Misanthrope as she was, perhaps she could still use a pack full of treasure. Or else being beholden to Kenlo ate at her soul worse than any spectre of Shyish could.

'I will mark you on the roster for one share,' he said. And if she'd asked for two, he'd have stretched to that. A scout's work entailed more risk, after all. But Stanner wasn't the negotiating type.

'I'll take the loot,' she told him. 'But maybe I just want to be there when you finally bite off more than you can swallow, quartermaster.' And she grinned, the sort of thin, sharp crescent best used for slitting throats. Kenlo held on to his shudder until she'd closed her lantern and gone.

By the end of the next day's march the woods were in sight for everyone, not just the advance scouts. Their sainted parent Sergeant Marinta had stinted in his descriptions to his children of his own travels there a generation before. Stanner hadn't been as forthcoming as she might have been the previous night, either. When Kenlo and Perlo had a chance to appreciate what they were looking at, the scout appeared like an apparition at their shoulders, sniggering at their discomfort.

'What's the matter?' came her unpleasantly soft voice. 'Nice walk in the woods. The blooming – what's the word, *verdancy*? – of nature. What's not to like?'

'Verdant,' Perlo said hollowly, 'means green.'

Stanner made an equivocal noise, as if to say that shades of grey and midnight purple were close enough.

The column itself was skirting the edge of the trees and keeping its distance, because Marshal Fenwech might not have been the brightest candle lit to Sigmar but he was no fool. The land beyond the clutch of the roots was barren and hard going, and Kenlo hadn't been joking about the bones, because there seemed to be a continuous layer of jumbled skeletons buried right beneath the surface. But better that than a whole army becoming disarticulated as it fought its way through *this*.

The trees grew crooked and close together, branches interlocked like bent elbows, and the knots in the trunks like faces. No, not *like* faces. Kenlo glanced at his sister, second thoughts rising up in his mind. The trees had faces, or at least the wood was clenched into recognisably human features. Not twisted in terror, not screaming, not rolling living eyes. Sad faces, sunken into a quiet, private misery.

The knotted network of roots that stretched off into the shadows of the trees looked more than a little like grasping hands. There were bones caught up in them, although for anyone who'd tramped the roads in Shyish that was no strange thing. There were stones, too. Worked by human hands, half sunken into the earth, half dragged to light by the roots. Grave markers, and more than a few that showed the hammer or the twin-tailed comet in their cracked outlines. The woods were a grave, but then the whole realm was a grave, and at least here it seemed the dead were quiet.

He'd expected to see Perlo shrinking back from the sight, but she was frowning. Even reaching into her long coat for notepaper. 'Sigmar knows what you're thinking,' he said, the old saying they'd grown up with, rapped out by stern tutors and suspicious Azyrite officers, now become a joke between them.

'We could build here,' she said. He had to ask her to repeat it, because the thought seemed anathema. 'Men like Fenwech still look to the light of Azyr or Hysh, or the green of Ghyran, when they picture the cities that honour Sigmar. But Lethis has found its peace with this realm, and I've heard there are cities elsewhere stranger still. Vindicarum, Excelsis, cities of fire, of monsters. This place is like a scar.'

'That's seldom a happy thought,' Kenlo pointed out.

'Better that than an open wound.' Her eyes, a mage's eyes, stared into the woods. 'This is a land of death come quietly, not blade or burning or strife. Except…'

'You feel it, don't you,' Stanner said, sounding more animated than Kenlo had ever known. 'The wrongness.'

'An intrusion. I can feel the place trying to… cover it up, so it can be forgotten. Like an old arrowhead where the skin's grown over. But it won't be. It resists, somehow. The land itches around it.'

'Well maybe when we relieve it of its treasures it'll rest easier,' Kenlo decided. A joke, of course, but Perlo actually nodded.

That night, Lofus pitched up with a squad of twenty men. Not the actual squad assigned to him as sergeant but twenty likely lads and lasses with empty packs and hungry fingers, and stout enough to risk a few nights in these off-limits woods with the ghosts. That Kenlo would lead them, they liked. He was the quartermaster, who could get what you needed if you had something to trade. His ability to weasel out of trouble was legendary, and they all planned to stay close enough to hold on to his tail. That Perlo was coming with them sparked even more smiles, because she might not be a full battlemage, but any student of magic was better than none. Even the least magician born to Shyish had a sense for the powers of death, and such learning had its place within the wider creed of Sigmar so long as it held within certain bounds of orthodoxy. The Soul Shepherds were not above consorting with a suitably penitent spectre or blessing the skulls of fallen martyrs with a whispering half-life. If the bones deeper in the trees were less quiet, perhaps Perlo would be able to tame them.

That Stanner would be their guide was more a cause for ambivalence. Nobody doubted the scout's skill, but even the other Wildercorps rangers tended to give the woman her space.

Kenlo distributed what he'd been able to skim off the top of stores: rations, digging tools, rope, spare blankets. Even, to spite Marshal

Fenwech's second, a couple of good pairs of boots. The bounty was doled out to grateful recipients. Men who would agree to this sort of foolery were not, by definition, well-heeled in any sense of the words. A little free donation from the army's wagons never went amiss.

'Sigmar,' Kenlo told them, 'would understand. Yes, it's all battles and glory the way they tell it, but we all know even he had his dark moments. And what we'll bring back will set the army straight for five years of campaigning. More than one way of being a hero, eh?'

He passed round a flask of the harsh spirit they called Stormcast Beer, because you couldn't, as the saying went, keep it down, and it had a habit of returning to the fray quickly.

'To gold,' Lofus said.

'To power,' Perlo added.

'To heroes,' added the skinny man at Lofus' elbow.

'To the bones,' Stanner said, snatching the flask off him. And yes, you always gave a nod to the realm when you raised a glass, lest the ghosts get jealous of your fortune, but in Stanner's whisper, it sounded like a curse.

CHAPTER THREE

IRIXI

In High Azyr, the skies were a panoply of stars set in an utter dark, flickering and coursing with restrained lightning. The bolts and searing fire of it coalesced below, within the clouds, tearing thunder out of the riven air in a constant accolade to the glory of gods that Irixi had no need to think of or name. Here, above the hurly-burly, was calm. Here was Irixi the Starseer's garden.

The chamber was a sphere. A perfect sphere, of course. The crew-congregation of the temple-vessel *Celestial Eye of Tepok* had, after all, been measuring and adjusting the great edifice's proportions for many centuries, and if there was a claw-point's width out of place then Irixi would have stern words for the seer-architect underclass whose responsibility it was.

Within the sphere, generations of Irixi's brood had installed concentric circles of planters, rising up from the eternal pool at the base all the way to the midline, and then ranks of hanging epiphytes above that, closing in on the sunwell that formed the room's apex. From this wealth of soil a thousand plants erupted, their vines and trailing roots and creepers interweaving across the golden stone of the walls until almost nothing but the living tracery of it could be seen. Flowers bloomed in countless shades, which only a Seraphon's keen eye for colour could have distinguished. There had been a human visitor once, a hundred years before, who had used crude phrases like 'crimson' and 'violet', and long-lived Irixi had listened and felt an odd pity at the creature's stunted senses.

And more, because the human had seen all this and thought it… decorative. Been envious, even, that the Seraphon devoted such time and space to some mere *pastime*. Irixi, who had been delegated the creature's liaison because of its past dealings with their kind, had found the misconceptions oddly endearing, like a trained beast that almost seemed to understand true language. Humans were, after all, a part of the greater plan of the universe, and doubtless would have their part to play at some key moment in the future. Such was the received wisdom, and surely it was the most ineffable part of the Old Ones' Great Plan that such clueless and impatient demi-sapients were necessary to return the realms to a balance free of Chaos. Irixi had listened to the thing jabber in its barking language, about the *beauty* of this, how *pleasant* that, and despaired of having the creature understand even an iota of how every aspect of the world worked towards the Great Plan. This garden, with its sun, its water, its flowers, was *not* just some place to sit and rest one's feet. Just as the planting of each seed had been conducted according to the most exacting prognostications, astronomical sightings in the skies of every realm and consultation with the currents of the Astromatrix, so the path of every vine and tendril and the opening of each flower was a message from the universe. Information, to be inscribed in the stone codex of the temple for future Starseers to use as the basis of their own predictions. In such a way were the missing passages of the Great Plan uncovered and returned to their places. All knew the great schema of the Old Ones had, in its inception, been perfect. All knew that the rise of Chaos had sundered it, obscured its parts, destroyed the painstakingly preserved records of the cosmic powers, so that the lords of ruin could stave off their own inevitable oblivion. It was a tenet of faith, though, for Irixi and for every one of the crew-congregation, that information could not be destroyed. Every secret of the Old Ones that had fallen away into the disorder of the realms was yet there to be uncovered, whether written on an ancient tablet or divined through the growth of flowers.

In the interim, in this vast but finite time between the rise of Chaos and its final defeat, Irixi planted and tended the garden, and went aloft to the *Celestial Eye of Tepok*'s crystal domes to measure the parameters of the heavens, and was content to fulfil a small and limited role. A life spent in such way, over the centuries that the temple-city's pure air and draughts of Aqua Ghyranis would pro-long Irixi's useful existence, would not be unwelcome. It was aware that briefer creatures might rush back and forth in clamour and fury, hunting some great significance that they could never truly achieve. If all Irixi left behind was a well-tended garden, then the Starseer would count itself fortunate.

Today, Irixi was to discover that this was not to be. The universe, and its masters, had other plans for it.

The message came in the way of such things. No fleet-footed skink with a missive graven in jade, no sound of drums echoing from the hollow heart of the floating city. Not even the presence of Sek'atta forcing itself into Irixi's narrow skull, so vast an intellect blazing like a star, like a third eye, imparting cryptic words of instruction. Instead, the great lord of the temple-ship made his will known by the withering of vines, the wilting of leaves. Irixi watched as a pattern of brownish ruin crept across a precise span of its work, a century of careful oracular planting gone to dried stalks and browned blooms. For the briefest of moments the Starseer was presumptive enough to feel dismay, that such hard work had been undone. A moment later, inwardly castigating itself, Irixi understood that this was *why* these plants had been grown. Why, a decade before, the seeds had been sown just so: in order that Sek'atta would have this means to summon it to his presence. The prescience of the act humbled Irixi, who measured the orbits of the stars and thought in terms of generations.

There were other ways to call... But the Starseer quashed the thought immediately, not least because Sek'atta would know of it, and none could be found wanting in the performance of the Old Ones' Great Plan. Even the least reservation could unbalance the whole. As below, so above, perfection was all.

The attendants were already waiting with the proper raiment. In the gardens, Irixi felt no need to wear the regalia of its station as Starseer. The trailing hems would drag over the seedlings, the jewellery accumulate dirt in its contours. One did not go before Sek'atta inadequately attired, though. It was not even that the ancient mage-priest would notice such worldly details, but the disrespect would haunt Irixi for a decade of shame. So it stalked swiftly through the carved corridors of the temple-ship, letting the votive images of the walls attune its thoughts to the proper pathways of receptive deference while a scurrying host of lesser skinks bustled on all sides. The twin-plumed tiara was set between Irixi's eyes and the ochre robes draped about the crest of its back and the arch of its tail. It held thin arms out for the angular armlets, and the most dextrous attendant secured the heavy pectoral about Irixi's neck, its weight of starmetal and gold and intricately incised greenstone. Even as the last tie was secured, the Starseer stepped from the crowd of them and into the pyramidal chamber of the mage-priest Sek'atta.

The sloping walls were inlaid with obsidian mirrors, granting dim reflections of the froglike being that fell away into infinity by way of strange angles, never quite what the eye anticipated. Many were blank sheets of gleaming stone, but perhaps half bore complex panels of inscription, snaking left and right across their smooth faces. The recovered sections of the Ninth Orchid Path of Tepok, the prophecy that permitted some small enlightenment of the Old Ones' plan.

Not the plan in its entirety, of course. There was not obsidian enough in the realms to bear such complexity. That small and bounded part of the plan that Sek'atta had devoted the long ages of his life to unravelling, though. Divined through the skies of every realm, through the motions of the herds of Ghur, the gleaming currents of Chamon's metal seas. And, most of all, the recovery of ancient prophetic texts.

Sek'atta himself was seated on a disc of black stone in the centre of the chamber, held effortlessly aloft by the same precisely calibrated force that held the temple-ship within the skies of Azyr. His was a huge toad-like form, skin mottled a poisonous yellow and black, festooned with countless strings of beads, amulets and plaques. The bulging globes of his eyes were closed and his mouth – broad enough to swallow the Starseer whole – was also closed.

Irixi crouched before his floating majesty and waited. Perhaps there would be instructions. Perhaps immediately, or Irixi might stay immobile for a day or more, while Sek'atta's monolithic thoughts gathered themselves. Perhaps, after that time, the Starseer would be dismissed back to the garden without instruction or explanation. That had happened before, and Irixi had only known that its presence there had been required by the plan for that span of time. Beyond that, Irixi's understanding was not required.

A pair of Sek'atta's attendants stepped forwards. One proffered a gold dish of crawling mealbugs, which the slann's webbed hand idly reached for. The other began to scatter white sand upon the black stone slab directly below the Starmaster. Abruptly Irixi was aware of Sek'atta's mind, the pressure of his thoughts like being at the bottom of the sea, or buried beneath great stones.

The pale sand swirled, clumped and formed shapes. The blocky contours of Seraphon architecture rose from it. A temple. A ship. Not the configuration of the *Celestial Eye of Tepok*, but another. Irixi gasped, recognising the pyramids and domes and spires. The name came from its throat unbidden.

'*Wings of Serendipitous Fire.*' Irixi cowered in case its words, uninvited, corrupted the working. A moment later it sensed the ponderous approval of the mage-priest, and knew that to speak those words, at that moment, had been part of the plan. Irixi had the sense of being close to the centre of all things, at the pivot point of the Eight Realms, where the careful adjustments of the slann could, properly informed by prophecy, guide the future.

The temple-ship *Wings of Serendipitous Fire* had been lost, whole ages of the world ago. At the high-water mark of the Chaos powers, when only the Old Ones' great servants had stood between them and the dissolution of all that there was. The ships of the Seraphon and their great masters, the slann, had been set across the realms like a constellation of stars, each one precisely placed, a pin in the fabric of the cosmos. Then had come the great wars. The gods of the fleeting warm-blooded creatures had rallied at last, unwittingly following the paths that the Old Ones had set them on. The realms had rung to the clash of powers, to a loss of life and an expenditure of energy that was unthinkably vast and yet calculable, for to the mage-priests of the Seraphon all things were calculable. All things could be made knowable; in such a way, the plan would be interpreted and moved forwards and the entirety of everything would be redeemed from Chaos.

Many of the temple-ships had been lost in those days, for the slann had been forced to place themselves and their vessels in hazard. The *Wings of Serendipitous Fire* had shattered in the skies over Shyish and fallen to earth. Sek'atta remembered, for he had been officiating within its halls and only his great power had saved him and his immediate retinue from the wrack.

Irixi watched the sand sculpture of the long-lost vessel grow and revolve in Sek'atta's shadow, conjured in immaculate detail from the priest's long-buried memories. The fallen ship had been a monument to the Nine Orchid Path, that strand of the Great Plan Sek'atta had committed himself to comprehending. Even observing the model's outward structure, Irixi felt connections and revelations flowering in its mind, teetering on the edge of a cosmic epiphany.

The sand convulsed. For a moment Irixi thought itself merely a witness to a re-enactment of the vessel's fall, but instead the sculpture turned itself inside out, so that the Starseer saw, from the outside, the inner structure. Its eyes watered with the mental exercise of comprehending what it was being shown.

There: the meditation chamber at the heart of the fallen temple. The sacred space within which Sek'atta himself would have contemplated the complexities of creation. One wall thereof: Irixi's focus was hooked by it, as though Sek'atta's hands were holding its head, directing its view. A tall panel, before which the Starmasters of old might have sat, attended by their myriad servants, to view… to view…

The sand model could not show the details, but Irixi felt the mind of Sek'atta thrust knowledge into its skull as though his clawed thumb had driven through its eye socket. The carvings of that wall – now shattered rubble in a fallen temple, if it persisted at all – had carried seven full passages of the Nine Orchid Path, meticulously cut into a great obsidian mirror. A span of the prophecy now lost to the records of the *Celestial Eye* and the timeworn and overburdened memories of Sek'atta himself. But present, in some ruined form, where the *Wings of Serendipitous Fire* had come down.

Irixi understood. Not a word had been spoken, but the thoughts of the slann were so vast that even the complex, subtle language of the Seraphon could seldom contain their full meaning. Instead, the concepts had been placed within the Starseer's head. Coarsened by the transfer, turned into the language of the young by comparison, but Irixi knew what must be done. The time had come for Sek'atta to recover the lost wisdom of the *Wings of Serendipitous Fire*, in whatever form it yet survived. And Irixi, the gardener, the viewer of stars, was the chosen tool for this task.

When Irixi left the mage-priest's chamber on trembling legs, a retinue was already being awoken, raised from the glimmering pools where they had slumbered out the ages. Some would be of this young generation, spawn of recent cycles of creation. Others had been preserved long ages within the bowels of the *Celestial Eye*, and one…

Irixi should, by rights, have returned to the garden, to brief its replacements there – for there was a significant chance it would not be returning alive from this task. Instead – a shocking deviation from the proper path – it descended into the deeper reaches of the ship to watch the awakening of the oldest of Sek'atta's surviving servants. The warrior who had, in those long-ago days, actually laid hands on the slick skin of the mage-priest, to carry him from the blades of his enemies. Who had stood and fended off the lightning-borne whose arrival had heralded the fall of the *Wings of Serendipitous Fire* – simultaneously preordained and lamented.

The warrior-champion of Sek'atta stirred and rose, gleaming Azyr-charged waters running from its scales, eyes flaring blue. Irixi saw a shudder go through the saurus warrior, rising from the ancient, slow dreams of an elder age.

Gokumet, champion of Sek'atta, the last survivor off the *Wings* before its final fall, stared. Its hulking, scaled form dwarfed Irixi, even as more skink attendants came with stone and starmetal armour, its wargear and weapons. *The master?* that stare said. *He calls?* Irixi could almost see Gokumet's last sight of the fallen temple-ship, still trapped in the reflections of its eyes.

'Gokumet,' the Starseer said, a precise series of syllables that were simultaneously a name and the precise relationship of their stations, 'you are called. Our master is sending you home.'

CHAPTER FOUR

STANNER

The priests always talked about Azyr as being the apex of creation, the Realm of Heavens where Sigmar dwelled in celestial majesty. To Stanner, Shyish had always been like a well, like the lowest point of the realms. Where ghosts were drawn, by an inexorable gravity. A decade and a half's campaigning with the armies of Sigmar had given her a good view of how the land had been organised once. Not nations, not physical boundaries like rivers or mountain ranges – or not necessarily. A land carved up by philosophy as much as topology. Without some other force intervening, Shyish was where the dead went, and each people, and each manner of individual, had a place prepared for them. A welcome, in a way. No other place in the eightfold realms was such a friend to all that it had your bed made for you after you died.

There was an island paradise for murderers, Stanner had heard, where they could shelter from the blood their lives had been steeped in, or else hunt one another forever through the streets of some knife-bristling city. There were molten pits where the spirits of smiths who had failed to create a masterpiece were melted down and recast. There were high castles where the spectres of vainglorious rulers howled out their demands to chambers empty of servants. A place for everyone, but so seldom a *nice* place.

And of course the dead were often poor neighbours. They were a constant peril across Shyish, whether slaves to some minion of Nagash or just mad monsters hungry for the life they could no longer enjoy. Here, though, the woods were almost quiet.

Quiet unless you counted Lofus and his impromptu squad, of course. Get fifteen Steelhelms and a few Fusiliers together and they'd not be sneaking past unnoticed if all the shadows of Ulgu descended to cloak them. One of them had even tried to start up a song not long before, although the character of the quiet beneath the trees put paid to it soon enough. A jealous silence, Stanner considered, but then she liked silence herself. Better than the sound of human voices, for sure.

It was how some of the Wildercorps got, sometimes. Send them out into the wilds of Shyish often enough, you had to prise a decent report out of them with hooks. A kind of sickness, almost, for which there was no cure. She'd seen it claim her own superior officers, her fellows. Those who ranged furthest and trod most subtly. Shyish was a terrible, cold place to roam, for a living human. It sapped something from you that you needed, to hold a conversation or enjoy a joke. At Stanner's back – thirty yards behind her through the trees – the others were all clustered together to avoid catching that sickness. She already had it, though. She'd caught the understanding that other humans were just noise and hot air and space taken up that could be better given over to dust and shadows.

Which gave rise to the two reasons she had agreed to Kenlo's idiot plan. Two reasons stemming from that selfsame malady but pulling her in opposite ways.

The first was that this was life. This disobedience, this profiteering. The gold, the glory, trading army discipline for greed and ambition. Like a votive candle lit in her: even if it was a guttering thing compared to the hunger in Kenlo or Lofus, it could still warm her a little. Remind her of being human. Why go scrounging for gold unless you were going to spend it, and what was there to spend it on but life? Good wine and fine food, negotiable company and everything that was a sop to the pains of existence. She would fill her boots with the legended loot of this place, like all the rest. It would remind her of the woman she'd been before the cold quiet had crept in.

But out here ahead of the others, she understood the other voice that had been calling her. The voice of these trees, this place. The dreadful one, which haunted her dreams. The calm and peaceful one, which spoke a language closer to her heart than mere human words. Because this wood was her place.

Probably once it had played host to some drifting population of ragged haunts that had lingered over the root-enshrined grave markers, wringing pallid hands and waiting to assail those visitors who lacked sufficient respect and reverence for the dead. Most likely, when Nagash had mustered his armies in his great crusade against the living realms, such ghosts had been stripped away to fill the ranks of the Nighthaunt, leaving the trees without protectors.

Or maybe the woods had always just been quiet and still. That would suit them. She understood what this place was, and knew that almost none of the others would. They'd likely not have come if they had.

Perlo knew, though. Stanner was sure of it. Perlo was just about the only one of them Stanner had any respect for, because you didn't turn down a good, pragmatic mage. Perlo would have looked at the stone markers caught up in the trees and seen that not a one of them had a name on them. Memorials to the anonymous, spaced out across this dense, gnarled wood where the trees seemed to grow into one other, to twist and knot together until she had to slide sideways between them, and every shadow seemed the pitch dark of a subterranean tomb.

This wood was the underworld of the lost. Those who died alone and far from friends. Not savaged by beasts or slaughtered by orruks but the slow deaths, the quiet deaths. Exhaustion, exposure, starvation. The death every scout courted when they left their fellows behind, which waited patiently out beyond the firelight for them, each time they returned. Stanner had walked alongside that death, stood in the shadows of its wings with her belly shrunken and her skin shivering. A friend, almost. In any other realm she'd be thought mad for saying it, but here in Shyish sometimes your death was the only friend who didn't abandon you, at the end.

She had come here to scavenge for more life. Or she had come to finally make peace with the death that had been a step behind her all her adult life. She didn't know which one. She was a woman caught between the two, life and death. One foot either side of the line, and no true place either in the grave or amongst her own kind. A lost soul, even though it was still attached to a breathing body.

One certainty, though: somehow Kenlo's idiot map had come through. She'd seen the scrawl of it, what he'd scratched down based on the rambling of his dead father. She'd not have given a bent coin for it being worth a damn, but ahead she could see the change in the land, just like the old man had told his son. Just like she'd scouted out for him, before.

And that carved tooth had to come from *somewhere*, right?

She found the first stone. Almost missed it in the gloom. The roots had clutched at it just like they did with the blank markers, and a blackish moss had furred it over, almost completely. The blockiness of it caught at her eye, though, telling her scout's senses, *This is wrong*. A great squarish lump thrust from the uneven ground. She took a knife out and scratched at it. Peeled the moss away until she could see below. Colour flashed at her, even in this poor light. Not the grey or bleach-white or near-black of Shyishan rock, no purplish marbling or the faded knots of fossil shells and bones as even the rocks themselves became riven through with the echoes of lost lives. She actually blinked at the sight: rock like the sun, golden as sand, and still carved. The details had been root-gouged and filled in with dirt as though the spirit of this place was offended by their obstinate existence, but she had a sense of bowed, inhuman figures, blocky script, the form of some unfamiliar long-tailed beast. All in an angular style unlike anything Stanner had ever seen, crude at first glance until she understood that what looked rough to her eyes was just adherence to an alien aesthetic of exacting angles and precise measurements.

Beyond, in her direction of travel, the ground was more and more heaped with obstruction, the work of the roots trying to drag it all down and break it apart. How long had these stones lain here? She had no way of guessing, but they were *old*, surely. Old when Kenlo and Perlo's dad had come by, and old a hundred years before that. Old when the king of the dead had turned on Sigmar. Old, yet not surrendered to the clutch of the forest.

There was light, visible through the trees ahead. Shyish's leaden radiance, of course, but still the glimmer of distant Hysh cutting past the ragged edge of the trees, where a great landscape of stone held off the forest's creeping reach. A whole ruin, more than mere tower or fortress. Like a shattered city hidden here in the heart of the wood.

Stanner felt the place then. Her death was held here, after all, promised to her by each lonely place she surveyed. The wood recognised her as gone half-native already, and spoke to her of the ancient loneliness of a ruin whose very script and meaning was lost to time. The stones might hold out against the forest's nature, but at the same time they had been conquered by it.

Like me, she thought, and shivered.

She crept ahead, and the only eyes on her – so she thought – were the hollow sockets of the faces within the trunks, or the carven skulls on the vacant grave markers.

Here was where the trees had been fought to a standstill by this intruding terrain. A vast field of broken stone, and whilst some was tumbled loose, here and there walls stood, and parts of statues, and the stumps of towers. Here was scaffolding gone green with verdigris that might once have supported soaring domes. Every face of stone was inscribed with a density of alien information, images and characters, and pictograms that were both – arranged in complex iterations that spoke eloquently of a meaning forever beyond her ability to appreciate, of an art meant for other eyes than hers. At Stanner's feet, she saw the gleams of precious metal set in patterns in the stone, or loose fragments of smashed treasures ripe for the open pouches of Kenlo's followers. She did not reach down for it. Her eyes were for the great expanse of ruination alone. It had a grandeur to it that spoke to her lonely, withered soul.

She had seen the works of civilisation cast down. Walls brought low by earthquake magic, by siege engine, by the loutish kicks of giants. A great coastal tower scattered along the strand by an arcane tidal wave conjured by aelven reavers. A town undermined by the armies of the ratmen and fallen into their festering burrows. This fit none of those patterns. Whatever had laid this place low was like no natural or military act she had ever seen.

'It fell,' said a metallic voice, as though the speaker had read her mind.

She cursed and leapt back from the sound. Her crossbow was out in an instant, hands moving before she thought of them, dragging the string back to the catch even as she levelled the weapon, a bolt in the slot and ready.

She had taken the figure for a tree, it had been standing so still. She had believed her own story of the forest being stripped even of ghosts. This masked face had become just one more morbid adornment of the wood.

A Stormcast. And not one of the Anvils of the Heldenhammer she knew from the streets of Lethis, or who marched with the army. No blacks and dull greys, washed-out reds and oranges. She saw armour of gold and blue that the flat light of Shyish fought to leach into dull brass and midnight. One of Sigmar's own champions, the Hammers.

'What,' she croaked, 'did you say?' Her voice was always soft, but in this forlorn place it sounded far too loud. 'Lordship,' she added, belatedly. One did *not* speak to the Stormcasts without the proper honours.

He reached up and unlatched his mask. The face beneath was long, angular, high-browed, and brutally carved up along one side, a jagged series of gouges like toothmarks that crossed the orbit of his eye.

'It fell,' he said. Without the mask, his voice was low, heavy with melancholy, like the bell that tolled for funeral rites back home. 'I remember.'

'Fell,' she repeated. 'It's a city. Or a castle. Or…' But the pattern of devastation spoke to her, and she found herself believing him. In all the Eight Realms, what, after all, was truly impossible?

The point of her bolt shook slightly. She registered, distantly, that it was still directed at his face, and forced herself to lower it, though her arm resisted. 'What are you here for, Chosen? If I might ask?'

His lips moved and lightning came and went in his eyes. 'I thought I would find…' he said, and then after a pause, 'something of myself.' So that she wasn't sure if the two halves made a sentence together or were orphans of separate thoughts.

At last he seemed to register the crossbow. 'You do not need that for me,' he told her. 'But for them.' His golden gauntlet pointed past her.

She swung round. She put space between herself and the Stormcast at the same time, being no fool, but he wasn't tricking her. Between the crooked trees, at the edge of the field of shattered stones, there was a wolf.

It lifted its head, and a howl rang out that sounded as though it came from three throats. She saw the ragged, rotten skin flutter over its flayed ribs and from the gap in its neck. It was a chorus of voices in itself.

Others joined it, echoing through the woods. The ghosts had gone, but the things that had harried their insubstantial forms between the trees had not, and they knew only the chase.

She loosed her bolt, taking the thing in the one eye that was not just empty socket. It sagged back and collapsed, seeming more in relief than pain. There were prayers she had carved into the shafts of her ammunition, to Sigmar and to Morrda. Wards against the dead that likely had no true power in the wider realms, save that in Shyish both the living and the dead believed in them.

Then she was running for the others, because those howls had been between her and them.

As she neared them she heard Lofus shout, 'Castle up!' Because being a venal bastard didn't make him a bad sergeant. The shields were pulling together as she came in sight of them, a circle anchored about the big pavises of the Fusiliers, with Kenlo and Perlo in the centre. The first cadaverous wolves were making exploratory lunges, testing the resolve of the Steelhelms. Stanner saw one practically come apart from a particularly well-targeted fusil shot, rib fragments and rotting flesh spraying from it.

She put on an extra burst of speed. Perlo spotted her and called out, 'Wildercorps coming home!' so the others would be ready for her. Not the first time the scouts of Lethis had been forced to make an unexpected return to the lines mid-fight.

She made for the Fusiliers' big shields, making brief eye contact with a stout woman whose name was Rengis or Ringis or something like that. Whatever her name was, the Fusilier nodded and took a step back, weapon still propped in the notch of her pavise. Stanner drew a deep breath and leapt, got a foot on the ironwork that topped the shield and vaulted clean over with teeth snapping at her heels. She came down next to Perlo, who was untangling strings of amulets. Lips moving with prayers or incantations, the mage leant forwards and garlanded each shield with a handful of charms. The hammer and the comet of Sigmar jostled with the spread wings of Morrda the raven and tiny writing that invoked divine protection or castigated the wild dead. A nonsense, a fiction, and yet the wolves whimpered and slunk back from the little medals of tin and brass, drawing together the rags of their courage before they could come close.

Stanner fitted another bolt to her crossbow. Perlo touched a charm to the head before she loosed it, and she fancied the wolf she hit suffered more for it.

Kenlo had attached an axe-head to his walking staff, the weapon cocked over his shoulder like a woodsman's, waiting to be useful. A cocked pistol was in his other hand, but he was saving his powder for now. 'Going to be much more of this?' he asked calmly. Because a hideous grave forest patrolled by rotting undead wolves was a day's work for Sigmar's army in Shyish.

'Not once we're past the trees, I'd guess,' Stanner reported. 'Can we push forwards? We're close to the ruin.'

'Lofus, ready to move? Follow Stanner's bearing,' Kenlo called. And Stanner didn't really like him, and Lofus not at all, but they were all army brats. Learned to march before they could walk, some of them. Everyone fell into line in a fight. It was when there was no visible enemy that the fractures showed.

Lofus barked out a handful of orders, organising them about the Fusiliers, who would be the slow, slogging vanguard of any move. 'Ready to advance, quart'master,' he told Kenlo.

The quartermaster opened his mouth to give the word, but what actually came out was, 'Who the hell is that?'

The Stormcast had followed her. She'd half thought his boots were grown over by the roots, the way he'd been standing. Here he came though, a gleaming behemoth out of the trees and his big hammer already coming down to smash one of the dead wolves to splinters. The others turned on him instantly, four or five trying to mob him, yanking at his cloak and going for his flanks. Stanner put a bolt in the haunches of one, and she saw a fusil ball shatter the skull of another. For that matter, she saw a fusil ball strike into the pauldrons of the Stormcast and ricochet off into the trees, leaving barely a scar. The man with the ravaged face just laid about him, patient and brutal as a siege engine, the hammer flashing sporadically with branching flares of blue-white power. After three strikes, the remaining dead wolves found their tormented existence preferable to oblivion under Sigmar's hammer, and fled.

In the echo of their whimpering flight, the Stormcast stood there, staring at the shields of Lethis' errant crusaders without recognition or humanity in his face.

'Oh, right,' Stanner said. 'I, ah, made a friend.'

CHAPTER FIVE

VAEL

Vael almost just hefted his hammer and kept up the fight, wolves or no wolves. It would have been simpler. It was the drive that blazed in him. Enemies of Sigmar, to be destroyed wherever they were found, unrelenting extermination of…

He stared at these shield-carriers, and image blurred over image until he couldn't say what was before him and what was dragged from the recesses of his mind. He knew the people of this land, from when he had fought here first. They were fallen from grace, crude warbands given over to the powers of Chaos. They were the followers of the Everchosen, like the tribe Vael himself had come from, and whom he had turned against when they had knelt before foul altars far back in the Age of Ruin. These here were just more of the same, they were…

He blinked away tears like angry stars. That had been long ago. That had been the time of the first forging, the height of the powers of Chaos. But who were these humans before him, frail and brief and weak? He remembered the men and women he'd marched alongside when Nagash had raised his necromantic hosts and sought to shackle every soul in the realms. Different clothes and colours and weapons, but they had died all the same, so how did it matter. Only Sigmar's chosen went on. Went on forever until that divine favour was no blessing, but punishment for some terrible crime buried at the bottom of his centuries-deep memory.

He tightened his grip on the haft of his hammer. Simpler to fight. Kill them, or let them kill him. To know certainty, if only in the fatal stroke.

One of them was talking. A bearded man, twisting the head of an axe until it came off the shaft and left him only with a stick. Vael caught the name of Sigmar, a greeting. Words. Words gone on the breeze.

They were asking him who he was.

He wasn't going to tell them at first. He owed them nothing. He wasn't going to fight them either, he discovered. He had planted the head of his hammer in the dirt, the last dust and ichor of the wolves sizzling quietly as it effervesced from the metal. In a moment he wouldn't even be able to tell that he'd fought here, and maybe he would forget that he had.

'Vael,' he told them. 'Called Scar-Helm.' The moniker still with him because his first true death had earned it. The death he remembered in such detail, and rewrote onto his face anew each time he died. The gold mask of his first armour, peeled back and ragged as the flesh beneath.

'Well, my lord, I am Quartermaster Kenlo Marinta.' And the man was wary, but not cravenly deferential as some of them were. They hadn't dropped from their shield circle either. 'We are on detachment from the Fifth Lethis, in this area.' And then, sidelong to the woman, the scout, 'He's your dog, that he followed you? What's going on?' in hushed tones this Kenlo probably thought Vael wouldn't hear.

The scout shrugged. 'He was just *there*. You didn't say anything about Stormcasts. We can hardly… you know, right under their *noses*.'

'What in the raven's name is wrong with his *face*?' hissed one of the others, staring.

'So, my lord, where might your own detachment be?' Kenlo called over, still overtly friendly, still bristling with suspicion.

Fight me. Attack me. Kill me if you can. It's easier that way. But Vael was beginning to understand. The nerves, the shuffling feet, their unhappiness with him being here, it wasn't just some squad of soldiers out on manoeuvres. They'd stood off the wolves stoutly enough, after all. *He*, Vael, worried them far more. Whatever it was they were doing out here, it wasn't entirely where they were supposed to be.

He felt that fire rise in him: here was a thing that did not serve Sigmar, therefore… But then the jagged skin of half his face pulled taut and reminded him that he was not serving Sigmar here either. He had come for reasons entirely personal, the last such motivations left to him. As though he was holding a wake for the last shreds of his remembered humanity.

'Do not question me,' he told them flatly. 'It is not your place.' And then, because he hadn't meant it like *that* – that was just how the words came out, a Stormcast speaking to regular humans – he added, 'Nor mine to question you. You have your task. I have mine.' *We are all beyond grace, in this moment.*

Kenlo seemed happy with that, and they all relaxed, slung shields, started cleaning out their powder weapons.

'We, ah,' the quartermaster said, 'we're sent to some manner of ruin they have in these parts. My scout here says the wolves won't come at it. If true, maybe we should move there.'

Vael stared at him for a moment, a moment of dislocation in which nothing about the man remained in his head, because none of it was part of Sigmar's cause or purpose. Then he caught hold of

the trailing edge of the last few minutes. Kenlo. Lethis. 'You are…
Dawnbringers.'

Kenlo frowned, a man whose conversational path was strewn
with unexpected pits. 'Yes, my lord…?'

Vael turned and walked away from them. Possibly they would
simply not be there when he looked back. Perhaps they never had,
and all this was just some encounter he'd passed through in another
life. But their gear and insignia seemed like the new wave of humans
who were spreading Sigmar's message across the realms. They had
clashed with the great upsurge of grots and orruks, and were now
entrenched against the festering eruptions of the rats. *So this is
now. This is real, then.* And when he set off back for the ruined
sky-temple, he heard the clank and rattle of them following at his
heels.

Halfway to the edge of the trees, the sky shivered. Not that the
quality of the Shyishan day had much to recommend it, but abruptly
a vast ripple seemed to pass across it, not an eclipse or a storm-cloud
so much as if it had been the surface of a clear pond and a pebble
had broken it. Vael stood, mind blank, unsure whether this was just
some feature of this part of Shyish until he heard the alarm of the
others. 'Castle up!' one of them shouted, and their shields clacked
together. A circle that did not include him. He just stood, hammer
loose in one hand, waiting.

Ahead, past the fringe of the trees and into the broken expanse
of stone, a beam of golden light fell, sun through clouds. Not the
lightning of Sigmar that must shoulder its way through the air
with main force but a soft shaft of sun, and then another, a brief
scintillation of warm rays issuing from a flat, leaden sky. Bizarre,
unheralded, yet strangely unobtrusive. As though it was simply
the way of things in some other country. Vael stared. If the others
hadn't reacted, he'd not have thought it real.

Slowly, the light leached back in, that leaden radiance that was all the skies of Shyish had to give. Ahead, the view seemed unchanged: the trees and then the ruin.

'I felt…' A woman's voice, the one who stood in the centre of their ring alongside Kenlo. A mage of some minor stamp, Vael guessed. 'As though a realmgate opened. But… I don't feel it now. There's no path there. Even closed I should sense something… But it *was*, just for a moment… Like…'

'Like a dream,' Vael finished for her. She stared at him. And true, he was no Knight-Arcanum to pluck at the strings of the universe, but he had seen magic of every affinity and shade in his time, from the crude smashing of Mork to the most subtly chosen lures of Chaos. 'It is a thing of the ruin,' he said. He hadn't even known it, before the words came out, but it felt right. Not the ruin as it was now, but the vessel-edifice it had once been. The thing he had stood and fought and died upon, even as it dropped from the skies.

They let him stride out of the trees first, needless to say, before trusting the open space themselves. He stared out at it. Just stones. Just a ruin that had been ancient before the first stones of Lethis were laid. Rubble that should have been buried and overgrown long before. Yet he took one more step and saw the tilting plaza *here*, where his boots had skidded as he parried the barbed club of the lizard-creature. And *there*, for a moment, not just a great mound of jumbled stone but an effigy thirty feet tall, a squatting frog-thing worked out of serpentine patterns of stone, its hide written over with sacred texts and studded with warts of ruby. Its open webbed hand lay near his feet, rendered in a style that was angular and yet vibrant with life. In the palm was carved a flower he didn't know, symbolic of some inhuman virtue he could not guess at.

'You said it fell.' The voice of the scout. He preferred it. Not brash and bullying through the air like all the others, but quiet, almost faded into nothing. He felt the same in his soul.

'Yes,' he said. He stepped over the broken hand. One of the soldiers had found some of the rubies amid the dust and was holding them up excitedly. Vael had been right, then, about their purpose here. But who was he to judge them, exactly? Was his own quest any less selfish?

'We fought here.' The words just came and went, as though he'd left the door of his memory open and lost the key. 'We came down in blazing fury, but they… were not supposed to be in our way. We shattered their stone and they swarmed out and we fought. It was…' *Terrible. Pitiful. Pointless.* 'Glorious.' For it had been that, too. *A bellowing monster charging down, hide scored with lightning as Crosillan's arcane power seared it. The metal voices of the Stormcasts and the roaring of the reptiles raised as though in common prayer. Vael's hammer thundering into the monster's armoured head, cracking its bony plating. The air busy with javelins and darts that lanced on him like rain.*

There, from that balcony, a host of little reptiles hurling missiles, spitting them from long pipes. The bows of the Judicators answering with cracking arrows, so that skinny bodies flew raggedly away, scorched and shattered.

'Lordship!' the scout hissed. Vael blinked. For a moment the crowd of little lizard monsters still danced in his view, their balcony vantage become a ragged high-water mark of fallen carving. The armoured beast was just its mail and its bones, the rest gone to drifting dust. Vael felt himself shaking, very slightly. It had been so real, his memories brought home. And either he would regain something of the man he had been or he would surrender all that was left of him and walk from here no more than Sigmar's servant, scoured clear of doubt. Either must be better than this terrible halfway state.

One of the lizards had not even vanished away into memory. It was very still, pressed against the inscribed slope of a wall so that he almost interpreted it as just one more carving or frieze. A thin green-blue lizard bleached almost grey in the light, one gold eye staring straight at him as he took another step towards it. In one hand it had a short weapon like a toothed axe. He could see so much detail, even in this stray memory. The shimmer of its fine scales, the slight flex of its spined crest, the way the weapon was worked to resemble a grotesque fish, the round eye a turquoise, the teeth stone barbs.

It shifted, and the scout hissed in sudden surprise, bringing around her crossbow. For a second Vael had no context for what was going on. The reptile could have leapt forwards and opened his throat.

It fled, dashing zigzag between the stones, and the scout's bolt clattered to one side of it. A moment later it was gone, leaving only human voices in its wake.

'What was that?' from Kenlo.

'Hold!' from the mage.

'Castle up!' from the big man who seemed to have command of the soldiers.

One of the powder weapons roared, the match touched so hastily that the ill-placed weapon jumped from the notch in its pavise. Out between the stones something bellowed, something far larger than the skittering creature just fled. Vael heard the crossbow clack again. Then one of the soldiers was down, clutching at a thorn that pierced her cheek, the skin already purpling angrily.

A lumbering scaled form, twice Vael's height, emerged from behind the half-walls and the rubble and the mess of fallen statues, hefting a ten-foot maul with a head of gold-and-black stone. At its back were lesser reptile warriors with spears and clubs, fanged jaws and lashing tails. Vael felt a physical kick inside him as memory and the moment fell into sync. He raised his hammer.

CHAPTER SIX

IRIXI

Irixi had been the least of its spawning. Skinks didn't vary much by size, but it had stepped from the pools the scrawniest specimen any of the tenders had ever seen. Soon after emergence, though, the tenders had discovered Irixi alone at one end of the spawning pool, the other young all clustered on the far side. A ring of water-flies had been dancing in the air over Irixi, flitting into strange configurations. A Starseer had been called and declared it the will of Tepok and Sek'atta – the two were seldom in disagreement – that this skink be trained in the priesthood.

Even now, a full adult, Irixi stood a little shorter at the shoulder than the other skinks of the expedition, made up for by the twin plumes of its headdress and the long drape of its cape, which dragged three-quarters of the way to its tail-tip.

The luminous transition that Sek'atta had decreed had passed, leaving them here amongst the ruins. No way back to the *Celestial Eye of Tepok* until the task was accomplished. Around Irixi, the bulk of the force mandated by the Starmaster's judgement was spreading out, ensuring there was no immediate threat to their leader's safety. The skinks were already overcoming their initial wariness, clambering and leaping on the stones, hunting out a good vantage point. Some were already pushing into the wreck of the *Wings of Serendipitous Fire*, memorising the tumbled layout of the place and hunting out anywhere the powers of Shyish had intruded. Oaxmal, the Chameleon scout, had probably slunk off into the ruin as well, following its own instincts because who would presume to teach a Chameleon its work? Or else it had stayed close and Irixi could simply not see it.

Nearby, Gokumet had the band of Starborne warriors arrayed in rigid order, after which they had settled into an almost stony immobility, spears straight, their scaly hides rippling softly with the celestial gleam of Azyr. They were true children of the high temples, born in the upper reaches of the realm of lightning and infused with its power. Irixi was vaguely aware that some cults and breeds of human also reached out to that realm for empowerment, with potent but unsophisticated results. The star dragon aspect they called Dracothion – known to the Seraphon by truer, older names – had taken pity on them and taught them some fragment of Azyr's secrets, Irixi understood. Raising them up from mere earth-made mortals prone to corruption and death and making of them something purer. A crude but effective tool against disorder.

The Starborne were steeped in the light of High Azyr. It glowed out from within them, limning each scale. They stood with a solid discipline, immune to distraction, able to go a week without drinking, a month without food in their slow, cold way, but ready to rouse to instant action if their charge was threatened or if Gokumet gave the command. Irixi shifted closer to them just for the security they represented. The Starseer had not been out of the *Celestial Eye* for a long time. To have one's claws digging into the earth of the realms was to be in danger. Even in so still a place as this.

Irixi had not seen the *Wings of Serendipitous Fire* aloft. The temple-ship had fallen to this ground long before the waters of the *Celestial Eye* had birthed it. Gokumet had, though. The pools which birthed the champion were buried beneath them even now, doubtless cracked open and choked with roots and bones. Irixi wanted to ask about those elder days, but saurus were not renowned for their descriptive abilities. Possibly the champion wouldn't even understand the question.

Irixi wondered if the first hint of Shyishan purple might be visible in the glimmer of Gokumet's scales. If these Starborne stood on this ground for long enough, the realm would begin to leach into them, making them more things of earth than of the stars. One more fragment of the native state of the Seraphon muddied by contact with the stuff of the world.

Looking across this stretch of ruin, Irixi tried to reconstruct how the *Wings* had seemed in its full majesty. Here was an observatory, surely, its crystal dome no more than sand but the curve of its walls still preserving familiar astronomical litanies. And that great heap of collapsed blocks – a discerning eye could reconstruct the tower that had once stood there, its core a spiral of braided gold like a barbel trailed in the fabric of the Astromatrix to detect the emanations of power. The gold would still be there, great arm-thick coils of it. Useless because the intricacies of its shape had been crushed out of it, the pictograms twisted and deformed.

At the back of its mind, Irixi felt a sense of loss at all this grandeur laid waste. The loss of a whole temple-ship! Hardly the only such disaster to occur back during the great heights of Chaos, when all things had teetered on the edge of oblivion. Then the Starseer shivered for more prosaic reasons and drew the cloak about itself, trying to husband the warmth brought from the *Celestial Eye*. Some of the other skinks had brought crystals that still scintillated with the fire of Azyr, setting them out to lend their heat to the saurus, and the lone, solemn Kroxigor who towered over even them. The Starseer gratefully stepped close to one, feeling its blood quicken a little.

There was something waiting in Irixi's mind, ready to descend should it be given the least chance of ingress. In a human it might be despair, for they were directionless things. Irixi *had* a direction. Sek'atta had entrusted it with a task vital to the comprehension of the plans of the Old Ones. It knew what it had to do.

It looked across the great landscape of half-walls and tower stumps and great loose scree slopes of stone. Within all of this had been a whole, intact passage of the Nine Orchid Path prophecy, a sequence of predictions and images that Sek'atta had found no record of anywhere else. Simple, then: Irixi must find it and record it, and then one more vital part of the plan would be recalled and the realms would be that much closer to perfection.

Somewhere within all this. And what state would that 'whole, intact passage' be in now, after the ship's fall and whatever ruin had been enacted below? Not despair, no, but for a moment Irixi felt like that undersized newborn again, facing the enormity of the world with no idea of how to overcome it.

Sek'atta had given the task to one specific servant. Therefore, that servant must be capable of performing the task. Any failure would be one of its own. The mage-priest's judgement could not be questioned.

Even so.

Irixi felt the gaze of Gokumet, implicitly trusting. The saurus warriors would all lunge into action at the least word, knowing implicitly that a Starseer's orders bore the authority and wisdom of Sek'atta. Their faith would be absolute.

Irixi felt very small.

Then Oaxmal was right there, skin shedding the shades of stone and dust as if removing a dull-hued cape. The Chameleon, leader of the scouts whom Irixi had sent to find a way below into the collapsed bowels of the ruin.

Irixi drew itself up to what height it had and rapped the ground with its staff, inviting Oaxmal to report. The purple crystal suspended in the crook of the stave's head sparked as the power around them earthed into it and was stored for future use.

Patterns shifted and flowed across the Chameleon's skin, a simple and efficient method of communication for those limited concepts they ever needed to pass on. Their jaws and tongues found the elegant sibilants of skink speech difficult. Instead, a flurry of colour and shade passed over Oaxmal's throat pouch and the curve of its crest, telling Irixi that the scout had successfully accessed the spaces below them. Irixi read additional markers there: an indication of incompleteness, a confirmation of mission. Much of the inner structure of the *Wings of Serendipitous Fire* must have survived the fall and been navigable – at least to a skink. Perhaps some parts of the prophecy remained intact on the walls of the inner sanctum? Oaxmal, without magical training, would not be able to answer – Irixi had to see with its own eyes. And most likely it was all cracked shards, but of course there was a plan for that. Sek'atta had foreseen the need, and placed the ritualistic details in his servant's head.

For which they would need… 'The pools?' Irixi prompted. Oaxmal's head bobbed, and its colours shifted and danced. Yes, the spawning pools remained intact below them, forming conduits of living water through the ruin. At a sequence of other prompts, Oaxmal confirmed that, yes, there was danger down there; yes, some of the sacred chambers had survived, though others were shattered into powder. A picture of the ruin beneath them emerged out of the pigments of the Chameleon's hide, and Irixi considered their situation could be worse.

At which point it became worse. One of the skink scouts came pelting back to them, eyes wide, clicking gutturally, *Danger! Danger!* As one, Gokumet's warriors shifted, one foot forwards, shields up. Irixi heard voices – out of sight around the mounds of stone but surely just in the next plaza. Not Seraphon voices, hence an intrusion to the plan. A destabilising force. Trouble.

A thunderous detonation sounded – not magic but some alchemical weapon. Irixi saw their Kroxigor had ambled forwards, reacting protectively to the alarm of the skink. Now it shuddered, a savage, blasted wound punched into its chest. It roared out a wordless complaint of pain.

Gokumet croaked out a command, deep and loud enough that Irixi felt it through the earth. The warriors rushed forwards, from dead still to full charge on the instant, getting their stone and starmetal shields between their leader and danger. Off the leash and enraged, the Kroxigor lumbered in the vanguard, maul upraised. Irixi heard more voices: alarmed, angry, human.

Humans. And while humans were surely part of the Old Ones' plan, they were not supposed to be *here.* A disruption, the introduction of unpredictable disorder. Not as if the Starseer *needed* any more obstacles given the scale of this task.

Let it be done quickly, it decided, and hurried at the heels of the warriors to give them its arcane support.

CHAPTER SEVEN

KENLO

He hadn't managed a good look at the little scurrying thing as it darted away. Honestly, his thoughts had gone to the ratmen. A swift-running creature smaller than a human, long tail whipping in its wake. And that would be the death of the expedition because nobody would be delving into the ruins for treasure if there could be a nest of Skaven down there.

When the big monster had lumbered out into sight, he'd been so sure of the problem that he'd taken it for a Rat Ogor first, one of those bulked-out rodent shieldbreakers who'd given them so much trouble in the first days of the Gnawtide. Then his eyes had caught up and he'd been looking at a twelve-foot-tall lizard-creature, a fortune in gold and precious stones hanging in amulets and medallions about its throat, and six hundredweight of mace raised above its head. And behind it were coming a host of armoured, spiky reptiles with spears and shields, a weird phantom luminescence clinging to them as though they were ghosts or conjured by magic.

The shields were drawn up before him, and he made sure to get Perlo at his back. The head of his axe was slotted back onto the haft – he'd long ago learned that a canny quartermaster had to walk into plenty of places where a weapon was bad manners but where someone was going to try and stab you eventually despite that. He planted the weapon in the ground for later use and took out his pistol. A masterwork weapon a mere Steelhelm shouldn't own, but it was a poor quartermaster who didn't supply himself as well as his army. Loosing it at the monster felt like spitting into the hurricane, but he let the weapon kick in his hand, seeing the ball impact in a spurt of weirdly luminescent bluish blood without slowing the beast remotely.

A crossbow bolt flowered in the creature's shoulder as it powered towards the line. Lofus was shouting at Vael, entreating the Storm-cast to get within the ring of shields, but the armoured figure was ignoring them. Staring at the reptilian advance as though it was a gift from Sigmar.

'My lord!' Kenlo added his voice. 'Stand with us!' Probably he should tug his forelock and say what an honour it would be, but who had breath for that?

The fusils sounded again, all three of them. He saw one of the lizard warriors take a backstep, a bright scar across the gold facing of its shield. *Gold!* Something in Kenlo kicked at the damage, feeling half the value of the piece torn away. Then the mace was coming down.

'Brace!' shouted Lofus, as though any mortal strength could have resisted the blow. The central Fusilier ducked down below her pavise, but the colossal descending blow tore through the iron-work atop the shield, smashed the stout planks below to kindling. The barrel of the fusil spun away and the jagged end of the shaft punched through the woman's thigh in a burst of arterial blood a fraction of a second before the strike of the maul shattered her every bone from skull to femur.

Lofus took his chance and thrust his sword at the thing's ribs, the force of the stroke skidding from its scaly hide. A spear-tip of greenish stone almost caught him in the face, but one of his squad's shields took it aside. Then Kenlo himself leapt forwards, finding himself standing over the smashed wreck of Fusilier and pavise, swinging his axe to carve a shallow gash in the monster's leg.

He looked up into its blunt turtle face. Calm, incurious, no more emotionally invested in this life-or-death struggle than the stone head of its weapon. *So this is how I die, is it?*

A bolt of spitting purple seared into the monster's chest from over his shoulder, Perlo putting her skills to use. Then an armoured form slammed into the monster's side, crackling hammer landing with a searing thunderclap. Vael had deigned to join them in the melee after all.

The monster staggered sideways, its vast bulk actually shifted by the strike. Lizard behemoth and Stormcast were abruptly off to one side, trading blows in a furious skirmish of their own, leaving the other reptiles' spears to test the shields. Kenlo fell back as one of the Steelhelms put himself between the two remaining Fusiliers to close up the gap, hunching against the jabbing stone points. Stanner popped up to shoot over the top into the snouts of the enemy, then ducked back down to reload. Perlo was shouting something, but then Perlo was always shouting something. One of the spears found a throat over the lip of a shield and a man went down, the wall crunching in to compensate. Kenlo set to reloading his pistol, wondering if the Stormcast was about to make another miraculous intervention.

VAEL

The reptilian giant stumbled back away from him, and Vael thought he'd overbalanced it. It caught itself with its tail, though, and then its own maul swept around at him. They were clear of the shield-wall, and just as well because that broad stroke could have shattered half a dozen in a single impact. The thought bloomed in his mind, for a moment making the regular humans a part of his strategy. Then they were gone from his sightline and he had forgotten them: just him and the monster, a duel to one more death.

He dropped, turning his charge into a skidding slide across the slanted stones of what had once been an ornamented square. As the teeth of broken stone chewed at his armour he had a moment's flash of vision: the same lines of wall and colonnade, but complete and bright, garlanded with a webwork of green vines that were parasite and part of the place all at once. An instant's flash and then all was ruin and dead stone around him, and he slid beneath the swing of the monster's club–

Not quite. The toothed edge caught the rim of his pauldron and hooked at it, a moment's pain across his upper arm as the straps bit tight and then snapped. The shock of impact – the slightest fraction of the monster's strength but enough to let him know how powerful it was – connected with his lost past. He saw the bright blooms, the panicked scattering of the birds, the lightning. The spears of Sigmar lancing down towards the unseen Chaotic host below, interrupted by this flying monument. The great beast bellowed in his face as he levered himself up to meet it, and he saw another such creature overlaid on it. A different pattern on its scales, other wounds, but the same breed of monster. *I have fought you,* Vael thought, and clung to the memory like a friend, like a drowning man with a plank. His hammer struck the monster across the jaw and one of its club fists smacked him in the breastplate, knocking him onto his back. The impacts – scales and stone – were bursts of colour in his mind. *It was so bright back then!* Understanding that it had not been the sunlight or the surroundings but his eyes that had changed. The life and *Vael-ness* hammered out of him with each successive turn on the Anvil until all was muted tones, the golds and bright blues faded. *I was so alive back then!*

The monster stood over him, maul held high to make as much a ruin of him as the fall had made of this flying temple. He dragged his short sword out from behind his back and rammed it upwards, driving it to the hilt in the reptile's belly. The wound went deep enough that when the bludgeon's blow came down, there was only a weak trickle of strength behind it. He took it on his other pauldron, feeling the weapon's teeth gouge his mail, then came up swinging. His hammer, with both arms' full might behind it, impacted against the side of the creature's head and it went down.

He was already wheeling for the next battle. In his eyes, the brightness of the past and the dull, leaden tones of the present chased one another's tails, not a distraction but an inspiration. He yearned for the way the fighting had felt back when he had been new to Sigmar's service. His felt his eyes and the jagged pattern of his scars blaze.

He rediscovered the Sigmarite shield-wall again, as it pushed back against the spears. The Dawnbringers momentarily bewildered him with their presence here, unwanted in his memories. Between them and him, already running at him, was one of the reptile warriors. A big one, its head-crest and scales bristling with spikes and adorned with gold and slate. In its hands…

He did not recognise the warrior, but the weapon. The square-sectioned club toothed with gleaming stone and reinforced with gold. A work of art. A thing from his memory. And he almost stood there too long, trying to sift past from present. Almost let his enemy gift him that weapon full force to the head, before understanding this was *here* and this was *now* and this *was* the enemy who had killed him that first time. Not the mortal death at the hands of his kin that Sigmar had stolen him from but his Stormcast reintroduction to mortality. The only one that had stayed in his mind.

He almost dropped his hammer. He *did* open his arms to the lizard-creature, and what mix of pain, loss and joy was on his face, he could not have said.

It slowed as it reached him, lambent blue-white eyes narrowing, looking for the trick.

'Come on!' Vael shouted at it, words the thing would surely not even understand. 'Fight me, brother! Fight me once more!' As though the creature was one of his fellows in Sigmar's service. 'I know you!' he called to it, feeling the mad grin dragging the corners of his mouth. 'We have unfinished business, you and I!'

And it knew him. He could read nothing in that reptile face, but he felt the jolt of connection like lightning in his chest. It saw the scars he had painstakingly preserved over all those centuries and deaths. The mark of its own teeth.

They could not smile, he thought, but he read it into the creature's jaws nonetheless.

GOKUMET

A long time, sleeping within New Home. To wiser minds, the *Celestial Eye of Tepok*, but always New Home to Gokumet. Sent out sometimes. Brought back. Held in readiness. A life apart from the world.

A long time in the service of Sek'atta the Starmaster, just one small servant of a great lord, as it should be. But hard, to know there had been another place, a *First Home*, now gone.

The pools of the champion's birthing, lost, shattered in the fall. The height of Chaos. The bright sear of the lightning. And Gokumet had felt the urge to stay and fight, back then. That was what a saurus was for. To hold the enemy while those more important to the plan survived. Born to service, to fight and to die. As it should be.

But Sek'atta had called his servant back. Called many back who should have stayed. Should have ridden their first home to the ground's embrace. And Gokumet had gone because, when the slann spoke, obedience was all.

And since then…

Since then…

The champion felt it had lived half a life, in New Home. But a part of its nature had fallen to earth here, and been lost. As though its shadow had been left behind, some ephemeral but essential part the saurus had no name for.

It saw the Golden One ahead, armour battered and hanging off it, turned pale brass by the dead light. The metal figure had its arms wide, that hammer held lightly in one hand, that had struck down the Kroxigor. Gokumet saw the pallid, flat human face. Blue-white fire outlined the marks of fangs and Gokumet *felt*, viscerally *felt*, how it had been to bite deep into that face. To avenge the Fall of First Home and First Siblings.

In that instant Gokumet had its shadow back and was whole.

The Golden One brought its hammer about as Gokumet charged in, but the Seraphon felt a new warmth within from the completeness, meeting the weapon's haft with the dense flesh of one arm and cracking across the metal warrior's armour with an upswing. The enemy's backplate slammed into the stones.

Gokumet's clawed hand gripped about the warrior's face, but a gilded gauntlet smashed across its snout, smashing loose two teeth. The saurus lunged forwards, jaws agape, trying to finish the work that was written in that pale flesh, but the Golden One threw it off, a prodigious feat of strength, casting Gokumet almost ten feet.

The champion rolled, caught itself, club drawn back to strike, to meet the hammer's thunderous downstroke. Meeting brute strength with brute strength, feeling both weapons flex with the impact.

The human's face was twisted in a wild expression, all its teeth bared. Gokumet had more teeth and larger and bared them right back.

* * *

PERLO

She had been shouting for them to hold since she'd seen the enemy. Like Kenlo, she'd thought *the rats* when she'd seen that fleeting long-tailed figure. Unlike Kenlo, she had read every book she'd ever got her hands on. Born out of the Reclaimed, army kids from their youngest years, that shouldn't have been many, but Perlo was gifted. She'd dogged the heels of every mage and priest who'd marched with them, run errands, done favours, all in exchange for scraps of teaching and lore. She'd learned half a dozen scripts by the age of ten; she'd copied and bartered and scrounged for scraps of arcane teaching. By age fifteen she'd stood behind the shield-wall and cast crude blasts of arcane power into the faces of orruks and ogors, or thrown up hasty shields against arrows and bolts. By eighteen she had started undoing the workings of enemy casters, tripping up their magics and calling out their locations to the sharpshoot-ers. She had threaded the needle between being so good they took her away for formal training and being so reckless that the witch hunters took an interest. She was Kenlo's secret weapon, to back up all his schemes and dealings, but she was also the one who *knew* things.

She had seen these creatures before. In books, histories of Sigmar's wars. Seraphon, they were called, and though they looked as mon-strous as half the servants of disorder or destruction, they were no friends of Chaos.

'Hold!' she shouted, pushing forwards and getting Lofus' elbow in her face for her pains. 'Wait, this isn't our fight!'

But there were deaths on both sides by then, and whoever's fight it had been before, it was theirs now. The reptile warriors weren't giving any quarter either, ramming at the shields with their spears or trying to stab past them, making the most of their reach and trying to take the missile-shot on their shields. The lesser Seraphon, the little scurrying ones with the bright crests, swarmed on either side, casting little javelins or spitting darts. They had more numbers, and if Perlo couldn't convince her *own* kind to step back, what could she do to persuade *them*.

She was going to have to do something rash. She opened herself to the arcane power of the place, expecting the bitter taste of Shyish that always resented obeying a living master. Instead, from the ruins beneath her feet, she felt a sudden upwelling of living power. For a moment her eyes were filled with wheeling stars and ancient ages and vast, mountain-sized monoliths grinding past one another. In the next instant she had the power – within her breast, between her hands – and was struggling to control it, a river where she had sought a meagre trickle. *This place! I had no idea!*

She could unleash it on the Seraphon, but it was their power, their place. She understood that, could almost see the tendrils of it rising up to invigorate them. Instead, she could...

She had to act right then, without any thought for the consequences. Another heartbeat and the power would escape her grasp, right here in the midst of the shields.

One hand on Kenlo's shoulder, another on Lofus', pushing herself between them. A foot on someone's shield. Launching herself up, a target for every javelin and spear, but the power, the *power*–

The magic exploded from her, not as force, not as fire or lightning, but as *light*. The clear, pure white of Hysh radiating from her body in all directions. She screamed with it too, feeling it radiate through her flesh, knowing that her very bones must be visible in the instant that she unleashed it.

She fell. Onto the spears, surely. Not even an act of war but of gravity. She braced for the pain.

There was pain, but not from impaling spearheads. Instead, she crashed to the ground, struck her knee, her hip, her arms, narrowly avoided opening her skull on the jagged base of a fallen statue.

She opened her eyes, feeling the last of the Hysh-light bleeding from them into Shyish's grey air.

The spearpoints were inches from her face. Close enough she had to blink to turn them from mere greenish blurs. That they were *that* far away meant the Seraphon had fallen back a good three feet. She craned back. The shield-wall slanted away from her at an alarming angle, and half the soldiers there were shaking their heads or had their hands to their eyes.

'Wait!' she cried out. 'Please!'

'Perlo, get behind the shields!' Kenlo snapped at her desperately. She levered herself to her feet unsteadily. The reptile warriors, their eyes already aglow, seemed less dazzled, but they weren't thrusting forwards to kill her. She tried to find some commonality in them, but there was nothing. They were like things of stone.

'Please,' she repeated to them. Then tried the same in the tongue of aelves and that of the duardin. None of the histories she'd read had said what Seraphon spoke, or even *if* they did.

And yet there was a voice. A high voice, the consonants clicking and popping in a way no human could have mimicked. More the piping of a frog than language, save there were words in it. 'You beg?' it said. 'Steal power from this ground and make light of it? What begging make you?'

The Seraphon warriors shifted. She was very aware of the tension in them, and in her fellows. A glance back showed Kenlo right at the shields, reaching desperately to drag her out of the way.

A creature appeared, actually clambering up the foremost warriors to be seen. A little thing, like a lizard's idea of a monkey, but fabulously adorned in gold and jade and feathers. It had a staff, and the magic of it made her neck hairs bristle even at this distance. A mage of the Seraphon, then, and a powerful one.

'I beg for peace,' she said carefully. 'We are not enemies.' And how long that would hold if they worked out Kenlo and company were here to loot their ruin, she couldn't know. But if there was any chance to get out of this without a fight to the death, she'd take it, because there were more Seraphon than in Kenlo's party and a solid shield-wall wasn't going to carry the day.

One of the Fusiliers was stealthily loading her piece, Perlo saw from the corner of her eye. Perhaps the lizard mage was too tempting a target. She jabbed a finger at the woman. 'Don't.' She got a rebellious look in return, but she got what she wanted. Perlo had proved herself to these people enough that they would follow her lead when faced with the unknown. And these Seraphon were certainly the unknown.

She looked back to the lizard mage. It had its head cocked to one side, a bright yellow eye scrutinising her.

'What, then?' it said clearly, a voice that came out of its throat without much help from lips to shape it. 'Sympathy, significance? Some reason, this place, this time?'

'I don't know what you mean,' Perlo said carefully, 'but please, let us talk, you and I. Let's find a way we don't have to kill one another.'

CHAPTER EIGHT

IRIXI

Something about the way the human had lain there, after that flash of light. Unexpected, momentarily discomfiting, but Irixi's eyes had membranes across them that had snapped shut, sparing it from some of the glare.

What had stirred in its mind, seeing the human mage prostrate between the lines? Not the act itself. Not the power invoked – the usual fumbling of inferior training. Not the creature's specific appearance. Certainly not its actions in interposing between the two sides. Altruism? A desperate bid for preservation? Perhaps Irixi's bodyguard intimidated it so much? From Irixi's viewpoint the outcome remained uncertain, especially given the presence of the god-forged warrior who had been struggling with Gokumet. The saurus veteran had taken a step back now, still facing off against the enemy, waiting for Irixi's word to continue the fight.

But this mage…

Seraphon memory could be slow. Irixi – by no means old by its own reckoning – had lived many human lifetimes, days filled with the complex minutiae of ritual performed towards distant ends understood only by the mage-priests. As well as the time in the gardens, it had also tended the great obsidian mirrors of Sek'atta's chamber where the Nine Orchid Path prophecy was assembled and displayed – those parts of it that had been recovered. Some sequences wound their serpentine way about the mirrors, showing precious elements of the Old Ones' Great Plan as it was intended to unfold. Others were orphaned images, ragged-edged, shorn of context and impossible to interpret. Irixi's memory supplied one such now. A single figure, lying flat, one arm extended, mostly swathed in a garment. The back half had been missing, and the figure's snout had been blunt, with a crease that might have been intended as a mammal nose. A human, or aelf – or even an orruk, for they were all very similar when depicted in the prophetic style. Impossible to surely identify the details of that blocky engraving with this human, save that the pose, the arm – they matched perfectly with this figure here, in this very moment when Irixi laid eyes on it. And Irixi was here to *recover* a missing section of the Nine Orchid Path, but the prophecy was perfectly capable of including *itself* within its own prophesying. The Old Ones had foreseen even the fallibility of their own message.

There was a connection here. For a moment Irixi felt a sense of vast wheels, the infinite interconnections of the Astromatrix binding everything of significance to the Great Plan. Itself, Sek'atta, the god-forged warrior, this mage…

Speaking like a human was difficult. Whilst the Starseer had learned their tongue, the language relied on a concentrated modulation of sounds unaided by skin pattern and tail motion. From past experience, one had to speak very carefully so the creatures could understand, yet quickly enough to stop them losing interest in their restless way. Irixi reviewed the mage's words and intoned a reply that hopefully meant something like: *Your right to petition me is granted, and you have some talent to modulate the latent potency of our temple for your own purposes, weaving the power of Hysh into your conjuring. Kindly specify what plea for clemency you wish to make.* Fighting over the weirdly fluid, consonant-filled words, aware that much of the meaning was coming out via pose and the flushing of its throat, which the human would be blind to.

The mage spoke. What it was petitioning for was 'peace', and Irixi would naturally have interpreted that as a wish for death, given how agitated and fleeting these mammal lives were. *I am understanding the words but not the meaning,* it knew. 'Clarify the meaning of your message,' it invited, falling into the tones appropriate for soliciting information from a Kroxigor or one of the denser saurus. 'So that I may weigh your meaning within the greater schema of the realms.' And again, what actually came out in human words was coarse and rudimentary, but then, so were humans. It would have to suffice.

Now the human was professing its own puzzlement. But the fighting, at least, had stopped. Irixi decided it preferred that. In the melee, the situation had felt quite out of control. The danger of an unpredicted outcome had loomed large.

The human seemed to agree, so Irixi ordered Gokumet to have their forces withdraw to one part-ruined hall, the jagged lines of rubble outlining a former barracks for the ceremonial temple guard, hence a proper place for them to reside. With a little gesturing, the Starseer had the mage send its own bodyguard back a similar distance. Between the two forces was a sad circular ridge that had once been a place of ritual cleansing for those about to enter the more sacred halls below. Now the jade font had cracked across, and the statue of Tepok was fallen, no longer focusing the minds of visitors on prudence and wisdom. It was, however, the most auspicious place for a diplomatic meeting, and perhaps some trace of the god's guidance would linger and aid in communication.

Rather than waiting for them to properly settle themselves across from one another in an appropriate attitude of patient listening, the human was talking all the way to where Irixi led it, and even made sounds through the abbreviated cleansing the Starseer performed in the ruin of the font. Nothing important, Irixi hoped, as little of it had been understood. It was some rambling anecdote concerning the human presence here, ending with a mention of a quest for things of value, presumably the wisdom held within the ruin of the *Wings of Serendipitous Fire*. For a moment Irixi even considered that the humans were also trying to reconstruct the Nine Orchid Path, which would be very impressive. Instead, more likely this mage had been drawn to the site by the lingering vestiges of power and fragmentary relics. That might or might not be a reason to recommence fighting, depending on whether they tried to claim objects of significance or just trash. In Irixi's experience, humans had no real capacity for judgement. Perhaps they might be steered to something suitably trivial and harmless.

'You must understand that we stand in the midst of the *Wings of Serendipitous Fire*, sacred domain of the Lord Sek'atta and receptable of prophecy, and many things here may not be fit for your unclean touch,' Irixi explained politely to the human, which scrunched up its face in that unpleasantly mobile way it had, making an odd little butterfly gesture with its hands.

'Sacred flight?' it asked, and then some more noises, but the Starseer stood suddenly. There had been a shift. The currents of power that informed its nose and tongue were abruptly different. It stared at the mage in case the creature had been trying some trick, but the power had a sharp, foul reek with nothing of the human to it. Irixi rapped its staff on the ground, a superior to a junior, ordering silence, but the human kept making its noises and the hostile, intrusive power was…

A terrible shrilling arose from all around them, out of the dark trees and across the ruin of the temple-ship. High, piercing, from many throats. The curdled taste on Irixi's flicking tongue coalesced into the bitterness of Chaos.

Even as it understood, there was a ragged tide of hairy, scurrying figures pouring out of the trees and up from between the stones. Rat-like things in ragged robes waving staves and cleavers or trailing thuribles that vomited stinking fumes. Ragged vermin with triangular shields of nailed-together boards waving pitted, rusty blades. The most wretched and despicable servants of the corrupting powers.

Both the Seraphon bodyguard and the mage's warriors were fighting, and Irixi saw its followers trying to reach their leader, wading into the sudden tide of vermin. They would not arrive in time. The rats were swifter.

Irixi might perhaps have run, despite its regalia, but humans were slow, and the mage *mattered*. The mage had a place in the prophecy and could not just be lost to Chaos.

The Starseer lunged forwards and grasped the human's wrist, feeling the soft skin yield unpleasantly. Because it had taken the time for a proper cleansing ritual, the latent power here was attuned to Irixi's wishes and told it of a vestry chamber below the font. At their feet, the stone shifted aside, showering dirt and debris into the blackness below. Oaxmal had said the internal structure was mostly intact, if not safe. Safer by far than the hospitality of the Skaven, though.

Irixi dropped inside and, though small, it was able to overbalance the mage and drag the human after. Above, the stone closed up once again, leaving the pair of them in the utter dark.

CHAPTER NINE

From the Scriptorium of Ferskine of the Eleventh Bell

Nownow slavescribe record faithfully these words of your better yes-yes?

Be it known that in this the time of great gnawing Lord Ferskine the wise the potent the festering, being unappreciated and unfairly schemed against by the infinite folly of those who style themselves his peers yes-yes, that lord, that wonderful inestimable and insuperably pestilent Lord Priest of Manifold Plagues His Foulness Lord Ferskine, yes, even he, has sniffed out the snuffling savour of a grandness fit for his use and possession and knowledge yes-yes only he.

Leaving the lesserkin to scramble and scuffle and scrape at the shields of the human army out beyond the trees it is only he himself great Ferskine the only, the majestic, may his incisors ever increase in length and sharpness, who has the wit and the boldness and the wisdom to seek this power. Let all his rivals and his inferiors know awe and dismay and respect and not to laugh at or demean or belittle him ever again, no-no, never.

This stone place this ruin place this snake-smelling place yes-yes, power buried here there is, and who but Ferskine, the unlimited, is to unlock it? Ferskine, who claims all these stones and ruins and dark places for the Horned Rat and the greater glory of the Clans that style themselves Pestilens yes!

So decrees Lord Ferskine: go forth and scour all that is not Rat from this place. Bring its flesh to the table of your lord! Bring prisoners! Bring entertainment! And power! All things that sniff and savour of it, bring to the tainted table that it may be smeared with the foetid and sacred exudations of the Rat and made into the possession and plaything and weapon of Ferskine, and let those who sneer at him be brought low and let the favour of the Rat be upon him forever and forever!

Part 2

BURIED IN EARTH

CHAPTER TEN

KENLO

Kenlo, no hero he. Sigmar's most prudent son, in any other circumstance. But Perlo, the well-meaning fool, had gone and put herself right out there in the open. The Steelhelms *here* and the lizard monsters – the *Seraphon* she'd called them – over *there* while she went and talked to the magisterial one in the elaborate headdress. And then the rats.

Nobody had been thinking about them. *Yes,* they were erupting across the realms right now. Yes, you heard nightmare stories through the realmgates to Aqshy or Ghyran. That was just how life was. The main army was even on its way to relieve settlements whose walls had gone from holding off scavenging bands of ghouls to full-on siege from Skaven raiders. But they were still in country that should have stood safe in the shadow of Lethis – nobody had even suggested the little vermin bastards had got so close! And what with the Shyishan woods and then these reptiles turning up, who'd looked for rats as well?

Only silver lining was that the lizard warriors obviously had it in for the rats as much as any solid Bringer of the Dawn. They'd laid into the squealing tide with a will, ramming those spears right in while the smaller reptiles went mad with their blowpipes and their bolas and all that weird kit they carried. And they were driving towards the centre to try and get their chief back, just like Kenlo was leading the charge to recover his sister. No 'Castle up!' and hold the line now, not with her out in the open. And the rats were going to get there first, and there wasn't a lot that Kenlo could do about that except hope she pulled some magic out of thin air to hold them off.

Then there were more Skaven scurrying in from the right, just seething up from between the stones, squeezing out of gaps a shadow shouldn't have been able to escape from. Stanner called out the warning, and Lofus had half their number throw a messy shield-wall together so the rats broke against it.

'Go!' he huffed to Kenlo. 'We'll hold 'em!'

There was already a scattering of rodent bodies between Kenlo and his goal. He had his axe to hand and just laid in, big two-handed strokes to scatter them. The edge bit – he felt it grate past rusty mail, then carve deep into rat flesh. He vaulted the shrilling victim, using the leverage to twist his weapon free and bring it down on the next. A filthy blade thrust at him, slashing his coat open but spending its force against the mail beneath.

Something eclipsed the sun. For a moment he thought it was that giant lizard champion back for more, but it was a rat. A rat like an ogor, his least favourite sort. It had one hand that was just a studded mace-head, and the other had yellow claws long as knives. Both were coming for him, and for a moment that was surely *it* for the quartermaster career of Kenlo Marinta. Then his ankle twisted in his headlong run and he actually headbutted the thing in the greasy expanse of its gut as he tripped forwards. The metal-shod butt of his axe somehow hit it in its brown and rotting teeth, cracking one incisor clear across, and he fell ignominiously at its feet.

He twisted round, looked up. The Rat Ogor's head, set ludicrously small within the bloated muscle of its torso and shoulders, hissed down at him, and it lifted up a pink, hand-like foot to stomp him into pulp.

The hammer arced out from past Kenlo's view, slamming into the Rat Ogor's open mouth and force-feeding it the rest of its teeth in jagged pieces. Vael Scar-Helm stepped over Kenlo, following up with a second strike and then a third, lightning sparking from the weapon and his eyes with each strike. The mad grin of before had gone. His ragged face was utterly devoid of expression – a Stormcast's golden mask would have had more personality to it.

Kenlo scrambled up, hacked down a sneaky rat who was trying to drive its blade into Vael's knee, and looked around frantically for Perlo.

Where his sister had stood with the little reptile leader there was just a swirling knot of rats, clawing and digging – or were they despoiling the bodies? Kenlo let out a howl of fury, but then Stanner was dragging him back.

'They went down!' the scout hissed right in his ear. 'Perlo and the lizard mage. Like a door opened and they dropped in. Kenlo, man, we've got to get clear!'

'No, we've got to get Perlo!' Kenlo insisted. But there was no Perlo, and the whole centre of the ruin was festering with rat-creatures. Across the plaza the Seraphon seemed baffled, fighting the rats that came at them but robbed of a plan by the disappearance of their leader.

'Perlo!' Kenlo yelled, attracting more rat attention than anyone was happy with.

'If she lives she'll come to us,' Stanner snapped, still dragging at him. 'Come *on*, man, or we're overwhelmed! Your lordship, champion, come with us!'

The look Vael turned back on her was devoid of humanity. The

Stormcast would stand and fight until the rats dragged him down, as eventually they must.

Kenlo made his decision. Stanner had to be right. Perlo would use her magic, would use her wits, would do *something*. This couldn't be the end for them.

'My lord!' he called to Vael, already backstepping towards Lofus and the others. He heard Stanner's crossbow snap once more, and then the woman took her hatchets out, hefting them grimly.

Vael's fire-eyed gaze seared across him, and he forced himself not to shrink from it.

'My lord,' he shouted. 'In Sigmar's name, with us! Come with us and we can strike back against this filth together!' The sort of motivating talk he'd heard from marshals and officers.

Vael's expression didn't shift. Another handful of rats dared his reach, and he slammed the hammer down amongst them seemingly without looking, crushing one and scattering the others. A moment later he was striding towards Kenlo, casual as though there was no battle at all. The vermin scurried from his shadow. The death of the Rat Ogor had taught them to fear Sigmar's champions.

Back with the shields, they retreated to the trees. Not that the rats would hesitate to brave the woods for a moment, but right now they seemed most keen to hold on to the ruins. *Thieving little bastards.*

'Reckon they've carved up those lizardmen?' Lofus asked.

'They have made their own withdrawal,' Vael said, his unexpected contribution shutting off whatever Kenlo might have had to say.

'You were, ah, serious about laying into them, before,' Kenlo noted warily. 'You've got history, I reckon, my lord?'

'A death is owed, between us,' Vael said. 'One way or another.' And smiled, the expression warping and twisting that scarred flesh, spilling little worms of lightning from the gouged lines. Kenlo shuddered at the sight. Right then, the reptiles would have looked more human.

They found a hollow with enough trees about that they could defend it with half their number, setting up the pavises to block two ways in and Lofus detailing triple duty for sentries. Everyone knew the Skaven were a stealthy bunch, and the gloom beneath the trees would be their ally.

'We wait,' Kenlo told them. 'I'll get a fire going.' Because no chance the rats would overlook them anyway, if the vermin came scouting, so might as well keep warm. 'We wait and Perlo will… She'll get to us, get word to us, something, somehow. She's smart. She'll find a way.' Looking round at their faces, ready to lay into any doubters, but they knew Perlo too. Having even a halfway-trained mage at their backs had saved plenty of them over the years. None of them was giving up on her.

One of Lofus' people, who was a halfway decent armourer, was fixing the broken straps of Vael's armour, wary eyes on the Storm-cast. The man stood there like a statue, not even seeming to notice the attention.

'I'll go see how the land lies,' Stanner said. 'Make a few rats scared of the dark, what d'you think?'

Kenlo didn't much like it, but they couldn't just sit here blind, and Stanner knew her trade. 'Don't get seen. Don't get caught.'

She made a disrespectful noise at that, and then Vael hefted his hammer up to his shoulder, the newly secured pauldron shifting on its makeshift strap.

'I shall accompany you.'

Stanner's eyes swivelled from him to Kenlo. 'All due respect, lord-ship, you're not the lightest of foot.'

'I find if the stick you carry is big enough, you don't need to walk softly,' the Stormcast said. His face was utterly deadpan again. Kenlo caught Lofus' eye.

'Was that…' he started, not quite sure he dared even complete the sentence, 'a… *joke*, my lord?'

Vael opened his mouth, and just stood there. For a moment he looked completely adrift, someone waking from a dream.

He doesn't know, Kenlo thought, feeling weirdly sick with it. *God, what a life.*

'Come on if you're coming,' said Stanner softly. Vael's face was all purpose again before she'd finished speaking. He nodded, and when she slipped out of the dell, he was striding after her. All that weight of metal on him, and yet only a little clink and clank despite it.

'Gives me the bloody shivers, that one,' Lofus said.

'Stanner or the Stormcast?' asked Regis, the Fusilier. She had her weapon off its mount, cleaning it with a filthy rag.

Lofus managed a hollow chuckle. 'Lovely couple. Maybe they'll wed.' He clapped Kenlo on the shoulder. 'Perlo's squirrelled out of worse, mate,' he said. 'She'll come back to us.'

Kenlo nodded, and began building up wood for a fire.

CHAPTER ELEVEN

GOKUMET

Gokumet had failed First Home. Not once but three times now. The feeling sat like a stone in its gut.

Once when the Men of Gold had come on their lightning and struck First Home from the sky. And could Gokumet have stopped them? Could the temple-ship have been saved? Surely the strongest saurus ever spawned could not have done it. And yet Gokumet had failed, and the failure was like teeth in its flesh.

And now two times more. It had failed because Irixi Starseer was not here and safe, but had vanished where Gokumet could not follow. Failure.

It had failed because it had not stood and fought the Skaven enemy until they were all dead or Gokumet was. The other Seraphon, after many had died, had fallen back into these bad trees. Gokumet, with no orders or direction, had gone with them. Had let the Skaven rats take First Home. Even ruined, it should not be made filthy by their feet and greasy fur. More failure.

Gokumet had been spawned for fighting. That was what a saurus knew. The alignment of the stars that had presided over its birthing pool had not picked the champion out for making weighty decisions, like *what to do now*. There was supposed to be someone to give instruction. To point the warriors in a direction and nominate an enemy, and thus ensure that Gokumet fulfilled a role in the Great Plan. But now there was just Gokumet, the champion of Tepok, to whom all the others looked, and who didn't know.

It had left the others behind. They were no good now it was dark and cold. They were clustered together with the last of the warming crystals, waiting for the morning. As if the coming of the misery-light of this realm would make anything clearer or better. Gokumet could feel this realm seeping into its flesh, touching the starfire that dwelled within its scales and bound it to High Azyr and the *Celestial Eye*. Its Starborne nature was infinitesimally bleeding away into the deathly clutch of this place.

Gokumet looked up. Above, the night sky was not even properly black, but a funereal grey as though even true darkness had died here. The moons that could be seen were pallid, weirdly phantasmal, the ghosts of celestial objects long deceased. The mark of the Lord of Death was on everything, a stamp of endless oppression and slavery. A plan for the realms that stood in opposition to the benign will of the Old Ones. The enemy. Gokumet was surrounded by the enemy, every root and branch, each blank panel of stone or faceless carved angel.

There were rats abroad in the trees. After they had smeared their foulness across the fallen stones of First Home, the Skaven had begun to range into the forest, seeking the Seraphon and the humans both. *That*, at least, meant that Gokumet had something it could do. While the others sheltered, it went hunting.

Too cold to prowl about the trees the way a warrior should, but a saurus had other means of hunting. It crept towards the skitter and squeak of the Skaven, then placed itself where they would pass. Nothing of fur could be as still as a Seraphon in waiting.

Husbanding the heat saved from the day, Gokumet let itself be like a stone, waiting in ambush for the first warm body to come within reach.

It was not something it had been told to do. It could not know if it was part of the plan. The act spoke to something deep in its reptile soul, though. The lurking, the anticipation, the sudden lunge, the brief squeal and blood on its teeth.

When the light returned – not even worth the name of morning – perhaps it would go and fight the rats. Lead the others into the ruin of First Home and kill Skaven until there were no more enemy, or until the enemy overcame them. As seemed likely, given their numbers. Was that what should be done?

Irixi Starseer would know. Irixi Starseer was supposed to be here to tell Gokumet how to further the plan. Not just Gokumet, with only its own thoughts. Heavy thoughts, cold like stones.

Simple pleasures, for a saurus: to know the warm sun, to fight the enemies of Order, to obey the words of wiser heads. All denied now.

In the morning they would indeed take the fight to the Skaven, and perhaps that was what the plan demanded. Gokumet would die to their unclean blades and teeth, but before that perhaps an end would be brought to some individual rat who otherwise might become or accomplish something. Maybe that was Gokumet's purpose in the realms: to deprive the powers of Chaos of one specific servant, whose later actions – or those of their progeny generations later – would endanger some aspect of the plan.

If only the truth could be known, the saurus would be content with that. It would be a life well spent, to advance the Old Ones' plan even to some tiny degree.

These thoughts passed like glaciers through Gokumet's mind as it waited and the Skaven band padded closer.

It let the first two pass, snapping at each other and squabbling over dominance, then let all that hoarded warmth and strength propel itself forwards, turning from stone and shadow into an unstoppable engine of scale and strength. Its club slammed down on the leader, crushing the thin metal of its helm and the skull below. Its jaws closed on the next and shook it, feeling spine shatter and flesh rupture between Seraphon fangs.

Another Skaven jabbed at Gokumet two-handed with an ugly little pike. The dull edge skidded off scales and the saurus lashed a gold-weighted tail into the creature's face, breaking bones. With a flick of its head the champion cast the broken body of its second victim aside and lunged for another, club laying about left and right with brutal efficiency.

For a moment the remaining Skaven were trying to stand, presenting flimsy shields and baring their incisors in desperate threat. Then the starmetal club crushed another with a single blow and the remainder fled. Gokumet caught the slowest couple with snaps of its jaws, whipping them about as fiercely as a crocodile and casting the corpses aside. Then it was after them, racing along on feet and one hand, club slanted over its back ready to strike.

They were fleet, though, bred from their first days to run away from danger, no heart in them. The Skaven scrambled through the trees, a good half a dozen of them still alive, and Gokumet knew only frustration that any of them would escape.

Ahead, through the dark of the trees, there came a sudden flash of blue-white. The lightning of Azyr! For a moment the saurus thought it must be reinforcements from New Home, because even this hunt must be a part of the Great Plan. Then it heard a voice cry out in triumph and it knew.

The fleeing Skaven had run straight into two of the other enemy. The human enemy. There was the Golden One, who had been at the ruin of First Home: the one with the remembrance of Gokumet's teeth cut into its face. Even as Gokumet clawed into sight, the Stormcast brought that hammer down onto the lead rat with a crackle of power. Behind it, another human lurked, hacking with axes at a Skaven trying to flank its companion.

It was the generosity of the gods, Gokumet decided, to provide a night with so many enemies to fight.

The vermin had skittered to a halt at the sight of the Golden One, meaning Gokumet caught up with them and tore into the rearmost without mercy. The Stormcast accounted for most of the rest, and a final running rat-form was taken by a bolt from the other human. Not one of them escaped to warn the others. That was good.

Gokumet stretched its neck and gaped its jaws at the Golden One, and the Stormcast bared small teeth right back, settling one foot back for balance and hefting its hammer. That was good too. That was something Gokumet could understand.

Then the other human was between them. Gokumet almost struck at them, cued by the movement, and the Golden One twitched in the same way. The same fight lived in both of them, desperate to be out in the open.

But the human was making noises, that human way of language that was dull and muffled to the holes of Gokumet's ears. Not like the pure, high tones of the skinks, supported by clear movements of body and shades of skin. Just noises that sounded more like the burbling of water or the clack of pebbles than real talk.

Gokumet tried to brush the human out of the way, but it had its hands up, and its voice was… not as abrasive and annoying as human voices could be. Not meaningful, but soft at least. The human was pointing at the dead rats, miming striking at them, even blowing water from its lips at them. Like a skink with a blowpipe, perhaps? Showing that even humans despised the Skaven.

Gokumet looked at the Golden One, who had its hammerhead to the ground now, hands resting on the haft. It seemed to Goku-met that the other human was making just as many sounds at the Stormcast. Trying to stop the fight that was between them.

Because the human was not being subtle, Gokumet lifted a foot and raked hindclaws across the Skaven bodies, to show understanding. Humans were enemies, but Skaven were also enemies to humans. Not exactly the sort of thinking a Starseer was needed for.

Good. That was out of the way. Gokumet readied itself to fight the Golden One again.

But the human kept making noises. Pointing towards the ruin of First Home, pointing at the dead Skaven, pointing at Gokumet, so much pointing. And now drawing things with a knife in the bark of trees. Gokumet stared blankly, wondering if the creature had gone mad or had been infected with some Skaven pestilence.

It drew a crude stick figure with a tail. Gokumet thought it meant more rats, but it was pointing at the saurus, then the carving, then back at the champion again. Then drawing more of the same, and then making sounds.

Are there more of you? It wanted to know if others had survived the rats. Why? So it could know if it could finish things with Gokumet's death, or if it would have to hunt more? But now it was back to making hacking motions at the dead Skaven with its axe, then pointing to the Golden One and itself, then to Gokumet and the scratched carving. Then pointing out towards the infested ruins.

Gokumet took a long, slow moment of consideration, but again the message didn't need a Starseer to interpret it.

Humans were not inherently opposed to the plan of the Old Ones, that much Gokumet knew. They were like beasts. They could be used, sometimes. Like a lever to shift a stone. Like a spear or a club.

Gokumet did not want to have to make this decision. Could only hope that when the Old Ones had foreseen these moments, they had known the poor, fallible tools that would be available to further their designs.

The saurus let out a rumble that any civilised creature would have understood as grudging acquiescence, and turned to stalk off back towards where the others were. At its back, after a second's uncertain pause, the Golden One and the other human followed.

CHAPTER TWELVE

PERLO

The dark.

For a long moment, after the stone closed up above them, Perlo just crouched there. She had been powerfully afraid of the dark as a child. A particular curse in the realm of Shyish, both because of the general gloom of the place and because the dark really *was* to be feared. But to be a servant of Sigmar you had to face it, not shy from it. It was one reason she'd had a powerful fascination with the arcane arts from a precocious age. The illumination of Hysh, channelled through a luminiferous engine at a battlemage's word, dispelling the dark and searing into the enemy battle-line: an early memory, a potent impression on a young mind.

Now her lips moved and her hands began to sweep through the passes that would call even a fickle light into this abyss, but she felt the pricking of the Seraphon's claws against her skin, stilling her fingers. A faint hiss of breath from the creature. 'Be sparing, the power is not for use.'

'I…' She heard her own voice shake a little. 'I need to see.' Because they were in the dark, and underground, and in Shyish. *You can fight Nagash for every inch of ground up above*, went the saying, *but down below, the Lord of Death has already won.* The realm was built on corpses, and anyone who ventured into the depths was bold indeed. She'd heard there was no profession riskier than mining the realmstone here. No riches of the earth not already clutched in a bony hand.

Another faint exhalation from the Seraphon, without words this time. And then a faint illumination, purplish and weirdly benthic, as though they were deep beneath the waves. The crystal that floated within the loop of the creature's staff was glowing, the radiance reaching out to touch them both and their immediate surroundings. Perlo saw her hands, washed with a pale bruise shade by the light. The buttons of her long coat glimmered like pearls. Crouched beside her, the diminutive Seraphon mage blinked in a complex way that used more than the usual number of eyelids. With somewhat wounded dignity, it adjusted the sit of its headdress. The light glittered in the depths of the one eye it turned towards her, slit pupil gone wide in the dimness. Probably the lizard-creatures could see better in the dark than she could.

Above them she saw – her heart lurched at the sight – a sagging ceiling of blocks, caked with dirt and wisps of plant fibre. There seemed to be precious little keeping the stones in their place up there beyond mere goodwill. Around them was a complex, jagged-angled space. Probably this had been some shaft, for access or lighting, but the walls had buckled in at random on all sides, making a crooked chimney of it. Every stone surface crawled with piecemeal, fractured carving, and she couldn't say what was picture and what was writing.

The Seraphon glanced up at the perilous ceiling. She couldn't read alarm into its hunched poise, but perhaps a little dejection. 'To progress,' it said, with that weird twitch and writhe she'd realised must be a part of its regular speech. Its crest and throat seemed to shift shade and pattern too, though in the dim light she couldn't be sure.

'You have a name?' she asked it, repeating, 'Name,' when it just stared. 'Perlo,' she explained. 'That's me. Perlo Marinta, out of Lethis.'

It blinked again, and remarked conversationally, 'One part of the plan was given to a humble servant, Irixi.'

'That's you? Irixi?'

Her mangling of the name was plainly not up to usual Seraphon standards, but it nodded.

'We're going to get out of here, Irixi? You took us down here, and I'm grateful the rats aren't gnawing our bones right now, but you've got a way out?'

'The Good Purpose is here,' Irixi said, investing the words with a peculiar significance. 'Come, we shall accomplish things.'

Abruptly it fell, or that was what she thought. She even snagged its cloak trying to save it, and there was an awkward moment when she was strangling Irixi with its own mantle. It bit her calf, not hard but enough to warn, and she let go and saw it descend the crooked chimney with impressive agility, staff held downwards to light the way and tail waving stiffly for balance.

She didn't much want to go down after it, not into the stone-choked depths of this place, but on the other hand, that was where the light was headed, and she wanted even less to be left in the dark.

What started off as an undignified scramble suddenly turned into a drop as she ran out of shaft, pitching the last ten feet onto a layer of clammy, slick moss, dead plant matter and…

Bones. And she didn't have any immediate revulsion about bones, because, living in Shyish, you'd go mad if you did. She picked herself up, seeing Irixi standing close, moving the staff's radiance about to explore the reaches of the chamber they found themselves in. Beneath her boots, brittle ribs crunched. Small bones, and for a moment she took them for Skaven, connecting them with the assault above. The skulls she saw lacked the prominent front teeth, though – showing just ranks of sharp little fangs. She saw ornaments there too: gold armlets and anklets, and the broken fragments of what had been beaded necklaces and pectorals. Not unlike simpler versions of Irixi's own.

'Oh,' she said. 'Oh, I'm sorry.'

'Regret is for what?' Irixi asked blankly.

'These are… your people.' The smaller kind of Seraphon, a whole host of them, their brittle remains mingled in with a mess of fallen stones, grown over by greenish-black lichen and the pale fronds of fungus.

Irixi made a noise that sounded noncommittal, certainly not mourning. It trod over the remnants of its kin without sentiment. Around them, the radiance of its staff showed what had once been a beehive-shaped chamber. One side of it had collapsed in and now formed much of the floor. The opposite side had bowed outwards, showing a ragged gap into darkness. The whole of it seemed twisted and… squeezed? *It fell,* she remembered. That was what the Stormcast, Vael, had said. A great structure crashing down from the dead skies of Shyish, its inner architecture rupturing and tearing in the instant of impact.

From somewhere distant, but not distant enough, she heard a distant shrilling and chittering. The high, ear-bothering voices of the ratfolk, and not from up above but coming to them through the jumbled spaces within the ruin. The Skaven had found a way down.

'It has weapon?' Irixi asked her. The staff it bore looked delicate, not suited for self-defence.

Nobody marched under Sigmar's banner without something that could brain a rat. Perlo hadn't spent much time learning fancy fencing, and her choice of weapon reflected that. She twitched back the hem of her coat to show Irixi the studded cudgel hanging from her belt. 'But I'm better with magic.'

'Unwise, not indicated, against augury,' Irixi said, and by now she could read the strong negative in its body language.

'Look, I've trained as a mage,' she said, although she felt she was overselling herself. 'If they come–'

'If we have Serendipity, there must be caution,' Irixi told her.

Perlo blinked. 'I don't understand. What is… serendipitous?' Although it had said the word with a peculiar formality, like a name.

'Some things are improper.' And the creature was trying very hard to communicate its meaning to her. It listened for a moment – the twitterings of the Skaven hadn't drawn nearer – and then waved its staff about at their surroundings. 'The Wings, the Serendipity' – definitely a name, she decided – 'come to death but is not dead. Broken but is not dead. The strength of such a thing cannot in mere fall be robbed from it. In Ghyran the fall, all such power is gone to growing things. In Ghur, ripped from it by savagery perhaps. In Aqshy, set alight, pillar of the flames, hundred feet, three days, then ash. Here, Death reigns. Death, you know it? Stands between Order and Chaos. You, mage-scholar, understand this?'

The more she heard, the more its speech made a kind of sense. 'Death can mean decay, but also preservation. Stasis.' Anathema to all the other powers of the realms, the eternal slavery that Nagash desired for all souls.

'Correct, Perlo the scholar,' Irixi confirmed. 'So is preserved the strength of Serendipity, in some part. Enough part? We must see!'

'You can use it to get us out of here? Get us back to the others?' she asked.

Irixi eyed her. 'To be used towards the Good Purpose of things,' it told her, and she wasn't sure if it was agreeing or not. 'But until the test is put, unfit for the use of improper magic, understood?'

She bristled a little at that. Oh, probably it meant that meddling with the powers of this place would be dangerous for anyone, but she couldn't quite escape the sense it meant she just wasn't mage enough, or maybe lizard enough, to be trusted with whatever still clung on here.

Still, she hefted her cudgel and followed the Seraphon as it cautiously reached the ruptured gap in the chamber and began descending further into the innards of the ruin.

From the crushed beehive chamber a stair of monolithic blocks led into a pillared space that must have been the belly of the original structure, whatever that had been. Irixi's light ventured out into great chasms of dark space on all sides. Perlo saw its reflection glinting weakly in water below. A scent came to her, of decay and something acrid and unfamiliar.

Irixi stopped at the lowest step, where the water lapped. Its staff was still held high, and Perlo's own descent slowed as she saw what lay heaped around them.

There had been great square pillars holding up this place. Some of them yet stood, buckled or leaning but still holding up incalculable tonnage of stone above. Each face of them was carved in that intricate style, as complex and detailed at the highest reaches the light touched as at any sensible eye level. It was not ordered like any script a human would set down. Panels of pictoglyphs interwove in angular, serpentine patterns with processions of sculpted side-on figures. Other images were shown as vastly out of scale: squatting toad-things, winged reptiles and effigies so stylised she couldn't make out what they represented at all. Everything was shaped to fit within squares and rectangles, and to fit exactly with no wasted space, so that her eye smarted with trying to understand what she was being shown. Her mage's senses were prickling, too. The slumbering power Irixi had spoken of suffused everything around them, yet went nowhere and did nothing, held in check by the moribund hand of Shyish and the cataclysm that had brought this place down to earth.

The staff's radiance reached one wall of the chamber, and the stones there were interwoven with pale, questing rootlets. Others descended from on high, prying between the stones even as they bound them together. The last few stairs at their feet showed the roots' clutching, too, along with more scabby grey lichen. Just as the old human saying went, Shyish had made far more inroads to the buried reaches of this place than it had up above.

Something brushed her hand and she drew it back with a hiss. A centipede as long as her arm snaked off down the side of the steps. The back of each segment was blotched with a skull-like imprint, like some necromantic warning colouration. She had a sense that the core nature of the edifice around them disdained such things as death, but over the aeons since it had fallen, that resistance had corroded away. The influence of Death's realm was gnawing steadily away at the foundations.

'Someday this whole place is going to just fall into the earth,' she guessed.

'Imperative it is, a nexus to be propitiated,' Irixi explained, without really adding to Perlo's understanding.

'That'll help us get out?' she pressed. 'Or fight the rats?'

'A Good Purpose will be served,' Irixi agreed, or she hoped it was agreeing with her.

The Seraphon didn't just drop into the water – it was blackish and of unclear depth – but found a bank of rubble to balance along. The stone was incised and cut, delicate as wickerwork, and Perlo reckoned some sort of ornamental screen had failed to survive the crash. What secrets it had held, in its pattern and inscriptions, they were ground beneath her boots as she did her best to follow. A best which was not good enough, as a wide section of the bank slid into the dark water and took her back foot with it.

She yelped and scrabbled for Irixi. The Seraphon planted its staff and its tail curved about her waist, rough scales biting under her shirt before its tip hooked her belt. By then she was in full descent, though, and the lizard-creature – half her weight – ended up yanked after her, both of them descending into what turned out to be no more than six inches of opaque, greasy-feeling liquid.

Perlo felt fragile things crunch beneath her as she fought her way back up the shifting bank. One hand came up with something thin-walled and hollow. *A skull*, she thought, and then, *A cup?* But it was neither. In her hand sat a broken egg, lozenge-shaped and as big as her fist. Through the end she'd smashed open she saw a curled-up lizard shape, large-headed, premature.

'Pools of breeding.' Irixi was wringing at its robe.

'I'm sorry.'

'For why?'

'Your… young. Your children, or…?' The thing in the egg certainly looked like it might have grown up into an Irixi. Or else just some big lizard. The whole thing seemed oddly heavy, and she realised it had been transmuted into or coated with stone. Some quality of the water, she guessed. Shyish, obsessively burying and fixing everything that came under the realm's aegis.

'Is not of children. Is of beast. Beast-servant.' The Seraphon looked from her to the egg. 'Divine Starborne, we form of the waters, of the magic, of the will of the Masters. Only lesser beings arise from egg or womb.'

That's put me in my place, Perlo thought. Did that mean the Seraphon weren't really… alive, like some magical construct? She felt an acute stab of alienation, trying to understand life without something as intrinsic as family, children.

Out across the water, at the far extent of the light, something grander had fallen. Perlo glimpsed it between the crooked bars of the pillars. The bones heaped out of the murk, fossilised before their time by petrified condensation. Ribs thicker about than Perlo's arm, a serpentine spine that arched twenty feet before being lost to the pools. A half-drowned skull still bared eight-inch teeth at the world. The whole monster would have been able to look a giant in the eye, and probably take its head off too. She tried to imagine this whole fortress airborne and filled with living behemoths, swarming with busy Seraphon, and couldn't. Too much, too inhuman. Sights not meant for the eyes of a mere self-taught mage.

'I'm sorry,' she told Irixi again, as the creature set off once more. 'You'd have been better off with the Stormcast. At least he could have' – she managed a wretched laugh – 'lifted heavy things for you. I'm just a mage who's not allowed to use magic.'

It cocked an eye back at her. 'All follows the plan,' it repeated.

She couldn't see that she was part of any plan, right then. Other than Kenlo's plan to get rich, which would hardly make her seem more worthy to this creature.

Something moved, out in the dark. She heard the slop of thick water, and then a low, gurgling rumble.

'That's… one of your friends, right?' she whispered.

Irixi had gone very still, holding out the light. A mosaic of pools caught the crystal's gleam and multiplied it without illuminating anything. And then two of the reflections moved, and she realised they were eyes.

Another gruff croak, and a bulky, splay-limbed beast sluiced over a gnarled ridge of white roots and into sight. A lizard-thing, horse-sized and sluggish, its hide a splotchy spattering of grey and white. Along its back, a great spined fin rippled and waved.

'Flight is augured,' Irixi said quietly.

The thing's jaws looked dangerous enough, but it seemed very slow, laboriously hauling itself towards them one limb at a time, wheezing like Sergeant Lofus after a brisk morning run. It was, she thought, almost comical.

Irixi was already pattering away, though. Perlo's good sense told her to follow, but the bank gave under her again and she slid back down to the water's edge, and abruptly that big blunt snout didn't seem so funny. Rather than get caught by it as she fought the disintegrating slope, she ran along the water's edge, trying not to wince as eggshell and brittle bone gave under her boots.

She heard the lizard take a deep breath, *exactly* like Sergeant Lofus if you told him he had to run all the way back. Then there was a hiss and spatter. Something stung the back of her hand, and abruptly there were half a dozen smoking holes in her coat. The air reeked of preserving balm, the stuff alchemists used to keep their pickled specimens free from rot.

Ahead, Irixi turned and presented its staff, lifted so the crystal waved over Perlo's head. A bolt of indigo energy crackled from it, and she heard the monster bellow in rage and pain.

'I thought you said no magic!' she yelled as she reached it.

'*You* no magic, *I* always the magic!' Irixi snapped back. 'However *you* and *I* also now run.' The arcana had done little more than briefly chastise the beast. She heard it roar and slosh forwards in the water, scrabbling and flailing itself along.

They fled, Irixi and its light leading the way. Any hope for delicacy of step was long gone. Perlo sloshed through the water, trampled bones and even clambered over a great tessellated shell where some prodigious turtle-beast had made its last stand against mortality. The sound of the spitting monster grew further away, though she wasn't convinced it ever really gave up on them. Then Irixi found one of the more intact square pillars and threw itself down in front of a… well, a stump, Perlo saw. A blocky carving of something that had possessed a loop of serpentine body, though both head and tail end were long gone. There was a jade dish carved as being supported by that loop, though. Like a begging bowl, to the eyes of a human girl who'd grown up poor in Lethis. Or like something meant for offerings…?

For a moment all those stories about the lizard people were true, and she'd only been brought along for some barbaric sacrifice. Irixi even had a knife out, a piece of razory black stone with a hilt of worked gold that Kenlo would have killed for. But the Seraphon was pricking at its own arm, not randomly but in an exacting pattern, touching blood to the rim of the bowl as it croaked and hissed some rhythmic utterance in its own tongue.

For a second Perlo was just a human, using mundane eyes and preconceptions, seeing the barbaric, some heathen practice that might invite who-knew-what power into the world. Then her arcane training resurfaced, and she felt the *precision*, as though the entire edifice around them, even broken, teetered on a fulcrum, and here was where even a light touch might shift its balance. Abruptly all that stilled power pulsed, like blood when the heart beats. Perlo's own heart thrilled to it. *Life*, even here with Death's hand three-quarters closed about the place. *Life returning*, flowing stone to stone along ancient conduits.

'Blessed Quetzl, serendipitous patron,' Irixi said, for her benefit. 'Guardian of the ways, preserver of past wisdom, most fit to mediate with the powers of stillness and death, granting access to sacred lines of influence. You possess understanding?'

'Yes,' Perlo breathed. 'I understand.' And it was gone, that understanding, just a moment later. Gone but leaving a hollow in its shape, in her mind, that she could feel around the edges of. An alien mathematics of magic, as old to the aelves as aelven calculation was to humans. And yet she'd felt it wake and move all around them. It had spoken to her. To *her*, Perlo the poor student!

She was simultaneously awestruck, terrified, wildly excited. She had fought every living day for an understanding of the arcane, scrounged, skivvied for mages, stolen moments with their books. Learned no single grand discipline but a patchwork of whatever she could scavenge. Trained herself to make use of any kind of power that came her way, which meant here, now, even *this* inhuman legacy was merely *outside her grasp* rather than an outright impossibility.

'Yes, good.' The lizard mage lashed its tail. 'The path of augury carries us–'

'Upwards,' Perlo finished for it.

Irixi fixed her with a look. There'd been a battlemage who'd taken her on as apprentice for one campaigning season, so long as she'd washed his clothes and darned his socks. He'd had nothing but disdain for her, almost all that time, but right as they were about to part company – to mutual relief, by then – she'd finally mastered a shielding ward he'd been despairing of teaching to her. Cast it once and then, without any intervening step, been able to conjure it safely and at will. The grudging look of appreciation she'd had from the old man was mirrored precisely in Irixi's reptilian regard now.

A bass croak rumbled out of the dark behind them. Irixi wiped a little spare blood from its pierced arm and then indicated with its staff. The next column over had toppled into a neighbour, obliterating whatever effigy had stood at its base. The slope of carved stone led to a jagged, root-crawling gap in the ceiling. *Upwards*.

Irixi scrabbled to the top effortlessly, then paused, looking back to make sure she was following. *Like I'm its dog*. Letting her cudgel dangle from its wrist strap, Perlo struggled up the slanted stone, fingers digging into who knew what sacred engravings. She could sense the webwork of arcane lines up above, though. The level over the pools was rich with them, sluggishly returning to some flicker of life.

There were nodes, she could sense. Points where the lines within the structure – the *temple*, she understood – intersected and strengthened one another. Had the place been whole, the building would have sung like the strings of a harp to a mage's senses, a constant chorus of wonder that a trained caster might have tapped into for all manner of miracles. Now she felt broken ends, severed connections where sheared and slipped stone had broken the flow. The architecture had been integral to the magic, and now that architecture was strewn across the heart of this Shyishan forest.

They came out on an upper level that had mostly joined the pools beneath, the floor sagging and ragged, slumping into a patchwork of holes and piecemeal edges as though eaten away by insects. Above, the ceiling was bowed and segmented, each stone shifted out of place but somehow not falling on them. The walls were close, buckled so that the whole chamber was probably half of its intended height. There had once been rich decoration there – plates of black-and-green stone worked with gold – but they had shattered into razor slivers as the space had been crushed. Across a yawning gash in the floor, another shrine hung at the very edge of a peeling fringe of stone blocks, each one heavy enough to kill Perlo if it fell on her. Irixi leaping over to it caused the whole sagging carpet to shift further, dust and fragments falling away towards the still water below. There was no way Perlo was going to follow *that*.

The lizard mage examined the broken shrine critically. There was even less to it than the last. Whatever icon had adorned its face was beaten into scars and stumps. Perlo could sense the webwork of dormant connections leading off from it, but there was no way for Irixi to perform its rituals here. The thin fingers of its free hand explored the stone, searching for some intact stub that it could dot with its blood. Within the stone, inaccessible, Perlo felt the sleeping focus of… a god? Some lizard deity, sacred to them as Morrda was to the people of Lethis? She felt she was both right and wrong. A god, but also a manifestation of cosmic rules, a convenient face and label given to some specific means by which the realms revolved and interrelated.

The stones beneath Irixi shifted again and the lizard froze. Past the stump of shrine, Perlo saw gleams and glints shifting in the gloom, catching the crystal light. *More lizard monsters?* For a moment she even thought it was some impossible survivors from the crash, some ancient kin of Irixi's here to welcome their cousin. Then the low, long-tailed bodies crept closer, and she spat out, 'Rats! Run, Irixi!'

Cued by her yell, the Skaven swarmed forwards. A harsh violet flash crackled from staff and shrine, and a couple of blackened rat bodies were flung back. The others surged on, pushed by those behind them, unable to retreat even if they hadn't been eager for the kill. At least one lost its footing and fell squealing to the pools below. Irixi sprang away from the shrine, out into open space, and Perlo snagged the Seraphon's robe, bundling it to her. Her cudgel lashed out and the keenest rat was caught mid-leap, knocked back into the abyss.

She could feel the power of the place all around her. Irixi had said not to, but she drew on it anyway. Perhaps it would have ignored her, in its native state, but the cold breath of Shyish had infiltrated the temple over the aeons, and that was magic she was used to working with. A crackling violet darkness leapt from the stones around her, from her hand, from the pallid roots and crawling skull-backed bugs. She felt it clench inside her, inside her ribs. Abruptly she couldn't breathe, her heart was still, death flowed through her like acid.

The power leapt across three or four of the rats, not blasting them apart but making dust and bones of them, armour and weapons falling to rust. As though she'd conjured the immense age of her surroundings and gifted it all at once to her enemies. A feat her own meagre study could never have achieved, but she'd reached out to this place and explained what she wanted from it, and it had moved for her. The death in it had stirred, shuddering the very stones into new alignments to do her bidding.

She realised she was still not breathing, and that some part of her had no problem with that, caught up with the thrill of mastering death. The necromancer's path, which saw the witch hunters sent after you, or had you end up as some vampire's lackey. With supreme will, she dragged air in, felt her heart shudder and pulse. *Too much, O Sigmar, too much!* Abruptly she was terrified of the temple around her, simply because of what she might become in its embrace.

The Skaven had eddied back, but now they were being pricked forwards by their fellows again. She looked for Irixi, but the light of its staff was already receding back down towards the pools again.

Next second Irixi was running right back up, yellow eyes wide. Without a word it vaulted past Perlo, clean back over the gap and scrabbling at the crumbling stone edge before the shrine, right in the face of the startled Skaven.

'Follow!' it barked out, and actually ran at the rats, practically onto their blades. Like a pack of dogs confronted by a furious cat, they fell back, but it would only take one of them to…

Something rumbled, loud and low, at Perlo's heels. She yelped and made the jump from a standing start. Half a dozen massive blocks just fell away from the edge as she landed there, and she actually snagged the front of a Skaven's rotting cowl to keep herself from falling. For a moment the thing was squalling into her face, trying to get its teeth into her, and then she yanked hard. She went forward onto stones that weren't trying to part company with their neighbours. The rat lurched past her, and she heard a shriek as it vanished into the dark.

Then she and Irixi were right there in front of the rest of them, a good dozen hunched rodent figures staring at this unexpected gift. If they'd just wanted a couple of corpses as trophies, Perlo and Irixi would have been carved up and bludgeoned in moments. She saw them fumbling for cords and manacles, though, and that was surely worse. Everyone knew that prisoners of the rats could look forward to any number of horrifying torments.

The fin-backed lizard monster erupted from below, where Perlo had been standing, clawing up the slanted pillar with a supreme scrabbling effort. Seeing such a wealth of prey so close, it let out a shrill hiss and redoubled its speed to vault the gap.

Perlo grabbed Irixi, intending to just run. There was an electric moment of contact, as though she had thrust her hands into a fire – her physical senses registering the small reptile body but some spiritual part of her screaming *sacrilege* as though she'd laid hands on the bones of a martyr. She let go instantly, feeling the *wrongness* of the act. Instead, she charged the startled Skaven, bowled into them, giving Irixi space to get clear. Beneath her feet, the stones shifted even *before* the beast crashed down on them.

She got a solid blow of her cudgel across the nose of the keenest rodent, smacked away the reaching paws of another and just pushed on through, hoping there weren't another hundred of the vermin choking the passageway beyond. Behind her, the monster landed. Incredibly, the carpet of root-bound stone didn't give. A glance back showed the shrine plummeting to a final resting place, a scatter of rats displaced into the void. Then the monster opened its jaws and vomited forth a spray of clear liquid that spattered across the dense pack of Skaven.

She was expecting corrosive acid, but the influence of Shyish had crept into this beast too. The sharp scent of preservative filled the air and the rats seemed to wither and brown, shrivelling into leathery corpses as the liquid desiccated and mummified them. Then the monster was chomping on the withered remains, its tail and haunches hanging off the perilously leaning stones.

Perlo ran, following the bobbing light of Irixi's crystal. Distantly she could hear more shrilling, Skaven drawn by the commotion. She hoped the monster ate them all.

Ahead, the square corridor they were pelting down ended suddenly. Irixi didn't hesitate, following some internal map denied to Perlo. The lizard mage jumped out into space, and by then Perlo was running so fast that she couldn't have halted if she'd wanted to.

They tumbled out into a high, vast chamber. *The heart,* she thought. All those lines her arcane senses were informing her of, they wrapped themselves in a web about this one place. The sacred focus of the temple. So did that make this the altar of their greatest god, some lizard Sigmar? She didn't think so. More that the deities themselves were subordinate to some grander purpose this room embodied. A purpose as shattered and lost as every other part of the temple.

Irixi was standing, walking forwards with what Perlo felt was a reverent air. The room was a ruin. Much of the ceiling had come down in massive blocks, and parts of the floor had followed suit, leaving a patchwork of gaps to the darker, half-flooded levels below. The roots swarmed underfoot like a plague of pale serpents, and there were great outcroppings of fungus: fans, bulbous caps and growths like human fingers, all faintly luminous in a spectrum of purples and pale blues and green-whites, the shades of Shyish. Perlo could make out a high dais at one wall, and wondered if some lizard regent had ruled from this place, or a high priest given sermons to a scaly congregation of hundreds. Again, she knew she was wrong. The architecture informed her of sanctity, quiet contemplation, a space to concentrate thought and wisdom.

Irixi had approached one wall. There had been something set into it, extending beyond the reach of the light in all directions. A kind of frieze, Perlo guessed. Several jagged cracks cut across it, and falling rock had wiped most of it away and ground it to dust. Here and there, some ragged-edged sections remained, though. Flat shards of black glass, incised with fine carving. The stylised artistry spoke to her human eyes now. She saw lizard warriors on the march, a mountain split with a horned figure breaking out of it, a centipede of ribs and limb bones with a crowned skull head that she somehow understood to be a Seraphon depiction of the Lord of Death. But all orphaned pieces, scattered islands of lost meaning across the defaced mural.

Irixi made a whimpering sound. It was crouching on its haunches, staring upwards. A human might have fallen to their knees, to the same effect.

'Nine Flower Path,' the Seraphon told her. 'This you appreciate?'

Perlo shook her head helplessly.

'The Good Purpose, this to be restored, now you see it?'

'I don't even see how you could start… restoring,' she said helplessly.

'But *see!*' The Seraphon grabbed her arm, all its inscrutable calm gone, practically shaking her. 'See! See or be blind!' Actually beating its staff on the stone so that the light of the crystal flickered. Directing her to…

One surviving scrap of the frieze in particular. A figure standing side-on, as all these depictions were. A figure in a robe – and without a tail, she realised. The head was tilted back, and it still looked lizard-like, but she understood that was just because it had been carved by those for whom 'lizard' was an aesthetic baseline. Less snout, a fold over the mouth that might be a separate nose. Its arms were thrust up and forwards, as though offering something, but everything from its elbows on had been lost to time and the wreck.

Not a robe, a coat, and at the figure's belt, a blocky weapon with a studded head, because the ancient masons had known how to depict clubs.

Irixi struck at the stone again, staring at her, demanding that she *see*. And she saw. She saw the image through the stylistic conventions of its crafters. The currents of power infusing every stone taught her how to read it.

She made her own little whimpering sound, taking a step back. Looking up the ancient, ruined wall at her own image.

CHAPTER THIRTEEN

VAEL

The scout woman was trying to keep one eye on him and one on the Seraphon warrior, meaning she ended up sidestepping along like a crab.

'Your lordship,' she said, 'if I can ask, Sigmar sent you here to fight the lizards?'

Vael's stare probably looked as though he was offended by her curiosity. Inside he was just… blank, vacant. Sigmar had not sent him. He had begged to be sent. Sent here, because all along the barren shore of his memory it was the one landmark remaining, and all else just driftwood and pieces. He had come to find the man he'd been, back in his first forging. The hard-edged bastion Sigmar had made him into.

And yes, he had come to relive his clash with the Seraphon, but only because it was the ragged edge of his story and he needed to tie it off. And somehow there were Seraphon here to fight, and yet…

'We were never supposed to fight them,' he said hollowly. An answer not to her but to his own thoughts. 'The Everchosen's host was below us. It was the apex of Chaos. Mistakes were made. Even by gods.' He felt the desperate yearning in him, to call for the Seraphon to turn and fight him. To end it. Win a victory or a new death, and either option as satisfactory as the other. *Lost, I am lost.* And the Seraphon had seemed lost too. *The war against disorder has scattered us across time, disjointed us from who we were and where we were meant to be.* Each time a squad of Stormcasts was broken up and died separately, they were Reforged piecemeal, sometimes even thrown into battle with new faces, new comrades, rather than left to sit idle in the halls of Azyr. Into a world of fresh enemies and a geography rewritten by mortal hands. New cities, new banners, new allies, even as their memories were eroded away by a constant personal attrition. Vael had struggled, death after death, to hold on to why they fought, who against, who alongside, what was won, what lost. Impossible. No wonder that so many of his fellows, perhaps the whole of the first forging of the Hammers, had abandoned all attempt to make sense of the fight. They had become nothing more than Sigmar's lightning in human form, no questions and no tolerance for dissent, consigned to the Ruination chambers. That was what awaited Vael the moment he let go of these last scraps of remembrance.

Isn't it better than this agony and doubt? But hidden within that agony and doubt were the last scraps of the human Vael, who had spent his mortal blood in fighting Chaos. Who had been stolen from true death by Sigmar, and made into something that never truly died but lived less and less with each remaking.

Ahead, the Seraphon stopped and turned, seeming just as oppressed by its own thoughts. Beyond it, through the trees, Vael could make out a cluster of its fellows gathered about a dim crystal. The lesser kind were in the centre, huddled close in the chill night as though the glowing thing were a fire. A circle of the bigger warriors surrounded them, squatting on their haunches and staring dully out at the dark, spears and clubs sloped over their shoulders. Easy to read human dejection into them, and easy as well to mark how few they were. He reckoned a good half must have fallen in the ruin when the rats attacked.

'You… going to fight them all now, your lordship? One at a time or all at once?' The scout was looking at him warily.

Was he? The prospect had simplicity to recommend it, but no more. 'There would be no meaning,' Vael told her. Just as the fight aboard the flying temple had possessed no meaning. Just one mistake in the confusion of the great war against Chaos. How the Everchosen must have laughed.

'Only I was thinking,' the scout murmured, and a hideous shrilling went up throughout the trees. Abruptly there was motion everywhere, a furry, bristling tide. There were more Skaven abroad than the isolated patrols Vael and Stanner had been fighting. They had spotted the Seraphon's camp.

They came swarming out of the dark, and in the first instant they seemed to completely overrun the reptiles, who reacted slowly, torpid in the cold. A moment later the great warriors had risen up, rats clinging to them that stabbed and bit and shrieked as they were plucked off and savaged in lizard jaws. The biggest warrior – Vael's nemesis, whom they'd followed here – let out a monstrous roar and lumbered into the fray, and Vael found himself following up automatically. As though the creature were his squadmate, his fellow champion of Sigmar. His feet, following some memory of their own, fighting some battle lost to the rest of him.

Stanner's crossbow snapped on one side, impossible to miss such a dense host of ratfolk as they swarmed the camp. The melee came down to teeth and claws on both sides as the smaller lizards tried to get out from the press to use their javelins and blowpipes.

Vael and the lizard champion tore into the rat pack together, club and hammer almost in sync. Lightning crackled and flared where he struck, and stabbed out from his eyes and the scars on his face. The Skaven fell back from him; their spears and crooked swords scraped from his mail and from the Seraphon's scaled hide. They were two juggernauts, wading into the mass of rats, scions of Order, indomitable.

Then one of the Skaven was on Vael's shoulders, fingers hooked about one pauldron as it sawed at his neck. He felt the edge grate across the scales of his mail shirt as the creature lurched left and right to evade his grasping hand. Its fur was standing out straight and dancing with blue fire, but it was viciously determined, refusing to be thrown off. A thrust of its blade opened a gash across his temple that bled blue light.

Vael lurched sideways as a new weight landed on his back. Another rat, surely. They were going to drag him down by sheer numbers. The first rat got another glancing blow across his brow and he went down, overburdened, hammer spinning from his grip. Spitting oaths, he tried to lever himself up and saw the point of the rat's blade right before his face, driving for his eye.

So be it. He feared the pain less than what the Reforging would take from him. It was the wounds Sigmar dealt that stayed with you from life to life.

The thing still on his back lunged forwards. He saw a reptile head jut into his eyeline, jaws open. A tongue flicked out, a foot's length of it, impacting straight into the rat's left eye. It squealed, and then the tongue snapped back into the lizard's jaws, leaving only a bloody socket in its wake. Kicking off from Vael's back, the little Seraphon leapt on the shrieking rat, one hand punching forwards with a fistful of dark needles. It drove them into the Skaven's throat with brutal efficiency, one turreted eye tilted to see if Vael was going to be trouble. A moment later it was gone. Not run off, just… faded into the general fray, impossible to keep track of.

Vael lurched to his feet, finding his hammer. His wounds burned, cauterising themselves with the fire of his blood. He felt detached from the fight, not sure if what he'd just seen was even real.

'Your lordship!' It was the scout, at his elbow again as she reloaded her crossbow. 'They're going, the rats are, but they're not going far. What's the plan?'

Her faith that he had one was one more burden. And if it had just been him then the plan would have been, *Fight until I die, after which it's in Sigmar's hands.* Easy for him to throw his life away. But if the rats killed this woman, or the Seraphon, there would be no Reforging for them.

He stared at her, and saw the exact moment when she understood he had no idea at all.

She nodded, as though the revelation was a kind of permission. The Seraphon had indeed thrown the Skaven back into the trees, but Vael could hear lots of chittering out there as the creatures regained their fickle courage.

'Listen here,' Stanner said urgently. 'Any of you speak a word of a decent language?'

One of the smaller kind stepped forwards. 'Ape-speak we hear,' it said. 'What does it speak, ape-speaker?'

The scout just nodded at that. 'Ape says this,' she told them. 'Rats're coming back. Stay here, your skins are cloaks and boots by morning. Our camp's better than this. You want to live, stick with us. We'll mess 'em up together.' That many words seemed to exhaust her. 'Or not,' she added. 'However you want.'

There was a lot of hissing and clicking between the Seraphon, as Vael watched furtive movement within the trees. Then the big one, their leader, walked up and pushed at his shoulder. Pushed hard, enough to topple a smaller man, and Vael thought, *So we do fight, then?* And knew a curious kind of relief that the decision had been made for him. But the lizard warrior wasn't raising its club, and he wondered if, instead, that hard shove was just a greeting amongst them. A handshake, a cheery salute.

'Gokumet says, you do what, Golden One?' said the little lizard interpreter.

Vael looked from one reptile face to the other. 'What?' he asked.

'You stand, you fight, all stand. To ape camp you go, also we go. Gokumet says, *you* do what?'

'Why?' Vael asked. *Gokumet.* His nemesis had a name.

'Gokumet, you he knows. Your flesh in his teeth,' the interpreter said.

'Your *what*?' Stanner hissed, and Vael found he was smiling at a joke that he shared with the Seraphon, that the human would never understand. Suddenly, he didn't want them all just to die here fighting rats, at night in this morbid forest. Let their final battle at least be in Shyish's pale daylight. Let them see one another clearly when the end came.

'We go,' he said. If there were tears in his eyes then they were lost in the lightning.

The Skaven tried another attack as they were moving out, but Vael and Gokumet held the rear as Stanner led the Seraphon away. Faced with the pair of them, fighting in lockstep, the rats' nerve broke again and they fell back. And it was good. Like fighting alongside his fellows in Sigmar's service. Good to look sidelong and see that brutal reptile profile, the glimmer of its scales. *You and I will fight, and you or I will die, but for now we will kill these servants of Chaos together.* Vael the man and Vael the Stormcast in momentary harmony.

Kenlo's people weren't expecting the reinforcements Stanner led to them. Vael found the whole business grimly amusing. The first sentries' challenges, followed by an escalating series of panicked exclamations as the entire reptilian convoy came into sight. The scout's hissed explanations, and the marching Seraphon simply refusing to stop and be challenged, until it was very nearly a whole new fight right there and then. Vael put himself between them, though, just holding his arms out as though restraining children, and by then Stanner had explained how the Skaven had been on the prowl out there. No news to Kenlo and the others, as it turned out, because they'd already turned away one attack by the rats.

They had a fire, too. The wood of Shyish burned with phantom flames of pale green and violet, casting no healthy light. It gave enough heat for the smaller Seraphon, though, who ended up clustered near it and elbowing the Steelhelms out of the way. Their interpreter was not endearing itself to anyone by calling them all apes, either. The alliance of convenience was off to a rocky start.

'But they're good for fighting rats, you say?' Kenlo noted. He and Stanner were sitting against a tree, and Vael lowered himself down to join them.

'They are warriors of Order. The rats are their enemies since the earliest days,' Vael said. He frowned at the thought: a fragment of memory, something he'd been told by someone wiser.

'Well then,' Kenlo said, 'I don't know that I'd have gone recruiting for them myself, but we can use them now they're here, lord. First light we're into the ruins and finding Perlo.'

'You think she lives?' Vael asked. An innocent enough question inside his head, but Kenlo tensed, hand clenched about the haft of his axe.

'She is my sister,' he spat. 'She can look after herself. She's fine. We'll find her. Find her, fill our bags, then get out, and the lizards and rats can fight over this cursed place forever for all I care.'

Stanner looked away, saying nothing. *She doesn't believe the mage lives either,* Vael understood. And he could see that the decent thing to do would be to tell Kenlo that, yes, obviously Perlo was fine and they'd somehow just chance across her in all the ruins, but neither he nor the scout had that kind of decency in them.

There was another burst of squabbling near the fire, as Sergeant Lofus tried to evict a couple of the lizards so he could sit down.

'What're they even here for?' Kenlo complained.

'This is their place,' Vael said.

'What, *now*? When our father came through he didn't say anything about the place crawling with lizards! Why now? Hey, you, the talker. You talk to me?'

The interpreter looked over. 'Apes need not the warmth,' it complained. 'The selfishness of apes shows no respect for need.'

'I see why they made that one the diplomat,' Kenlo muttered to himself. 'What are your people here for?' he said out loud. 'You came to fight the rats?'

'Irixi Starseer has come for the Good Purpose, proclaimed by Sek'atta Mage-Priest,' the interpreter said. 'Purpose beyond the wisdom of apes.' Then another lizard was at its shoulder – suddenly enough that all of them started. The creature with the long tongue and the pivoting eyes that Vael had seen during the fight. He watched, fascinated, as the firelight chased across its skin and was chased in turn by a wave of swirling pattern, the outlines of the creature simultaneously there and not there as though it were made of smoke.

It flashed angry patterns at the translator, ending with a hiss that was plainly a threat. The interpreter flinched and ducked its head, flushing dark.

'Someone got told off,' Stanner remarked quietly. It was the first suggestion of disagreement he'd seen between the Seraphon. Then she frowned. 'What's that light?'

She wasn't the only one to have noticed it. A pale indigo radiance was forming in the air above the fire. Steelhelms leapt up, scrabbling for their shields and weapons, but the Seraphon were all attentively still.

'Hold!' Vael called. From a dim glow, the light stretched and fragmented, forming a constellation of star-motes that shaped a head. For a moment it was a lizard head, crowned with two feathers. Blocky and stylised but animated, moving as though it were living. Pictograms bloomed and faded around the image.

'What is this?' Kenlo demanded, but even as he spoke, the image broke apart into firefly motes and then reformed: a human-seeming visage, as though some lizard artist had tried to capture Perlo's likeness.

'Kenlo?' Her voice echoed to them as though from some vast chasm. 'We're in trouble. You have to come and get us.'

CHAPTER FOURTEEN

IRIXI

The human, Perlo, made sounds again. By now, Irixi was familiar enough with the rhythms and fluting of its voice to understand the meaning: 'It's me. How is it me?'

And it was, and the fact that human eyes had recognised the fact showed the wisdom and foresight of the original frieze-carvers because Irixi could recognise the effort that had gone into making the image as human-like as possible, pushing the boundaries of the accepted sacred form. When the ancient mage-priests had dreamed this vision and decreed it to be set down for posterity, they had known that it was important even a human could interpret this specific panel.

What, then, was the carved Perlo proffering, that the ruin of the temple had erased? Irixi felt a spike of hope: perhaps this panel depicted the very moment that the carving itself was restored. Why else would events have conspired to place humans in the ruin of the *Wings of Serendipitous Fire* unless their presence could assist in Irixi's mission? Of course the full record of the Nine Orchid Path included the story of its own restoration. Irixi felt a flutter of awe in its heart at the magnificent prescience of the Old Ones.

Now was the time to explain. Perlo was a part of the Nine Orchid visions, and so the human must be made to understand.

'You must know that in the dawn of time the Old Ones foresaw the rise of Chaos and the disordering of the cosmos,' Irixi began, because surely even infant humans were taught as much. Perlo was listening attentively, face screwed up in concentration, doing a human's best to grasp the concepts. That was gratifying.

'The Old Ones formulated a plan by which the cosmos could be restored to its proper order, all things in their place.' Irixi made the proper gesture of hands, crest and tail, to indicate the supreme desirability of such a state. Lost on Perlo, but it was force of habit by now. 'Then they passed the responsibility of carrying out the plan to their greatest servants, the supreme arcane authorities of the universe, the Starmasters, of that exalted people whom some call slann.' Irixi searched the human's face and body for signs of understanding. Perlo was doing its best, the Starseer judged, which would have to suffice.

'All forms of life have their role in the plan,' it explained magnanimously. 'Of course, we Seraphon are to be trusted with the most important elements, but other servants of Order will play their parts, the aelves, the duardin, the humans. When the plan calls for some obstruction to be torn down, that is why there are orruks and ogors in the realms. When something must be preserved in cold stillness, the forces of Death shall play their role. Sometimes even the agents of Chaos itself shall take a hand in their own downfall, so all-encompassing is the plan of the Old Ones.' Irixi hoped Perlo understood the great honour paid to all humanity by being permitted to play its part.

'Alas, the machinations of Chaos, the tides of strife and time, mean that much of the plan has been obscured,' it went on. This was how one taught skinks new from the waters, those who would in time progress into the study of such things. 'To enact its details, we must uncover each part of it and piece together the whole. In such a way the cosmos shall be returned to its proper order. Here in this chamber was once recorded one small loop of the coils of prophecy, known to us as the Nine Orchid Path. Over time, all other record of this wisdom has been taken from us, but here it is preserved.'

Perlo blinked. For a moment Irixi thought that the whole exercise had been for nothing, and that human minds were simply not acute enough to grasp the breadth of the Old Ones' foresight. But then the human said, 'But it… hasn't been preserved.'

Irixi felt a weird pride, as if some skink fresh from the pools had piped up with some sensible words before its time. 'That is why the beneficent Sek'atta, wise beyond comprehension, has sent me. That is the task you have been placed here to assist with. We are to restore the record of prophecy that once stood here, so that our understanding of the Great Plan may be made more complete.'

'But…' Perlo looked about at the utter ruin of the chamber. The carven obsidian of the prophecy frieze, which was now mostly shards beneath their feet. 'You can't mean… just sort all the pieces and put it back together? That would take a thousand years!'

'What are years for, if not to dedicate to the plan?' Irixi asked. The Starseer wasn't actually sure what humans *did* with the little time they had, but surely it couldn't be *that* important compared to restoring the entire cosmos. 'But there are other ways. Come, we must–'

A sound came to them, from quite close by. A muted, metallic *clonk*. Not familiar. Not of the ruins. Irixi turned.

The Skaven with the bell looked almost embarrassed. It had a hand to the clapper, stilling the motion. The other Skaven – a whole bristling host of them – had frozen at the sound. They had been creeping up in the dark all this time, following the crystal's light and Irixi's voice.

Perlo spat a human word that must have been a curse.

The tide of rats, discovered, surged forwards. Irixi had the arcane strands of their surroundings at its claw-tips, though. Whilst much of the ceiling had come down, there were perilously balanced stones above them that yet owed a duty to the Great Plan. A few words of entreaty and they fell, crashing down amongst the rats and sending them scattering in all directions. At the same time Perlo dropped to a knee, digging fingers into the mounded debris of the ground. Beneath the Skaven's feet, the webwork of roots writhed, winding about rat feet and ankles.

'Run!' the human said, following its own suggestion. The pair of them dashed across the chamber, but Irixi's light picked out a host of beady little rat eyes there as well, and at least one much larger form looming from the shadows. The Skaven were all around them.

One of the rats leapt out of the dark and bowled the Starseer over. Instantly there were more, the fleetest, the most eager. Irixi felt teeth worrying at its robes, claws scraping its scales. Perlo lashed at them, first with the club, and then a blunt scouring of magic like caustic salts that withered their rat bodies. Although it was not becoming for a Starseer, Irixi got its own jaws into the neck of the most aggressive of them, grinding small teeth into its throat until it let go. Perlo tried to haul the skink away, but more rats were scrabbling at them with their unclean hands. Irixi felt a fierce stab of pain as one got its teeth hooked into the Starseer's flesh.

A moment of regret. A mark of shame to be worn for many moons.

Irixi was abruptly free, dragged along by Perlo, retreating from each new front of rats that scurried out of the dark. Behind them, a writhing lizard tail whipped back and forth in the jaws of a rat, which spat it out disgustedly. Irixi felt a little blood leak from the stump before the vessels sealed themselves. Abruptly its balance was off, constantly pitching forwards like an animal. Leaning heavily on Perlo, the Starseer shoved the human towards the dais.

Its heart was in its mouth, because it was about to enact a piece of sacrilege. Upon its return to the *Celestial Eye*, prostrate before the mage-priest, Irixi would beg his forgiveness and only hope that necessity blunted the ferocity of the penance to be carried out. For now, the Starmaster's instrument must live so that the prophecy could be restored. If Sek'atta struck his servant dead once the task was done, that would be a satisfactory and appropriate conclusion.

Irixi scrambled up the steps of the dais, Perlo a heartbeat behind and the rats scurrying right after, chittering and screeching in their hunger for blood. When the *Wings of Serendipitous Fire* had been whole, this was where Sek'atta himself had sat, pondering the intricacies of the Nine Orchid Path. It was not fit for a mere Starseer to defile the podium with its meagre presence, but the Starmaster had left behind something that yet held his ancient power.

Not a weapon – no blasting rod or mighty sceptre. Just a convenience and comfort for the Old Ones' greatest servant. There, lying at an angle and scarred by falling debris, was Sek'atta's throne. A wide stone seat, the back worked into a great fan of stylised feathers ornamented with topaz and jade and turquoise like the spread wings of Coatl. Irixi leapt up to it and dragged Perlo after, already reaching for the precise series of arcane conduits within the stone.

The Skaven surged forwards, a tide of blades, teeth, greasy fur and mad little eyes. The worst filth of Chaos, the gnawing corruption who undermined the precise architecture of the plan with their mindless burrowing. The most despised enemy of the Seraphon. Surely Sek'atta would forgive this theft of his privilege?

Perlo let out a yell of surprise as the throne lifted into the air, the ancient arcane modulators within renegotiating its proper place in the world. From fallen masonry to floating podium, a fitting seat for a great mage-priest. The keenest of the Skaven scrabbled at the lip of the seat and arms, snarling and frothing as they tried to retain their hold. Perlo lashed at them with its cudgel, sending them tumbling away.

For a moment the throne tilted and trembled in the air, about to crash down just as precipitately, but then Irixi had completed the proper reverences – hurriedly and in its head, rather than properly acted out and spoken, but needs must – and the throne renewed its connection to the greater channels of power across the shattered temple. A woefully incomplete network, but enough to keep them aloft. And enough to…

Below, the Skaven had been clambering one atop another, fighting each other to reach their prey. Abruptly, a pinkish globe of power crackled into being all around the throne. The most basic protection that a mage-priest could call upon, to exclude distractions that might disturb their placid contemplation. Enough to incinerate the most eager of the ratfolk who tried to leap past its borders, though, and that in turn was sufficient to discourage the rest. The Skaven fell back in a circle about the steps of the dais, staring upwards. A few slung stones or threw filth, but the barrier turned their missiles back with ease.

Perlo sagged back, staring down at them. The rats weren't going anywhere. The light of the barrier reflected in dozens of pairs of bulging rodent eyes.

'How long can you keep this up?' the human asked.

The Starseer thought about explaining that this was no Starseer's working, that the ancient workings of Sek'atta within throne and temple remained true to their ancient covenant with the realms – and incidentally allowed them this respite. It seemed too complex a matter to reduce to human terms. And also Irixi didn't *know* how long, honestly. The temple was fractured in so many ways. It could only hope the barrier would remain for long enough that its task could be fulfilled. Which would be easiest to accomplish if it and this human weren't trapped within the midst of a host of Skaven.

Gokumet and the bodyguard must be out there on the surface. Perhaps Irixi could find a connection to them. Maddeningly, it could detect their presence, like a dim pressure out past the rubble fringes of the wreck. A clenched fist of Order, embattled by Death and Chaos but holding out. None of the lines of power it could touch led to them, though. Irixi could not bridge the gap to establish a link. *Gokumet!* it tried, but it lacked sufficient connection. There was none amongst the guard who had come from the same pool, or had any sympathetic bond that a Starseer might exploit.

Yet there was something. The broken shell of the temple was a kind of ear, which a deft Starseer might use to listen to the ebb and flow of realmic power, to hear the fine, high sound of intact lines of connection. In amongst the great sombre susurrus of Shyish itself, gnawed at by the corrosive static of the Skaven presence, Irixi could detect a single fragile thread from *here* to…

'You have a broodmate within your bodyguard,' it said.

Perlo frowned. Beyond the barrier, the Skaven seethed and squabbled.

'You have… a fellow from the same birthing, a pool-sibling.' Human life cycles were different, of course, messy and unhygienic. 'Family, that is what you call it.'

The human's eyes went wide. 'Kenlo? My brother? What about him?'

Irixi couldn't remember what *brother* actually denoted, in human relationships. It was enough, though. They were connected.

The Starseer murmured a proper prayer to Tepok, who saw clearly how the cosmos was ordered, and Quetzl, whose bright wings preserved and protected the connections between kin. Like an architect constructing an edifice, Irixi fitted the invocations together, then joined Sotek, the Serpent, who had ever been the enemy of rats, and whose twisting path could circumvent all obstacles. For a brief moment, fatigue and fear rose at the sheer enormity of ever accomplishing this mission, and the throne trembled, the barrier flickering. There was strength to be taken from the wisdom of Sek'atta, though, who would not have entrusted his servant with a task beyond its powers. Irixi reached out and found the node of connection that was Perlo, a curious muddle of powers, Hysh and Shyish and a melange of other lores all smudged together, and followed it to…

The throne hummed with power, for a moment as balanced and content as though its true master sat in it, and a disc of pale light swirled into being before them. Through it, picked out in a spectral tracery, were human faces. Perlo gasped in recognition.

'Speak,' Irixi directed. 'Instruct your guard.' Marvelling again at the completeness of the Old Ones' plan, for beyond the humans could be seen familiar faces: Gokumet, Oaxmal, ready to obey.

Perlo began speaking urgently, telling its followers what they had to do.

In the darkness around them, the rats watched keenly, more of them now, waiting with a patience Irixi didn't like.

CHAPTER FIFTEEN

OAXMAL

That morning Oaxmal had opened its eyes to the lacklustre dawn and rummaged in its bag for a fresh frog, a bright one of black and angry red, the colours of Huanchi. Dispatching the frog with the correct prayers, it tied the expired amphibian to the cord of its belt and filled the creature's open mouth with fresh darts, letting each steep in the curdling venom of the creature's flesh. Each one lethal from a scratch, at least to a rat. Or a human. That done, Oaxmal had left the camp to do its job, wondering if today would see its long-overdue death.

It was the last of its clutch, because they had been the tip of the javelin since they came of age. A costly currency spent by the *Celestial Eye of Tepok* when presented with something that the temple's regular *eyes* couldn't see. Tip of the javelin, not the spear, because their role was to land deep within the midst of the enemy to scout, not merely jab about its edges. Oaxmal and its Chameleon siblings were hunters of relics and foes both, the stealthiest of all things that crept on a scaled belly.

Irixi's bodyguard and the mob of humans were behind, waiting. Oaxmal was already deep into the ruins of the dead temple, investigating each pit and crevice, learning the land. Learning a way *down*. Irixi was below, in the earth, and so were many of the Skaven, always happiest in burrows and holes. Oaxmal was more than happy to slither its way in and kill them there. Each death a sacrifice to Huanchi, the Jaguar. Only a shame the rats were such unworthy prey.

Oaxmal had worked with its siblings, back when they had lived. One by one Sek'atta's tasks had seen them fall, each one a necessary sacrifice. Until Oaxmal worked alone, knowing only the silence and the stillness and the sudden strike.

It had grown used to solitude. Now it had a shadow. Oaxmal's skin had argued against it, but the humans wouldn't trust Seraphon scouting, more fools they. They had given it one of their own to follow in Oaxmal's noiseless footsteps. And while Oaxmal had chided the speaker, Zitzel, for calling them apes to their ape faces, being shackled to one while on the hunt was…

Should have been a hindrance, or else perhaps a distraction. Lose the human in the stones, let its blundering draw the rats, sneak past behind them to the buried places. But thus far the human hadn't been lost. Had trod in Oaxmal's shadow with only a little scuff and scrape of its shod feet. When they had found a sullen pair of rats keeping watch from atop a broken pillar, there had even been a moment when Oaxmal had taken out its blowpipe, and the human had followed suit with its own weapon, the device like a little bow on a stick. They had struck together, the envenomed dart and the little javelin arrow each finding their mark, the rats toppling from their roost with no more sound than the wet impact of their corpses on the stones.

Oaxmal padded forwards, step and pause, step and pause, a rhythmless, swaying advance that would look like shadows and the breeze to any watcher. When it took one of the bodies, the human had the other and they hauled both into cover. The rats were an unruly presence. They'd think their sentries had grown bored, perhaps.

The first descent into the ruin met only with root growth and fallen stone, the interior structure of the temple quite collapsed. The human was already pulling back before Oaxmal. Its eyes weren't so good in the dark, but it had a little lantern it could open and close, lit by a shard of glowing realmstone: smokeless, scentless, absolutely dark when its cover was down. A toy Oaxmal admired.

There was a big pack of rats in the centre of the ruins, two score at least, with a pair of the huge rat-Kroxigor roaming restlessly around. Oaxmal noted their leaders: rats with crested helms and the pick of their ragged armour. There were others in grey robes, too, who had authority: the plague mystics. Oaxmal had killed them before. Least favourite of all its past prey, if only because of the putrefying stink and taste of them. Better to be a human with a dull nose and tongue.

On their third excursion below ground they found a network of slanting, crazed passageways big enough for a saurus. Venturing forwards a few steps at a time, hearing the chitter and yip of rats ahead and all around. Each temple-ship was different, but Oaxmal had explored several, whole and ruined, and guided its companion on a crooked path towards the heart. The chamber of meditation, sacred place of worship and prophecy. Profaned now, ruined and then befouled by the rats, but easy enough to find an intact path leading to it.

They stayed there, watching, for a handful of heartbeats, Oaxmal and the human hunter. There was the radiant sphere of divine protection, and within it Irixi. And the human mage, if that was important, but Irixi at least. Sitting awkwardly, short a tail. And obviously Oaxmal knew only profound respect for all Starseers and would never find such discomfort a little amusing, in a skink who had spent its whole life being tended to hand and foot.

Oaxmal cocked an eye at its companion. The human met its gaze and nodded. Around the enthroned Starseer was a whole other host of Skaven: monks, armoured warriors and a festering horde of vermin rabble. The rank stench of them was like bile in the mouth.

Carefully, they withdrew and traced a course back to the surface, then back to the camp, killing every watching rat they could find on the way.

KENLO

Stanner's report was typically laconic. Yes, they'd laid eyes on Perlo. Yes, they could get in, even Vael and the big lizard lads. The scout laid out a roundabout route through the ruins that would avoid the main rat camp up above, but once they were down below, the alarm would be sounded sooner or later. No way to just sneak Perlo out under the rodents' noses.

'We're going to need a rearguard to hold the entrance,' he told Lofus.

'Fusils plus a handful of shields to back them,' the sergeant said.

'You do it,' Kenlo said. 'We'll let the lizards be the vanguard. Probably my lord champion as well, not like we could stop him. You hold up top and I'll run things below.'

There was a little relief in Lofus' face, not a man fond of enclosed spaces. 'Right you are, quartermaster.'

The lizard interpreter had its reptilian bestiary lined up and ready to go, the big warriors and the little ones. Kenlo stared sourly at them. 'Will you stand alongside us, or will you just charge in there?'

'Irixi Starseer shall be brought out of chaos, above all,' the creature informed him. 'No purpose greater.'

'Keep telling yourself that,' Kenlo muttered. *And hold out, Perlo. Just keep making that magic happen, however you're doing it.* 'Right.' He checked the mechanism of his pistol, then loaded it. 'We go in, we get them, we get out. No human left behind, but nobody better *dawdle*, right?'

A chorus of muttered agreement. They were scared, and it was a good job they'd all had their arses saved by Perlo's magecraft at one time or another or he might be facing some mutiny over this. His sister had proved herself on the battle-line, though. They all owed her.

'Let's go,' Vael said, and suited actions to words. A moment later they were all at his back: Stormcast, Steelhelms, Seraphon and all.

Stanner guided them through the ruins, constantly vanishing off into the maze of fractured stonework and then ghosting out in front of them again, warning of sentries or unsafe ground. The high-pitched clamour of the Skaven camp was loud as sacrilege across the ruin, and Kenlo ground his teeth, imagining the rats pillaging the best of the treasure from the place. *His* treasure, the trove his father had found a fraction of all those years ago, and squandered his share of. Well, when Perlo was back with them, maybe they could throw the last of the lizards at the rats and then fill their boots while the creatures fought one another. That sounded like his kind of plan.

Speaking of plans, this particular scheme was going perfectly right up until the moment they found the root-edged sinkhole Stanner had picked for them to descend into, to discover the Skaven had found it first.

They came out just as Kenlo was about to go in: a dozen rats, and the foremost couple wearing banded steel mail that had actually been halfway taken care of. For a second everyone just stood and stared. Then one of the rats let out a keening screech and the big lizard warrior bellowed back and they were at each other in a fury.

GOKUMET

This was what Gokumet understood.

The scouts and the lesser creatures melted away as the Skaven rushed headlong. Gokumet rammed its shield forwards, taking the lead rat's pike with so much force the weapon's shaft splintered. The starmetal club came down hard, stone teeth hooking the plates of the Skaven's armour and tearing them from their leather backing one after another, like unshelling a crab. Satisfying.

The teeth of the club were still snagged in the rat's armour and flesh. Not a problem but leverage. Gokumet hauled the creature to itself, took the blow of a pike shaft across the thick scales of its shoulder and closed its jaws about the Skaven's head, buckling the rat's helm, snapping the crest from it, feeling the narrow skull give beneath its teeth. Satisfying. Then the club was free to smash a shield. Irixi Starseer was below. Gokumet would save its leader. At last the champion knew what was going on.

At its side, the Golden One was fighting. Not like a fellow saurus, the cold fire and steady advance into the teeth of the enemy. The Golden One fought like someone trying to die. Not even fighting to win, save the lightning that moved it would not let it just bare its throat to the teeth of the rats. The Stormcast threw itself at their blades as though cursing the strength of its own mail. As though daring them to wound it. Gokumet knew desperation, but that was the last of all resorts for the Seraphon. If Irixi was dead, and if the others were dead, and if Sek'atta cast his servant off and if the balm of the gods was withheld, then Gokumet might have nothing but hollowness left in its heart. *Then* it would give itself to despair and fight like the Golden One. When there was no more to it than which death might be won.

Die, then. But the Golden One *had* died. Gokumet had killed it.

The pair of them shoved forwards, forcing the rats back down into their hole, hammer and club like two sticks beating the same drum. Gokumet felt teeth, claws and blades try its shield and hide, drawing no more than a little blood. Then another pike lanced out from the pack of them, piercing the skin of its chest, skidding off bony nodules beneath. The pain was distant, because when saurus fought, the pain could wait. The champion lunged forwards and took the pike in its teeth, trying to break the shaft. The Golden One paused in its beating, swung sideways to smash the weapon, then drove onwards again. Blue-white fire lit their way as they chased the rats all the way back down into the depths.

The rats made a stand there, where the stone chambers widened. Shields on shields, and spears over them. In the dark, in a corner, even rats could be fierce. Gokumet appreciated that. The grind and shove of shield against shield was something it understood.

For a moment the bottleneck of Skaven held the champion and the Golden One both, cowering beneath the blows but digging in, stabbing over and under and around the rough wood of their shields. Gokumet took a broad, shallow slash to the leg, a gouge to the arm, pushing the pain away until there was time to feel it. The Golden One lost a hip-plate entirely, hacked away and straps severed. Another rat was digging behind the man's leg armour, working a dagger under the plates. Gokumet stamped down on the creature, clawed foot raking, feeling bones crunch. Satisfying.

Then Oaxmal and the skinks had found a way round and come at the rats from behind. Darts and javelins whispered out of the dark and the rat line gave, each rodent scrambling for its own life, so none of them lived. None escaped to fetch more or give warning. Yet the sound of the fight must have pricked up dozens of rat ears here in the depths. It was time to move forwards. Time to save Irixi.

STANNER

She was ranging ahead of the shields again, her proper place. Just her and the lizard whose skin shifted like smoke. She'd been properly spooked at first, working alongside the thing. Just appeared and disappeared like a conjured daemon. Except it was just a sneak.

A good sneak, but she knew sneaking. Her eyes had grown used to looking for it, parsing its shape from the background. The little frog it had with it helped, a marker for her to pick out the rest of it. The frog full of needles, weirdly amusing until you saw what those needles *did* to the lizard's victims.

Stanner didn't have those kind of lizard tricks on her side, but she'd been doing this for good chunk of her life. That was the thing about ranging ahead of the Dawnbringer Crusades or scouring a city's hinterlands for enemies. You had yourself and your weapons. There had been a dog once. Arnulf, a mongrel hound who'd been gentle as kittens with her and savage as Sigmar with any grot or orruk he could get his teeth into. He'd given his life for her, in the end. Practically eviscerated a big brute of an ogor that had her on the ground. Wouldn't give up, fought with bloody jaws until the hulking brute had finally got his hands on the mutt and crushed. Giving her the chance to reload her bow and put a bolt in its eye to finish it off. Arnulf's death had hit her harder than the loss of any human she'd ever known. He was the only thing in all the realms she really missed.

She might miss this lizard when all this was done. It was a handy creature to have alongside you. And Arnulf had been sharp, followed her hand signals and always known the score, but this lizard was teaching *her* tricks.

The weird mishmash shield-wall was following up behind them, making about as good a pace as they could. Amazing Kenlo hadn't stabbed one of the lizards or that big scaly monster hadn't eaten someone. Once Perlo was back with them, Stanner reckoned it was going to happen one way or another. Not like there was any love lost there. Allies of convenience only.

Ahead of her, the smoke-skinned lizard stopped, one eye swivelling back to look at her, the other still on the tunnel ahead. *That* was a handy little trick as well. Be a grand thing for Stanner to be able to do, save they'd probably burn her as Chaos-touched if she managed it. She didn't chuckle – unprofessional, and she wasn't the chuckling sort – but a little dart of humour jabbed at her.

They were close to the big room where the ring of rats had been camped about Perlo's magic shield. The squad of rats they'd just annihilated seemed to have been the only sentries, and the sound of the fighting had somehow not drawn another score of rodent warriors out from the camp. All to the good.

She thought so, anyway. That it just meant the rats weren't keeping a decent guard. She hadn't thought that they might just have more important things to be doing.

The sound of dull bells echoed to them as they drew close. Small wonder the fighting hadn't tipped off any ears; they were having a celebration over something. The lizard scout crept to the jagged fissure in the stone which gave on to the chamber, eyes narrowing against the pale radiance of the magic shield that bathed everything within. It went still, and a sequence of colours moved across the side of its body facing Stanner. Reds and oranges and blacks, the warning stripes of a poisonous animal.

Stanner crept on her belly until she could see. And swore inwardly, eyes wide. The rats had been busy. Mostly they'd been busy calling in all their friends and relations.

There must have been twice as many Skaven down below. The newcomers were mostly the grey-robed, bandaged-up monks that every follower of Sigmar had learned to despise. Plague-bringers, poison-spreaders, fanatics, and very obviously in charge down there. All the others, the rabble of shield-bearers, were bowing and scraping before them, and any who were slow about it got a slap from the half a dozen ogor-rats who'd turned up as well. One in particular was bigger than the rest – bigger in the massively bulked-out body, anyway, though the rodent head almost lost between its shoulders was the usual size, wildly out of proportion. There was a wooden frame about its shoulders, and on its back…

It should have seemed ridiculous, like a baby being carried about on a hulking mother's back. Instead, the arrangement had the weird dignity of a high priest in a pulpit. Up on the great ogor-rat's back was a Skaven almost the size of a human, swathed in layers of rotting grey cloth, gripping the rail with one hand as it lurched about, chittering and waving a staff in pestilent benediction. A brass thurible swung from the stave's end, leaving circling trails of greenish smoke that hung heavy in the air. There were two sawn-off stumps jutting from the rat priest's head, bony where projections had been brutally removed, but to make up for it the creature wore a whole twisted crown of crooked horns. Probably it had revisited the indignity on its rivals with extreme prejudice. Stanner wasn't learned in the hierarchies of the rats, but she knew bad news when she saw it.

She looked at the lizard. It was still making colours run down its skin at her. A wordless message, like the hand signs she'd used with Arnulf. She squinted, let the shades and patterns pass into her mind in search of meaning to connect to.

She jerked a thumb back the way they'd come, widening her eyes. Human markers, but the lizard understood her. She felt as though they were building their own common language as they went. Its patterning shifted, stilled, washed back and forth. *Wait.*

She nodded, and it was gone. A moment later she caught it again, like a shadow down below, drifting about the edge of the rats. A couple of them lifted their snouts in the air, scenting something amiss, but the arrival of their leader was plainly cause enough for festivities that they had other priorities.

Heart in her mouth, Stanner tracked the lizard scout across the cavern's perimeter. It was at the rat's baggage, she thought – a mound of sacks and rags. Was it going to poison their supplies or...? But no, it had spotted something there that it wanted. A weird, curled thing, like a horn or... Stanner frowned. A tail. It was a reptilian tail. And yes, the lizard mage on the throne was definitely missing one. She wasn't sure that was a prize worth risking the rats for. Would she have done the same if Perlo had lost a leg or something? She would not.

Then the lizard scout was back with her, its grisly trophy held close to its body. Carefully, the pair of them slunk backwards and then hurried towards the advancing shields.

KENLO

They were picking up speed. No ambushes, no traps, the worst danger just a twisted ankle from the broken-up stones beneath them. A pack of dead rats behind and ahead…

He had his lantern part open, enough light to see the footing. The violent illumination ahead didn't look like Perlo's usual tricks, but she'd said the lizard mage was helping. Up on a flying chair, Stanner had claimed. The sort of thing that would make a good *Do you remember when…?* story for future nights around the fire, once he'd got her back from the teeth of the rats.

He could almost smell the anticipation about the Stormcast, Vael, and the big lizard champion too. They were just desperate to bludgeon some more rats, and he was happy to let them. Honestly, if he came out of this place with Perlo and without either of them, that would only simplify his life. Let all the lizards throw themselves on rat swords to make a path to his sister! He'd heard the whole talk about where they fit in the great wheel of who hated who, and come out of it only with the understanding that he was a quartermaster, not a philosopher. Right now they were useful, but he reckoned they'd have something to say about him walking away with their golden trinkets, and then they'd all have a disagreement again. Hence the more of them who died killing rats for him, the better.

By the time Stanner got back, Vael was so keen for rat blood that the Stormcast almost trampled her down. She practically climbed over the man's golden shoulder to make her report.

'Back,' she got out. 'Back right now. There's a whole load more and they've got some big priest-mage type with them, and a lot of the ogor types.'

Kenlo felt a fist close in his chest. 'No,' he said.

'Seriously, Kenlo,' Stanner hissed, low and urgent. 'We can't, not even if we caught every one of them on the hop. There's two score mad monks working themselves into a frenzy down there, all with their sacrificing knives out and ready.'

'We push on,' Kenlo told her. 'It's Perlo down there, Stanner. It's my sister. That's why we're *here*! Let the lizards take point and we'll go round the side and ger her, easy as that.'

'It's not going to work,' Stanner said, but he was already telling the Steelhelms to shove forwards, practically rapping on Vael's backplate to get the Stormcast moving again. For a moment the lizardmen weren't going with them, warned by their own little lizard sneak, but then their champion obviously wasn't going to be outdone by Vael and hustled forwards to keep up, and the plan was back on.

Briefly on.

He saw her. That was the worst of it. The rats let them get just far enough that Kenlo could stare out of that gaping crack in the stone, into the sundered, deformed space of the chamber. The floating chair – *Oh yes, such an anecdote, how we'll laugh about it later*, but suddenly not funny. A desperate little lifeboat bobbing in a great sea of seething rat flesh. Reinforced, like Stanner had said, twice, three times as many. A globe of magical shielding, and within it the floating stone throne, on which Perlo and the lizard mage were crouched.

And silence. All those rats, all right there, but still and silent. Reverent.

Kenlo looked out across the mass of them and met the gaze of their priest. Its mad eyes, glowing green beneath its crown of horns. Its clawed, pinkish hands clutching the rail of its mobile pulpit, pox-scarred and missing some fingers. At its side, a stunted little white rat clutched a grand book, frantically scribing as though every breath and deed of its master must be recorded for posterity.

The priest reached out, almost delicately, and flicked a bronze bell that hung from its pulpit. The sound – sonorous, mournful – rang out across the fractured chamber and twisted Kenlo's gut.

Then every rat there was shrieking, each voice piercing the ear like a nail and dozens of them all at once, each a discord amongst its neighbours. They rang bells and clashed blades together and just shrilled until the whole chamber was crammed with their noise. A cacophony that forced its way into the skull and left no room for thoughts. Kenlo saw at least one Steelhelm drop their sword and clutch at their head. He felt as though a hundred drills were biting into his mind.

The lizard champion bellowed like a bull. Their ears were duller, maybe; the assault of sound seemed to slant off the creatures. When the rats boiled up from the chamber at them, it was the reptiles' readiness that saved them in the first instant. A great grey-swathed tide of Skaven waving knives and staves, gnawing, frothing, clutching ragged scraps of filthy scripture.

He felt the shock of impact, and for a moment Vael and the lizard champion were holding the breach, bottling them up in the chamber. They crawled over one another, though, mounding up until they were striking *down* at their enemies, mouths full of curses and infected spittle. A Steelhelm fell to their blades, and then one of the big lizard warriors went down to some kind of withering magic, a plague caught and running its lethal course in an instant, leaving the creature's corpse flyblown and rotten.

'Kenlo!' Stanner hissed in his ear. He tried to find Perlo past the tide of rats, but they were pressed together right to the top of the fissure now, a ravening wall of them trying to force their way through.

'Back!' he shouted, the word like bile in his mouth. 'Keep your shields up and fall back!' Saw another woman fall to the blades and get dragged down under the pestilent surge of rodent bodies.

I'll get to you! he promised Perlo in his head, but right then he was despairing because he couldn't see how.

CHAPTER SIXTEEN

PERLO

She thought she saw Kenlo, just for a moment, at the high tide of the rescue attempt.

Since the Skaven priest had arrived she'd been trying to get Irixi to contact him and warn him. The Seraphon had seemed to be saying that it couldn't create the connection again. Something about the rat priest's influence, and Perlo could certainly feel the creature's presence fouling the flow of power around them. Deep in her heart, a treacherous part of her still wanted Kenlo to try despite the new odds. Wanted to know that she hadn't just been abandoned, and who knew? Enough of a surprise attack, backed by some Seraphon magic, maybe even this force of Skaven could be driven back? Certainly they were all making enough noise with the squealing and the bells. You could have marched an army of ogors through without a rat of them noticing.

But the Skaven leader had been entirely aware of what was going on. The rats had stopped their party altogether at some signal from the crowned creature, just turned towards the crack in the wall that Kenlo and the others were about to appear at. That brief glimpse of Kenlo was all she got before the would-be rescuers were forced away, doubtless to be harried all the way back to the surface.

They were dragging bodies back into the chamber now, just a handful. Seraphon and human. She couldn't make herself look too closely.

'An approach is occurring,' Irixi said quietly. The little lizard mage was crouching on its haunches, leaning forwards on its staff to make up for the lost counterweight of its tail. Easy to read her own dejection into its slumped stance, and what else would any creature feel in this situation, exactly?

The 'approach' was the Skaven leader, of course. That festering priest of theirs. It rocked and lurched in its basket on the Rat Ogor's back, still chittering to its little amanuensis, which diligently scratched every word down. Skaven writing was spiky and jagged, Perlo saw, each character seeming to wound the eye.

The priest examined the curve of their shield. One of its eyes was half closed by inflammation about the stumps of its lost horns. The other, as if to compensate, bulged too wide, looking constantly outraged. More Skaven writing ran in a vertical strip down the length of its brown incisors. She'd heard those teeth grew at a fearsome rate, having to be put to constant use to gnaw them down to a manageable size. Some rodent scrimshander must be engraving an eternal chronicle marching down those teeth to oblivion.

The priest locked eyes with her. Perlo recoiled from its gaze. Green-eyed, luminous, mad, but then what was insanity to a human was just a day's business to the Skaven. Wicked, cunning, amused. She felt queasy that she could read the mood in the thing's rat face far more easily than she could in Irixi's reptile countenance.

Its hand – long-fingered, long-nailed, weirdly delicate for so monstrous a creature – reached out and tapped the bell hung from its carrying frame. Immediately one of the robed rat monks, crouched in utter obeisance nearby, leapt up and ran at the shield full tilt, waving a staff. She heard a war cry at the very edge of human hearing, and the thing hurled itself at the barrier of crackling energy. There was a flash and a shrill scream, and then a charred body rebounded back, robes spitting and crackling with violet flame.

Beside her, Irixi had flinched ever so slightly. Perlo hoped the rats had been too focused on the fire to notice. Using the shield was taking something out of the little Seraphon – or else drawing from a finite well of power in their surroundings. If the rats came en masse then eventually they'd get through. And their leader plainly didn't care much for their lives.

The enthroned rat began some sort of twittering oration, high and ear-scraping. There were words there – all the languages of the realms had traded terms back and forth with the movement of armies and powers over the centuries – but the speech was so rapid and high that she couldn't catch any.

It saw the blankness in her face, no doubt. Mammal to mammal, a kinship she absolutely didn't want. Impatiently, it rang at the bell on its pulpit and chittered some orders, before settling back to a little self-indulgent dictation to its secretary.

Shortly after, they brought up the corpse.

Most of a corpse. It had belonged to a man named Groslyn, one of Lofus' cronies. Not actually the most pleasant person Perlo knew from the army, but he'd deserved a better fate than this after death. Much below the ribs had already gone, the skin and innards ragged with the marks of rodent teeth. In place of that stolen flesh were a fistful of crudely stitched leather tubes rammed up into his chest cavity. Behind the propped-up corpse she saw bellows, with a team of rat monks already labouring over them.

Groslyn's mouth dropped open, dead lips quivering. When the rat priest spoke again, a hollow, terrible voice issued from the man's throat. Hollow because it was absolutely not that of a living man, terrible because it was still, somehow, Groslyn's.

'The great and terrible Ferskine, High Plague Priest of the Clans Pestilens, he who is most irresistible, most contagious, bids you welcome to his new den, may his wisdom and his issue fester and increase.' Probably the valedictions were supposed to be triumphant, but in that ghastly voice they sounded like lamentation.

Groslyn stopped speaking – or being spoken through – and a thin, high whine like far-off screaming issued from his open mouth as his puppeted lungs deflated. The monks laboured at the bellows to give him more artificial breath.

'To you, the human neophyte, know that Ferskine the worshipful, the magnanimous, the infinitely trustworthy, offers you your life in service to he, the majestic, the entropic, the master of decay and breeder of plagues. Know that to live in chains at the feet of such a lord is honour and freedom beyond all the rigid walls of your cities. To earn so prestigious a reward, know that you need only strangle that miserable scaled anathema crouching beside you and drive your thumbs into its accursed eyes.'

Perlo blinked. Possibly they'd drag half a dead Seraphon up and make a similar offer to Irixi, but she didn't think so. There was an enmity between the lizards and the rats that cut far deeper even than her own people's loathing of the enemies of Sigmar's crusade.

She wondered if the whole thing was just mockery, but the mad fervour of the rat priest suggested otherwise. To the Skaven, this was a good and genuine offer. Slavery at the festering feet of this thing, as a *reward*.

Compared to the fate of most who fell into the hands of the rats, it probably was. Since the resurgence of the ratfolk, she'd seen plenty of evidence. The surgeries, the experiments, cells crammed with prisoners infested with parasites and plague, bodies stitched together or spliced with animals. Oh, she'd seen the victims of orruk torture, back when the creatures had been on the rampage, and that had been bad. What the Skaven left behind them was worse, though. Not because they were *cruel*, but because everything about their leavings spoke to an all-consuming and amoral *curiosity*.

She cleared her throat, and the whole broken chamber went silent to hear her, save for the faint squeal of air leaving Groslyn's chest.

'O great Ferskine,' she said carefully, and saw the little rat scribe briskly setting down her words for posterity, 'your generosity is without limit.'

Irixi was looking at her suspiciously, and she wondered if the Seraphon simply didn't *lie* much. She'd have to hope the lizard caught on and didn't think she was actually betraying it.

'I am obviously humbled and awed by such a gracious offer. I am, just as obviously, not worthy of it, and if I were to accept I would…' How to buy time? 'I would have to cleanse – no, uncleanse, befoul myself. I would have to… rid myself of this stink of Order that surrounds me. I… ah… There are rituals I must perform, before I am worthy to enter the service of so grand a magister of your clan.'

Honestly, she was larding it on so heavily by the end that even Irixi understood. But the Skaven lord was plainly very fond of itself, and so just maybe that level of obsequious buttering was what it was used to.

The creature made a languid gesture and sat back in its pulpit. The monks worked the bellows again and Groslyn's half-corpse shuddered.

'The triumphant and puissant Ferskine, whose very fleas are themselves potent with fecund power, notes the very proper and appreciated respect in your crude human mouthings,' came the voice, using words that the living Groslyn probably hadn't even known. 'So be it that Ferskine, acute of senses and encrusted with knowledge, wishes you to know that the sufferings you shall endure for your duplicity shall be slightly leavened because of your respectful and pleasing utterances.'

The bell rang again and a good score of monks surged instantly up the stairs and into the barrier.

Beside her, Irixi stiffened. One clawed hand clutched at Perlo's arm, and she felt the Seraphon desperately reaching for the strength of their surroundings. All around them, the network of connections and conduits that ran in broken lines through the ruin blazed in her sight. No, in her mind: when she screwed her eyes shut they were still there, wheeling constellations, piecemeal and incomplete, dancing in her brain. She could see how they linked – and where they no longer did – and how Irixi was drawing from them to keep the throne's shield active.

She lent her little power to the fight – small, but she had grown up in Shyish, a child of Lethis. You learned some tricks. The realm had infiltrated this place in a thousand small ways, through root and spore and grave dirt. Weak, but pervasive, and a source of strength that Irixi had no connection to.

She felt a shudder all around them, dust sifting down from the ceiling, stone grinding against stone as the invasive roots crept forwards. There was a fulcrum point of the arcane here, where the alien, ancient mathematics of the Seraphon met the inexorable encroach of death to make some new thing, some grand potential. She heard Irixi draw in a shocked breath – shocked, but perhaps hopeful. Its grip tightened on her arm.

She opened her eyes. Charred rat bodies lay strewn back down the stairs. The violet radiance of the shield was now marbled with a deeper black-purple, deathly swirls of Shyish eddying across its surface. But it held.

Ferskine steepled its fingers, not furious but fascinated. She had the sickly feeling that the rat priest was actually enjoying itself. Curiosity: a virtue that, in Skaven, became the worst of vices.

'If you have a plan,' she said to Irixi out of the corner of her mouth, 'you'd better hurry it up.'

'A plan is unfolding,' the Seraphon replied quietly. 'Our allies, their venture, not without merit. The Good Purpose can be achieved now.'

'You mean getting us out, right?' And Irixi seemed calm – even optimistic, unless that was just her reading human feelings into a lizard face. And surely that meant a way out, a chance to live. What, after all, was more important?

Her eyes strayed to the great wall where this Orchid prophecy had once been recorded, that was now just shards and dust. Her own image there, truncated arms raised. She very much hoped the original image hadn't been her begging for her life before some rat priest.

CHAPTER SEVENTEEN

From the Scriptorium of Ferskine of the Eleventh Bell

Nownow slavescribe record faithfully these words of your better yes-yes?

Let it be known by the countless generations that shall come after and gnaw at the underside of the realms and sing shrill chorus of the virtues of Ferskine, the potent, the pestilent, the plague-begetter. This place of the snake-enemy, the hunters in the tunnels, the scaled ones, is in the grasp of none other than he, the triumphant, the terrible, Ferskine, none other, yes-yes!

Plainly there is none other fit within the ranks of our supreme Clans Pestilens, nor any of the lesser servants of the Horned Rat, may his fecund progeny ever increase until all the realms are consumed and corrupted, none other than he, great Ferskine, who could claim such a place for the furtherance of the gnawing tide. None other who could have sniffed out the luscious power still held within these stones. None other who can claim them from the Realm of Death and from their dull makers and repurpose them to corruption. Breed hosts of new kindred in their pools, cut our teeth on the bones of their beasts, sing our plagues into their flowing waters until all this place runs green and overbursting with rat and rot.

Be it known that, under the guidance and intellect and erudition of the most knowledgeable Ferskine, the true and proper feculence of the Horned Rat's chosen shall creep into the moribund stone of this place and overcome the sleeping power of the scaled ones, and in that union a sickness shall be born of death and of lizard-rot and of Rat Triumphant that shall be spread to all the places of our enemies. For this ruin is theirs, and it is a part of their world, and all their places, their temples by land and water and sky, are touched by it. Be it known that Ferskine, only he, the most magnificent and unequalled, shall make this place a breeding ground for plagues against all the foes of the rat, that shall devour scale and skin and sicken the very stars. We shall blind their prophecies. We shall gnaw out their eyes. Only by Ferskine shall this be achieved, the unparalleled, the most noxious, may the favour of the Horned Rat be upon him forever and forever!

Part 3

WRITTEN IN DARKNESS

CHAPTER EIGHTEEN

KENLO

The Skaven had harried them all the way back into the trees. Kenlo had been hoping the lizards would just stand and get hacked down to give his people a clean getaway, but instead the little ones ran ahead, a determined sprint for shelter, while the big ones lumbered along and trusted to their armoured backs to shrug off the stones the Skaven slung at them. All sense of cohesion had gone, and it had been the Steelhelms bringing up the rear, shields high in a bitter fighting withdrawal. Bitter because of the blood they'd lost in the venture. Bitter because Perlo was still down there.

They'd left four dead. Three in the tunnels, and one of Lofus' people, because they'd had a pack of rats ambush the group holding the tunnel mouth while Kenlo had been below. For a group of chancers who'd come here expecting a quick looting trip, the venture had been slapped with a savage cost. The last thing Kenlo felt like doing was glad-handing and backslapping and telling them all how rich they were about to be. If he just let them fester they'd quit, though. Meaning he'd never get Perlo out. The magic would falter and then she'd be prey for whatever abomination the Skaven had planned for her.

He put on his best face to meet their glowering.

'Look, this pack of rats isn't just out on a jolly of its own,' he tried. 'You can bet the marshal's facing their main force now. It's not like you're eating different to everyone back at the main camp.'

Regis the Fusilier gave him a level look. 'All the same with you, I'd rather be on the line than whittled down out here. You never said lizards, quartermaster. You never said rats.'

'I mean, I reckon we're glad we've got a few lizards to put between us and them,' Kenlo argued. 'You mind 'em taking a spear for you now? You're too good to have a big star-behemoth get gutted in your place?' He weighed them up, trying to work out how it *did* sit with them, because Morrda knew the lizards were an uncanny bunch, and 'better than rats' was a low bar.

Stanner was watching him with those cold eyes of hers. He looked at her, made her a part of the conversation in case she was about to leap to his defence, but she just kept her thin lips shut. Probably enjoying seeing him on the back foot.

'You'd rather be back taking the marshal's orders right now?' he challenged Regis. 'When we could go back to the lines with some magic loot our mages could throw into the fight? Plus your bags stuffed with gems?'

'Like the rats are going to let us have a sniff of them!' she snapped. 'And who says there's enough out there to pay for a round of drinks? This place was picked clean long before your bloody dad found it.'

Lofus cleared his throat, pulling rank. Regis scowled at him, and then her eyes widened. The sergeant was holding up a weird kind of mask. A lizard mask, for one of the small sort. Kenlo could see the slot where its crest would fit, and how the object would sit on top of its head, almost to the end of its snout. There were solid bulges moulded over the eyes, meaning the creature would be blind when wearing it, but then he was no judge of reptile fashion. A few strands and tatters showed there had been more to it, now fallen away, but what was left was very clearly gold, finely worked and inscribed with hundreds of little pictures, plates of topaz and bloodstone alternating in a neat border around its edge. It wasn't necessarily the single most valuable artefact Kenlo had ever seen up close, but it was surely the most precious thing that anyone of his acquaintance had ever just picked up off the ground.

'Did a bit of digging while we were waiting,' Lofus said mildly, as if it was nothing. 'Picked clean? Not hardly.' He looked over at Kenlo, not challenging but not friendly either. 'I reckon we start making patrols. Get in and out quick, couple of hours scavenging, lookouts for the rats.' He clapped a hand on Kenlo's shoulder. 'We figure out some miracle plan to get her back, quartermaster, then you count me in. But as matters stand, I reckon we grab what we can and get back to the army. Flash them just enough relics or magic so they decide we were out here following orders, and then we're rich and I'll raise a mug to Perlo's name next taproom we find ourselves in.'

Kenlo opened his mouth to object, and Lofus added pointedly, 'And to the rest that died. And we'll all consider ourselves lucky not to be amongst them.'

'Sergeant…' Kenlo looked around at the others and saw that Lofus had them. They weren't just going to leave, but that was the most he was going to get out of them. If Perlo was to be saved, it was up to him.

Him and maybe Stanner. He eyed the scout, who was watching them all as though they were mildly interesting bugs on a twig. Before he could ask where she stood, though, there was some manner of hissing, croaking exclamation amongst the lizards, who'd been huddling at the fire.

The smaller ones had sprung apart into a circle. One of them, the one with the weird, shifting skin and the mobile eyes, had dumped something on the ground there. Kenlo peered over their heads and then grimaced as he saw it was a severed lizard tail.

'Sigmar's spit, what's that about?' he demanded.

Stanner was abruptly at his shoulder, making him jump. 'It's from their magus,' she said. 'The rats cut it off or something. The lizard scout nicked off with it when we were down there.'

'With a *tail*?' Kenlo asked incredulously. The lizard scout was making quite a song and dance about it, maybe retelling the whole grand adventure in mime. The tail itself didn't even seem to be quite dead. It was writhing slowly, like a stubby serpent, colours blooming and rippling along it. It all seemed absurdly barbaric, and he wondered if they would ceremonially burn it or eat it or something. He looked to make some scathing remark to Stanner, but the scout was frowning.

'It's like…' she murmured, 'talking.'

'What?' Kenlo asked blankly.

'You never see how they talk? It's like it's with their whole bodies, too. Like hand-sign. They're watching the tail and it's talking to them.'

'What would a *tail* have to say?' he demanded, and, at her shrug, pushed her forwards. 'Go ask them.'

'Why me?'

'Who else is there? They've got some scheme, we need to know before it bites us. They've got a way to get… below…' *If they want to rescue their chief still, maybe I've got a chance.* 'Stanner, just *ask* them, if you know so much about it.'

She looked mutinous, but after a moment's hard staring she turned to approach the ring of lizards. Nearby, Lofus chuckled.

'Cold enough to be half lizard herself, that one,' the sergeant observed, and Kenlo recalled vaguely that Stanner had slapped the man down that one time, when he'd drunkenly come on to her.

Stanner plainly overhead it, and shot Lofus a petrifying look, then turned her back on the pair of them and crouched down where the lizards were. Kenlo expected them to close ranks against her, but a hiss from their own scout had them shuffling round to make space. The stuck-up interpreter, which had been peering closely at the tail, now looked up.

'Starseer puissance, forging sympathies, flesh to flesh, a path of words to be made,' it said, which sounded like a lot of gibberish to Kenlo, but then it added, 'For the Good Purpose, a return below must be made,' and he felt a stab of hope.

Stanner looked over her shoulder at Lofus and the rest. 'I don't reckon they're keen,' she said.

The interpreter looked from her to Kenlo and Lofus, and then to the lizard scout.

'They are unfit,' it said, and then jabbed Stanner in the shoulder. 'Oaxmal says *you*.'

CHAPTER NINETEEN

OAXMAL

The tail was writhing. Writhing but also *writing*. Oaxmal concentrated, feeling as though it had become a surrogate seer in this moment. Divining how things would be from the alignment of the stars or the flight of birds. Or the convulsing twitchings of a severed tail.

The tail was Irixi. If Oaxmal had been trained in the arcane rituals – under the auspices of some other guide than Huanchi the Jaguar – then probably its eyes would see the strands of connection stretching from this trophy out into the depths beneath the ruins, to where the imprisoned Starseer endured. Irixi's flesh, and so through a Starseer's arts Irixi's words.

The Good Purpose may still be achieved, said the convulsions of the tail, said the flushed patterns of its colouration. Zitzel interpreted for the other skinks, and then, pompously, for the human. The Useful Human, as Oaxmal had come to think of it. The one that could keep up, and not announce its presence to every living thing in a hundred yards.

The human was asking if that meant they could rescue Irixi and their own lost mage. 'All things are possible,' Zitzel told it grandly. The interpreter had a particularly sage nod, learned from watching wiser heads. Oaxmal rolled its eyes, a very literal act.

The tail threw itself into another series of twists, and momentary clumps of colour bloomed and faded across its length. Oaxmal didn't know how long Irixi could continue to perform this working. Surely the severed thing would die sooner rather than later? The Chameleon fixed both eyes on it, reading the desperate, curtailed messages being mimed out.

'We must return to the inner halls of the *Wings of Serendipitous Fire*,' Zitzel stated. Plain enough to Oaxmal's eyes, though most of the rest seemed to need the interpretation. Then came, through a fresh set of spasms, 'The Starseer being temporarily engaged, correct ritual actions may be undertaken in these circumstances by another.'

A current of trepidation went through the skinks. Perhaps Zitzel itself had been admitted to the absolute lowest levels of the priest bureaucracy that dominated Seraphon life, but as no more than the meanest scribe. To step outside the bounds of their lifelong role and assume the mantle of Starseer, even in the least possible way, was sacrilege, surely? Yet Irixi must know what was being asked of them.

The useful human spoke, once that had been translated, in that voice which didn't clamour at the ears the way the others' did. Zitzel gave its words as 'Back into the ruins? Or *under* the ruins? The rats would be on us the moment they heard a clink of mail.'

Oaxmal agreed. Another assault below would see them all surrounded and the strength of the saurus and the humans' shields wouldn't be enough to get them out alive. The rats had a stranglehold on the spaces below the fallen temple.

The skinks murmured and whispered, one to another. Obviously the command of Irixi must be obeyed, but they were weak and scared creatures, out here in this chill wood with nobody to lead them. And Gokumet and the saurus warriors would certainly just march to their deaths at the Starseer's word, but what would that accomplish?

Gokumet could walk softly. Oaxmal had seen it. Not just a warrior but a hunter. Huanchi did not often bless the saurus, but the Chameleon felt that its patron would spare a nod of approval for the champion. A warrior who knew how to lurk and ambush as well as just stride in and fight. But the rest of them, Irixi's bodyguard? Unsubtle tools, all of them.

Oaxmal tilted one eye back across the camp. The humans were arguing. They never seemed to stop making noise of one kind or another, as though to make up for the muteness of their skins. Their metal warrior, the Golden One, stood aloof from them. Another strong fighter who could be very still, and who trod surprisingly softly for all that weight of metal.

None of that was the deciding factor, of course. Destiny was written in the fact that Oaxmal did not need Zitzel's translation of Irixi's messages. They were written for the Chameleon's mobile eyes, speaking straight to its sneaking soul.

It placed a hand on the interpreter's arm, halting it mid-pontification.

Zitzel stiffened at the interruption. 'You presume.'

Oaxmal composed its skin. A warning that Zitzel not overstep its role. An assertion that this task belonged to the Chameleon and Huanchi. Patterns of skin pigmentation spelled out the simple blocks of a scout's language. *Force will be defeated. The host of the Enemy.* That concept given its very specific shade to show Oaxmal meant the hated rats. There was a skink tale about how the Skaven were the Ruinous Powers' attempts to recreate the perfection of the Seraphon. A fiction, but one that expressed their horror of the rats.

Zitzel, being argumentative by nature, had some scathing rejoinder prepared, but let it die on the tongue. 'Knowing that threat, you offer yourself,' it said at last. Was that grudging respect, from the realms' most junior seer for a mere hunter? Probably not, but at least the interpreter had stopped puffing itself up with its own importance.

Oaxmal let its mind speak on its hide. *Huanchi blesses. A time to strike, a time to walk softly.* There was a third part of the hunter's mantra it didn't feel the need to act out. *A time to die*, the axiom all its broodmates had proved the truth of, one after another. *Perhaps this will be my time.* A death in the dark, amongst the rats. Oaxmal shifted its skin perfectly grey and plain. It would not do to show Zitzel and the others how it felt, just then.

It jabbed a thumb at the useful human. *This one also.*

'It shall be so instructed.' Zitzel flushed with self-important colours and raised its crest at the chance to order a human around.

Oaxmal's hand clenched tighter, making the skink wince. *Humility,* said its skin, meaning, *Do not tell – ask.*

'If it is decreed in the Great Plan that–' Zitzel started, but Oaxmal made a warning hiss deep in its throat, and the haughty words were bitten back.

After the translator had asked the question, the useful human looked to Oaxmal. That rubbery, naked face was hard to read, in all its contortions, but the Chameleon reckoned it was as unhappy with the prospect as Oaxmal itself.

It pinched Zitzel again and indicated Gokumet.

Zitzel glared, but Oaxmal was the chosen tool of Irixi now, and that conferred authority. 'Champion, Shield of Sek'atta,' the interpreter addressed Gokumet. 'Your strength would be welcomed in this venture.' Not a command, because who was the most junior of priests to give orders to Irixi's protector? Yet the saurus agreed swiftly enough.

The useful human spoke a few quiet words, looking from face to scaled face. Asking, Oaxmal thought, if they had a plan. The

Chameleon recognised someone working themselves towards a decision. The human wouldn't want to die to rat teeth down there, any more than Oaxmal did. The human's hands picked out Oaxmal, Gokumet and itself as it spoke again, then made a gesture like a spider creeping. *We three, in the shadows.* It gave a wary look at the looming saurus.

'It is the will of the Starseer this be done,' Zitzel proclaimed. 'Only in such ways can the Good Purpose be fulfilled.' Which was not, of course, the rescue of their mage, or even of Irixi itself. There were more important matters.

The useful human closed its eyes for a moment and let out a long breath. Expelling all the imperfections of its kind, the fear and the indiscipline. Holding in only the courage. It bobbed its head, which in a Seraphon meant obedience but in a human, Oaxmal recalled, was agreement.

CHAPTER TWENTY

STANNER

'The lizards want you with them? What, as a mascot?' Lofus asked her. 'Going to tie you to a stick and use you as a standard? Or put a rope round your ankle and go trawling for rats?'

'It's not "the lizards",' Stanner said quietly. 'They're staying here, most of them. It's that one.' She pointed out the scout and watched them all squint a bit before finding the creature's camouflaged shape amongst the trees. 'That one and the big one. They've got some scheme.'

Kenlo was watching her very intently. 'To get their leader back.'

Easier, far easier, to just say yes. To let him hear what he wanted to hear. But Stanner had never been a good liar. 'Maybe. Some plan, anyway.' She hadn't followed the details, and their translator hadn't been interested in explaining, but it seemed more complicated than just grabbing the lizard mage and running. 'Any of you have a plan? No? Then I guess this is what we've got.'

'If it isn't getting Perlo back,' Lofus said, 'and it isn't getting rich, I don't see what's in it for you.'

And Kenlo rounded on the sergeant, because Kenlo had obviously decided it *was* getting Perlo back, because the woman was his sister and he was desperate, and desperate people heard what they wanted to hear out of any offer you put to them. Just ask half the fools lost to Chaos if that wasn't true. Stanner reckoned if one of the Dark Gods turned up now and offered Kenlo a hand, he'd take it. She let them bicker, exploring the hollow parts inside herself for the answer. What *was* in it for her, exactly? She did like Perlo, but not enough to trade places with her. The riches, then? A pouch full of loot solved many of life's problems, in Stanner's experience.

Solidarity, maybe, and a pride in her tradecraft. There was one thing in the world she did well, and that was scout. Get in and out, see and not be seen, tread softly, strike sure. Time had stripped her of her Wildercorps fellows and even her dog, but left her that. And the lizard scout, Oaxmal – she wrestled the sounds in her head, fighting to make a proper name of them – had seen that in her. Their mage had told them, through that grotesque trophy, that some serious sneak-work was needed, and rather than turning to one of its diminutive fellows, the creature had asked her.

Stanner had always valued the cold deadness inside of her. The way that all she'd lost had been like a callus to the soul, so that she stopped feeling the bite of it, at last. Like an old wound whose scar leaves you numb where the hurt used to be. The exercise of her skill in Sigmar's service had become all that was left to her, and what little joy she took, she took in that. But now, like an unexpected shoot pushing through the dead earth of Shyish, she felt a touch of that old camaraderie. It had been a long time since she'd had anyone who could keep up with her. Not since Arnulf got himself killed by the ogor. And maybe that was enough.

For a moment she felt horribly scared. The possibility that a loss might actually get through to her, make her grieve again. And now stupid, that she wouldn't waste a tear over Kenlo's corpse, or Lofus, but with this reptile, just maybe.

'I'm going,' she told Lofus. 'What's your problem? Nobody's asking *you*.'

He held his hands up, disavowing any responsibility. 'You go feed yourself head first to the rats for all I care. In the meantime we're going to pick some golden flowers up on the surface. You know, where the rats mostly *aren't*. I'll save some for you. If you come back.'

She turned away, but Kenlo grabbed her arm, face naked with desperation. 'Stanner...'

'Whatever can be done,' she said. Noncommittal, but he plainly saw it as a binding promise.

There was a clang of metal from across the camp. She saw Vael stumble back a step, facing off against Gokumet, the big lizard warrior. Who'd just shoved the Stormcast hard in the shoulder, apparently.

'Not *now*,' she said, because the pair of them had been on the edge of fighting even when they met in the forest, and it hadn't gone away despite all the *actual* fighting that had happened in the interim.

Vael plainly wasn't sure what was going on either. He had his hammer ready – the thing never seemed to leave his hands – but Gokumet wasn't squaring off against him, just waiting expectantly. Stanner dodged through the crowd of gawping humans to get to them.

'I am ready,' the Stormcast said. Stanner wished he'd put his mask back on. The distant golden perfection would be preferable. Not that the man had a bad face by nature – a bit long, a bit pale maybe, but the way it was all chewed up made her shudder. Not the scars – you got used to all kinds of damage marching under the Dawnbringer banner – but the way he bore them. Like an anchor, as though they were the only thing keeping him in place.

'Your lordship?' she asked.

'He wants a fight, I am ready.' And even as the Stormcast spoke, the lizard warrior reached forwards and pushed him again, in the chest. Not a serious shove, but enough force to knock Vael back a step.

'I think it's… "hello", your lordship. Just a way they do it, amongst themselves,' Stanner said. 'Or maybe "goodbye".'

Vael's look was utterly blank. He'd just been stood there while all the planning went on, and she guessed he hadn't taken it in. Mind on other matters, praying to Sigmar, who knew?

'We're off, lordship. Into the tunnels,' she said. 'Doing… a lizard plan. Him, me, their scout type.'

'I accept,' said Vael.

'Your lordship?' Then she got his meaning. 'No, he wasn't asking you to…' And she stopped, because the man was exactly right, and she'd got it wrong. She pictured some lizard battle muster, their reptile sergeant going down the line, picking its squad with a wordless shove at each, and them all falling into step behind it.

'All right then,' she said. And the thought of a Stormcast at her back if they got into trouble down there was actually reassuring. Normally you didn't want to stand too close, because they were always in the worst of the fighting and sometimes that lightning of theirs wasn't so discriminating. Given she was going into the worst place around already, though, she didn't see the downside right now.

Oaxmal was taking the tail, she saw. Just looping the thing about its waist as though it was a thick belt. Stanner had seen plenty of her fellows go into battle with a skull or fingerbones or some other hero's relic, but a still-living-and-moving body part was a step beyond even that tradition. Not as though you could get it to stay in a reliquary, she considered with a suppressed snort of amusement.

She avoided meeting Kenlo's gaze on the way out towards the shattered temple. Perlo would live or Perlo would die, but Stanner didn't reckon she'd have much influence on which.

They didn't go in the same way, and probably that was just as well because Stanner guessed the rats had their previous entrance staked out. The ruins were riven with holes and cracks, though. The interior of the place had been honeycombed with chambers and passageways, and now it was a whole broken egg of scrambled spaces and rubble down there. Plenty of ways a small, determined party could skulk into the dark without attracting notice. The way the tail apparently directed them to was choked with rubble, but Gokumet and Vael cleared that away quickly and quietly. It would be darkly funny, Stanner considered, if the pair of elite champions had come along purely to do the manual labour.

The way cleared, they crept into the dark.

She reckoned it would have been more efficient if the tail had literally just pointed the way at each juncture, but of course nothing was as simple as that. Every time there was a choice of descent, Oaxmal had to place the thing on the floor and interpret its writhings, like a squadmate she'd once had who'd thrown a handful of knucklebones before each mission to determine Morrda's favour. One time he'd tried it and gone very quiet and solemn, and that had been the job he'd not come back from. She could only hope Oaxmal was receiving better omens.

It led them down through crooked shafts and perilously slanting tunnels that contained only the skitter of little things, anyway. Stanner's half-hooded lantern caught pale serpents and toads and skull-backed bugs the size of her hand, all creeping about amongst twining roots that had forced themselves in between the stones and hung in dank curtains from the ceiling. Nothing wholesome, everything touched by Shyish's insidious hand, but none of it was going to kill them. The sound of Skaven chittering came to them in distant echoes, but for a long while that was all the sign they had of the rats' presence.

Then the tail spasmed fiercely about Oaxmal, practically dragging the lizard to a crooked fracture that would be just wide enough for Gokumet to squeeze its bulk through. From below came more of the skritch and shrill of rat voices. Oaxmal tilted its head sideways, one eye tilting back and forth as it studied what lay below. It beckoned them close and indicated down. Their goal was below, and the Skaven had found it already.

Oaxmal slipped into the crevice, its own tail coiled and grasping for purchase. Without a word, Stanner reached forwards and let her arm be its anchor so the lizard could hang from her. The weight of it wrenched at her shoulder and she clenched her teeth against it. Vael, who could probably have performed the same service for Gokumet if the creature had felt acrobatically inclined, just stood there, of course, living face as blank as his gold mask had been, seeming to see some other vista than the jumbled innards of the ruin.

Oaxmal had its blowpipe out but was just hanging there thoughtfully. Stanner peered past it. Below it was gloomy but not pitch dark. Great leathery florets of pallid fungus thrust up between the tilted stones, giving out a sickly violet light that reminded Stanner of the dead glow of Shyish's moons. There were half a dozen of the more wretched-looking Skaven there, crawling all over some kind of statuary that sat sheared into two leaning halves. Hard to see what it represented in the gloom, but the rats were prising gems and inlay out with an avarice that would have done Lofus and Kenlo proud.

She'd thought Oaxmal would just start spitting darts, but the lizard plainly didn't want to risk sending the Skaven scattering into the dark. With steady, patient movements, Oaxmal reached out and caught hold of root after root with hands and feet, making its way upside down across the ceiling. After three steps, and despite her best efforts, Stanner couldn't make her ally out from the dim grey of its surroundings.

The other two, Gokumet and Vael, had noticed something was going on, and were pressing closer. Stanner, with a certain foreboding, loaded her crossbow and sighted up.

The slab beneath her trembled. With her free hand she waved frantically back at the pair of them. Yes, this ruin had sat here for countless ages, but that didn't mean it was stable…

With a thunderous grinding sound, the whole section of floor beneath them came apart and dumped them downwards into the space below.

Stanner had, at least, been ready for it, by her usual maxim of *Expect the worst when the heavy mob come through*. She landed on her feet and put a bolt into one of the rats on general principles. They were already leaping away from the pillaged statue, scrambling to pick up their weapons and shields.

Vael was on one knee, still straightening up. Gokumet had dropped to all fours, club spun away into the darkness. The Skaven paused for a heartbeat, weighing the odds, then charged.

Stanner reloaded, focusing on that sole task because that was how it went if you didn't want to end up running from every threat in the realms. When she glanced up, the rat at the back had dropped, twitching and shivering. She knew Oaxmal was out there, but she couldn't see where the darts were coming from. The rats just fell in reverse order, one, two, three, even as the pack of them surged forwards.

Stanner tensioned the string and levelled her bow. The lead Skaven had its shield high against a blow from Vael, so she ducked low and practically put the point of the bolt up the creature's nose before pulling the trigger. The impact knocked it head over tail past its sole remaining ally, which was only just working out that it was on its own.

It fled, throwing itself into a skidding turn and dashing off amongst the glowing fungi. Vael shouldered past Stanner on one side and Gokumet on the other, but the rat dropped before they could catch it, just one more meagre bundle in the shadows.

Carefully, Oaxmal let itself down to the ground, thrusting its pipe through the strip of hide it used for a belt. It directed an eye at the two returning warriors and flashed some jarring colours at Stanner. *These loud boys, why'd we bring them?*

Stanner found herself grinning. Oh, she couldn't be sure she'd understood that signal, but she reckoned she wasn't far off. It was good to be around someone who understood the trade again.

They let the silence creep back in, in case another pack of rats was on its way. They were in a room that had been a domed hemisphere before half the ceiling had fallen in. The walls were inlaid with concentric bands of turquoise and gold depicting something astronomical. Not stars and moon, Stanner reckoned, but the rising and setting of the sun. Holes here and there had maybe let the outside light in at particular times and dates. She'd heard of such things. The cracked-in-half statue or altar or fountain had been in the centre, where those beams of sunlight would have touched. It was big and blocky, with carvings on each face that she reckoned represented a stylised Seraphon with maybe a sun rising behind it, or maybe just a really elaborate headpiece. Some ancient mason had put a great deal of detail and work into a likeness that didn't speak to Stanner at all. Whatever was there wasn't intended for human eyes.

The rest of the chamber was a whole topography of fallen stone and ruin – in some places great stepped mounds where sections of several upper floors had fallen in, in others pits of dark water where pallid frogs and translucent-bodied fish lived sightless lives. There were bones, too. Thin ones that looked like they came from creatures like Oaxmal, and a scattering of greater relics from beasts, or perhaps just really big Seraphon. The former inhabitants of the ruin. Vael regarded them darkly.

Oaxmal had the severed tail laid beside the statue and was staring at it keenly with one eye, while the other looked the statue up and down. 'Chotec,' Gokumet rumbled softly. Just a sound, but then Stanner understood it was a name.

'Your god?' she asked.

Oaxmal flashed warm yellow-orange colours at her, and one hand described an arc that followed the curve of the surviving ceiling.

Chotec. The sun. She tried to see the meaning in that lizard statue, in the whole chamber as it had been, but it was too alien to her. She just nodded. 'You know what you've got to do?'

Oaxmal took a blade of dark stone and studied its own hand, then referred to the tail again, reading the slow, oracular convulsions. With a deft motion, it pricked at its skin until the blood welled, then anointed precise spots about the base of the statue. Gokumet's croaking voice ran through some flat recital that Stanner guessed must be a prayer to this sun god of theirs.

It was warmer. Paradoxically, Stanner shivered. The statue itself wasn't giving off heat like a fire, but the air in the chamber seemed close, almost stuffy. The dead Skaven – not fragrant at the best of times – abruptly seemed ranker, as though they'd been left out on a hot day.

There were shafts of light in the gloom. Stanner flinched, because those channels surely no longer led outside, and the fickle Shyish light wasn't golden like that. And some of those beams came from parts of the ceiling that had long collapsed and taken their lightwells with them. She was seeing the ghost of a sun long gone, creeping into this buried place, touching the walls. And the walls it illuminated were not the cracked and root-webbed stones of the ruin. They were brightly painted, set with gold and polished slabs of chalcedony and rose quartz. Shadows danced there: crested lizards come bearing offerings, great plodding beasts of burden. Stanner caught her breath.

Vael made a sound, shuddering. His eyes were wide. Not fear – everyone knew Sigmar beat that out of the Stormcasts with a vengeance – but something existential.

'I see...' he said hoarsely. 'Do you... see?'

From out in the darkness, there was a grinding crash of displaced stone. Stanner saw a minor avalanche of broken masonry shouldered aside, and something shook itself and lurched forwards. She thought it was a crab at first. A crab the size of a hut. It had a great rounded shell, as though its scales had grown thick as planks and merged together into an overarching shield across all its body. A lizard or a turtle, she saw. A vast armoured reptile on four stocky legs, and behind it, a tail capped with a spiked club like the fist of a giant. It had just been there, under the stone. But how…

Stanner blinked and blinked again. It was a living reptile monster; then it was just shell and bones wreathed with the residual power of Shyish that had been seeping into this place for hundreds of years. Every step it took shifted the beast from living to animate dead, just as the phantom sun coursed into the chamber from aeons past and all around them the phantasms of ancient votaries danced.

The beast bellowed, the sound coming to them like an echo, distant and wavering. But when it charged, Stanner felt it would crush them flat whether it was really there or not. She couldn't even move. The thing seemed to fill the entire chamber.

Vael stepped before her, hammer raised, one shoulder forwards as though even a Stormcast could have received that charge and not been flung across the room. His voice sang out, a battle cry, not a song to Sigmar so much as to his own death. Stanner dropped, hands over her head, waiting for the crash.

There was nothing. The space about them was dark and cold, blotched by the ghostly fungal light. Before them was just an assemblage of bones and curved sections of shell, dusty and brittle, as though they'd lain there since the dawn of the realms.

Stanner stood slowly. She could hear Vael's breath rasping, and his eyes glimmered with frustrated lightning. Gokumet inhaled vastly and then let the air out, snout high as though seeking the scent of the vanished monster.

'Was that… real?' Stanner asked slowly.

Vael let out a dreadful, despairing sound. Only after its echoes had faded did she identify it as a laugh.

Oaxmal stepped back from the statue, cradling the tail. Patterns coursed across its skin: motion, forwards, upwards. Its eyes tilted towards the ceiling.

Suits me fine, Stanner thought as she looked for a path to climb through the rubble. Whatever it had once been, the buried sun shrine was a good place to be out of as far as she was concerned.

Their route back up through the compacted layers of the temple was a different one, and she was waiting for Oaxmal to lead them sideways off to some other half-crushed shrine. Instead, after a hard climb up a near-vertical shaft, they emerged into the flat, hard light of day. Not the sun that had been resurrected into that chamber below but Shyishan skies, which could feel overcast without a cloud in sight.

She found an intact pillar and shinned up it, fingers crooked into the intricate carvings. Her best guess was that they were somewhere in the heart of the ruin – the Skaven holdout above ground was some distance away, though not so far that their scouts might not be all over this place. The structures here were more intact – few roofs but plenty of partial walls. She could see what had once been a grand flight of steps but was now just a broken serpent of disarticulated stone. It led to where they were, though, and immediately below her was a mess of fallen statuary, all of it shattered past any hope of knowing what the original images had been. *I hope one of those isn't what Oaxmal's after.* But the lizard scout passed between the colonnade of fallen images towards what had once been a solid, heavily ornamented building and was now just three jagged-topped walls and a reaching talon left over from a domed bronze roof.

She slipped back down, and the three of them followed Oaxmal into the shadow of those walls. One was weirdly melted and blackened in a vertical band down its centre. Vael stopped dead at the sight of it, face blank again, gone away to whatever lost world claimed him. Stanner regarded him warily in case some fit came over him, but he just stood, features slack. Tiny arcs of blue-white power danced across his scars and between the plates of his armour.

At the far end of the broken eggshell of a structure was what remained of a shrine. Stanner recognised the style now. This statue was mostly whole and set into the wall, a great serpent ascending in blocky, tessellated coils to a head that the fall of the ceiling had smashed half away. In the wall behind it were carved in relief a multitude of arms and a great arching set of batlike wings. The many hands held forked swords and maces and jagged bolts of lightning. Parts of it had been adorned with precious metals, but some past heat had set them running in rivulets of molten finery that had crept into all the contours of the carving, limning its outlines in a tracery of silver and gold.

Gazing on it, Stanner was struck with an inexplicable feeling of familiarity. The previous shrine had excluded her in its design and symbolism, but something here spoke to her. Or it was simply that something she had seen – in a very similar setting, her memory nagged at her – resembled this. A commonality of reverence. A point in the cosmos where lizard and human dreams touched.

Gokumet had crouched before the scarred effigy, hands flat on the floor, head tilted back to look at that ruined head. A serpent's head, Stanner presumed, though she saw the stumps of horns jutting from behind it. The great forked tongue that still hung from those jaws looked to be solid gold, enough to enrich everyone in Lofus' squad twice over.

'Sotek,' breathed the big lizard warrior, its voice trembling a little. The divine name whispered out into the deity's dead temple.

On the surviving section of wall, either side of the shrine, ranks of figures were carved in bustling motion. Stanner felt her eyes were becoming more lizard, in the way they read the art. She saw vast armies of Seraphon streaming away from the god, doing battle with hunched, long-tailed enemies that were surely Skaven. She saw streaks of stars overhead, joined by lines to make strange patterns – was that Sigmar's comet, or just the forked tongue once again? She saw what she realised were great cities or temples, borne aloft amongst circling pictograms. *It fell,* Vael had said. And here she had just the faintest suggestion of what the ruin had looked like when it had flown.

Oaxmal had its little flint blade out again and was dotting the shrine with more of its dark blood. Stanner looked nervously about, waiting to see how their surroundings would react, and whether the rats would notice. She backed off from the statue in case it became a real giant snake and wanted to cause trouble, and almost ran into Vael.

He was staring up at the broken icon and the great span of time-worn carving behind it, lips moving. Stanner didn't want to talk to him, really, still less hear what he had to say, but there was such a look of revelation on the Stormcast's face that her curiosity wouldn't let her just turn away.

'What?' she asked. 'What do you see, your lordship?'

'Dracothion,' he whispered.

She twitched. 'Lordship?'

'Do you not…? Sigmar's ally, the father of dragons, the lord of Azyr's sky… How is he here? How is he…?' His eyes were dragged to the line of melted stone.

Oaxmal touched a final blood spot onto the stone and stepped back. Stanner braced herself.

Nothing happened.

Oaxmal's puzzlement was clear to human eyes. It consulted the tail again, as Stanner might have rechecked a map if the terrain turned out to be wildly different. She saw its hand pass over each bloody mark in turn, a ring around the cracked remnant of an offering bowl before the statue. Complex, angry patterns danced across its skin. Gokumet let out a deep, wordless sound.

'What?' Stanner asked.

Oaxmal had retreated from the shrine. Whatever the tail was trying to communicate was plainly no help.

'Do we need to… fix it up, the statue?' Stanner asked. It seemed in better shape than the Chotec shrine below had been.

'No,' Vael said hollowly. Gokumet was asking Oaxmal something now, in its guttural voice. Uncertain patterns glimmered on the lizard scout's flanks.

Vael sighed and stepped forwards. The two lizards froze. *Sacrilege!* Stanner recognised. They were tensed, eyes on the Stormcast, ready to go for him if he tried something with their holy of holies. 'Lordship,' she hissed in warning. 'Maybe don't–'

'I understand.' Vael's voice was like lead. 'I was here.'

'Lordship, *what*?'

Vael hauled off one gauntlet. The hand beneath was pale, pristine. In the shadow of the statue his flesh seemed to glow faintly, like the fungi had. A repository for lightning. 'We were here. It was an error. A terrible, pointless thing.' His voice was shaking, which Stanner found profoundly unnerving in one of Sigmar's chosen champions. Had the man been anything else, she'd have expected him to weep.

Vael slipped a knife from his belt, and Stanner saw the two lizards tighten another notch, staring. This was going to go badly, but she couldn't exactly tackle Vael to the ground, nor stand in their way if they decided to attack.

'In this way I atone,' Vael said, 'for the destruction we caused, in our eagerness for the fight. In this way I make my first death *mean* something.' A wildness in his voice, growing with every word.

Viciously, he gashed at his hand, making Stanner wince for the chance of severed tendons and ruined fingers.

'Take it,' spat Vael, and crackling blue-white fire blossomed from his hand where blood should have been, dancing about his fingers and refusing to fall. 'Take it!' he said, shaking his fingers over the bloodied bowl, but the lightning clung to them like serpents, refusing to be dislodged.

'*Take it!*' he shouted, loud enough to reach the rat camp by Stanner's guess. He actually pressed his gashed hand to the stone, but the dancing energy evaporated from his flesh before he touched it, leaving no mark. Refusing him. Vael made a sound, hollow, grieving, like a sob. He crashed to his knees before the icon. 'Dracothion,' he got out. '*Please*, do not turn from me.'

'It's not Dracothion, lordship, it's… Sotek, some lizard god, some snake god.' And yes, there was a touch of the dragon to that image, and maybe that was what spoke to her. But it was a coincidence of iconography, no more.

From somewhere too close she heard a shrill twittering. Some band of rat scavengers drawn by the shouting. 'Oaxmal,' she said. 'You'd better do your thing.'

The scout indicated the tail, its cut hand, the marked bowl. Its *thing* had been done, and nothing had happened.

'We defiled the temple with our arrival,' Vael said, head bowed. 'We brought our lightning, and it seeped into the stones, even as Shyish did below. This is my fault.'

Stanner closed her eyes. If there was one thing she could never stand, it was self-pity. It was no more appealing in Stormcasts than in regular mortals.

'Right,' she said. 'Oaxmal, you keep your darts and your friend back. I don't mean any disrespect, but this is my turn, right?'

The lizard eyed her warily, but at least it didn't get any more twitchy when she went to stand beside Vael, taking out her own knife. *Lightning in the stone,* according to Vael, and, before, he'd said, *It fell.* She was putting together a picture of just what had happened between the Stormcast and this place. She was no great divine champion, of course, but she had fought for Sigmar's cause. She had made a pledge, embodied in what she'd worn around her neck since she'd taken it at age fifteen.

The Coin Malleus, a hammer on one side, the two-tailed comet on the other that looked so like the statue's forked tongue. She placed it in the bowl as though this effigy of alien divinity was a beggar at Lethis' gates. She took her knife and put it not to the fingers but to the back of her arm, because *that* was where sensible people drew blood, if they weren't lizards or immortal Stormcasts. Dabbling her fingers in the cut, she made a red smear everywhere that Oaxmal had. *Look at me, doing magic. Does that mean I get more pay when I'm back at camp?*

Only when she'd made the last mark did she understand that the ruined shrine, the whole ruin maybe, had been holding its breath.

A voice, in her head. A voice in her imagination, surely. A child's idea of what a dragon might sound like. *Child of Sigmar, walker with the Seraphon.* Stanner felt a stab of fear far keener than anything the Skaven could put into her.

Thunder rumbled above, in Shyish's clear grey sky. A shudder rippled through the stones beneath them, the sense of *movement,* ponderous and stately as a great ship.

What did I do? She got back from the statue in case it fell on her. Oaxmal and Gokumet were crouched, ready for catastrophe. Suddenly the ruins around them seemed busy, seething with frantic motion. *The rats? No–*

A pack of small Seraphon dashed past her, some in trailing robes. Phantoms. She saw the broken stones through them. Nearby something bellowed. A huge three-horned beast, ornamented with a fortune in gold. On its back a trio of lizard mahouts shrilled and waved goads. Scaled warriors were pushing past, heading somewhere at a run. From nearby there was a flash, and she felt the ground shudder like an animal in pain.

Vael cried out, staggering back from the statue. Its complete, horned head regarded him, eyes blazing with Azyr's pure fire.

In the next second: a ruin, dead for centuries, grown cracked and dark with Shyish's encroach. She stared at Oaxmal, who stared right back, as spooked as she was.

Another flash, a searing column that left afterimages on the eye and yet was entirely in her mind. She had a sense of massive gold-armoured figures, head and shoulders above a regular human. Shields lifted high to display the hammer and lightning of Sigmar. Reptile warriors answering like the thunder, wielding spears and clubs. And still the lightning came, bolt after vertical bolt, and each one leaving another metal-clad form to join the fray. A cataclysmic coming together of force, Stormcasts and Seraphon, and all around them the cracking of walls and the sundering of causeways. Her feet felt solid ground beneath them but her stomach lurched from the sudden drop. *It fell,* Vael said.

Sigmar help us, they brought it down. He'd told her over and over, but she hadn't understood.

Another moment's clarity, nothing but the ravaged shrine. Vael had his hands to his head, to his face, digging at his scars. He was howling and his eyes were two storms. In another moment he had taken up his hammer, one hand still bare and bleeding lightning, and was fighting – she couldn't tell who he was fighting. Ghosts, yes, but the ghosts of the lizard defenders or of his own companions. Or perhaps himself.

'Lordship!' she called. 'Lordship, no, the rats!' But he couldn't hear her and she couldn't get near him. That great two-handed hammer whirled all about him, swifter than she could have moved a sword, striking at stones and at air and at enemies only in the man's head.

He was shouting, begging maybe. She heard Sigmar's name there, and others that might have been his comrades of past aeons. Arcs of white fire danced from his armour to the masonry and bloomed within his skin. She wondered if he was just going to explode in Sigmar's holy power there and then, an end even a Stormcast might not return from.

How do you stop a Stormcast gone mad? But a god had put all his power and ingenuity into making them as hard to stop as possible, and surely no mere Wildercorps scout was going to manage it.

'We need to get out of here,' she told the lizards. 'We have to leave him. We've done the thing, right? Only, the rats are going to be here any moment.'

Oaxmal was already backing off, plainly of the same mind, but Gokumet disagreed. Gokumet was, Stanner thought with sinking heart, a warrior. Here was their temple reliving its own sundering, and here was the man who had been a part of it. In the big Seraphon's mind there was probably only one course of action.

It hefted its club and bellowed out its own war cry to answer Vael's shouting, then charged forwards.

CHAPTER TWENTY-ONE

IRIXI

For an instant it seemed that every block and column of the *Wings of Serendipitous Fire* shifted around them. The host of rat monks encamped around Sek'atta's throne shrilled and leapt up, ringing bells and shaking scripture-studded staves. Irixi watched them, narrow-eyed, thinking, *You may well fear.* The Starseer's followers were following the prescribed steps, which meant simultaneously that they were following the Old Ones' plan. Or so it was to be hoped.

I am presumptuous. Forgive me my self-importance. And yet surely this must be what the great powers of the cosmos had ordained, before they were severed from their chosen servants, the slann and the Seraphon. Perhaps, when – *if? No, when!* – the Nine Orchid Path was restored, Irixi would even see itself depicted there, crouching with the human on this throne, within the circle of Sek'atta's protective power.

Irixi could reach out, with that wisdom Sek'atta had caused to bloom, and sense the balance of the ruin tilt around them. Not physically, although a very definite shudder had passed through every part of the place. The balance between life and death, the living temple against the dead land. The balance between decay and preservation as the *Wings* rested within the cupped hands of Shyish. The balance between the past, what the temple-ship had once been, and the future, that it might become.

Work still to be completed, but at least the other Seraphon were capable of it. Irixi had despaired when the Plagueseer's forces had turned the rescuers back, but only because it had misunderstood the plan. When it had assisted Perlo in calling out to the human's broodmate, Irixi had assumed it was to allow the mage's bodyguard and Irixi's own to come and defeat the rats. Instead it had been so Oaxmal could retrieve that severed tail. Better even than a link between kin was the link between a Starseer and its own flesh.

Although, truth be told, communicating complex arcane wisdom through such a medium was taxing, and Irixi hadn't been convinced of the Chameleon's ability to comprehend and follow complex instructions. Oaxmal was a swift student, though. It was common for most skinks to think of the Chameleon as simpler creatures, mute and clannish as they were. Easy to overlook that their usual tasks took them deep into hostile country where they had no ally but their own resourcefulness. Of course Oaxmal was equal to the responsibility. Irixi should have had more faith.

Now a certain malicious satisfaction could be felt, observing the rats scurrying back and forth in panic.

'You're doing this, aren't you?' Perlo said. The human had been meditating, contributing its little stock of strength to their shield in a way that showed considerable finesse. Seraphon students of the arcane were usually highly trained in very narrow fields, each to a particular task, and Irixi had thought humans would be the same. Perlo seemed to have a broad but shallow learning that could work with whatever it came across, even the leftover echoes of Sek'atta's own workings. Small wonder the human had won itself a place in the prophecy. Who knew what great work such a one might make some small contribution to?

'The Good Purpose is being accomplished, by small but steady steps,' Irixi said. 'That it also confounds our enemies is tangential, but not unappreciated.' Hard to properly demonstrate amusement without the usual curling of the tail, but then the nuance would be lost, of course, to human eyes.

'This will let them rescue us?' Perlo pressed.

'When the Purpose is complete, word must be carried to Sek'atta,' Irixi said. A little obfuscatory, it knew. If the secrets of the Path could be restored, then Sek'atta's residual power here might be spent to place the knowledge in the mage-priest's mind, for this place was a conduit to the ancient slann, as sure as Irixi was to its own tail. That accomplished, it wouldn't actually matter if a rescue happened or not. The task would be concluded, and so might be the usefulness of Sek'atta's servants to the Old Ones' plan. It was right and proper that Irixi accept its fate.

Preferring an outcome where the Old Ones had some further use for a poor Starseer was not proper, but it couldn't entirely banish the thought. *I am an imperfect tool,* it supposed. And if the human also survived to escape the rats' clutches, that would not be unwelcome, and would bring further dismay to the egg-stealers, surely a small good in itself.

Perlo grimaced and nodded. Irixi saw the Skaven Plagueseer approaching them with its unpleasant interpreter. A pair of monks set to the bellows again, and as the crowned rat chittered from atop its pulpit, the half-corpse's mouth gaped to force out new words.

'O cold-blooded apostate, wretched belly-crawler, do not think that your intentions are hidden from the keen eye of Ferskine, the perspicacious, the all-seeing, the chosen receptacle for all the pestilential blessings of the Horned Rat,' droned the corpse. It was actually easier for Irixi to understand than a living human: the words came out slower and flatter, shorn of all that gabble of emotion that made their normal speech so hard to follow.

The Plagueseer made an expansive gesture with its staff, leaving an arc of foul smoke in the air.

'The most erudite Ferskine, lord of arcane mysteries, sees your feeble efforts to wrest this place from the death-blighted paralysis of this realm,' the corpse exhaled. 'Doubtless you believe, in your feeble scheming, that such an act must thwart the grand and most intricate ambitions of Ferskine the Far-Sighted, master of machinations. For even as you lever apart the stones of this place, what should seep in but blessed corruption, the very pus from the boils of the Horned Rat!'

Irixi narrowed its eyes.

'Does that mean they're on to you?' Perlo whispered. The human was putting on a defiant face – insofar as Irixi was any judge – but its voice sounded worried.

'The vermin lord gives itself many titles, but true deserving is judged by those above,' Irixi said reassuringly.

'Just hot air, then?' Perlo was biting at its lip, looking at the ghastly translator.

'No more than the shed skin of truth, which seems to have its shape but has nothing within it,' Irixi said. Better that the human had fewer worries, or it might get agitated and do something unwise. Inside, though, Irixi felt a creeping worm of fear. Yes, the Skaven had their own ritual-working: all those monks praying and squealing and ringing their accursed, discordant bells. They were about some piece of plaguery, and the Starseer could feel their toxic influence creeping like mould between the stones of the *Wings of Serendipitous Fire*. A most infectious ritual. The Plagueseer might not deserve all the plaudits it heaped upon itself, but it was a potent foe to Order nonetheless. Irixi had a queasy feeling that if it was able to gain complete mastery of the ruin, it might try to spread its filth even to Sek'atta and the *Celestial Eye of Tepok*. Not that such a wretched creature could hope to contend with the august mage-priest, but…

Irixi had just one strand to cling to. *Wrest this place from the death-blighted paralysis of this realm,* the Plagueseer had said. And maybe that was just its florid language or a mangling in the translation, but there was just the slightest chance that the Skaven priest had not entirely understood the great working Sek'atta had ordained. Looking into its razor stare, Irixi wasn't sure. There was madness in those warpstone eyes, certainly, but it brought a great deal of cunning with it. A mind that could gnaw even into the secrets of the slann.

Had another Seraphon been there, they would have seen Irixi's worry through pose and skin tone. Just as well Perlo was blind to such things.

Irixi looked the Plagueseer in the eye and was dismayed to see an all-too-evident glee there. *It* saw, sure enough. When it yattered to its scribe again, the corpse translator remained blessedly silent, but the Seraphon was grimly sure it was saying, *Set down that the lizard-creature fears our power,* and it wouldn't be wrong.

Oaxmal, you must hurry to complete the working, before the rats corrupt it. Before they corrupt a great many things.

CHAPTER TWENTY-TWO

VAEL

The lightning seared through air and stone and they came down. Sigmar's champions, the first forging, deployed by divine fiat to smite the armies of Chaos and turn the tide of entropy. Around Vael, the supplicants of the temple surged, taking up weapons never far from their scaled hands. Rising up to meet this desecration of their holy places. Surely the greatest symptoms of the Age of Ruin, that the servants of Order should be pitted mindlessly against one another by mere mischance!

The golden-armoured figures blazing into being, each at the heart of a column of raging blue-white fire that melted stone and seared flesh. Sigmar's warriors, forged by Grungni with superhuman craft. The perfect, the majestic, the indomitable, misdeployed here in the heart of battle. Javelins and darts scattered off pristine mail still bright from the armouries of Azyr. Each took a fraction of a second to grasp their surroundings – their comrades, their foes – and then they were charging forwards, coming together with shield and spear and hammer, unstoppable, glorious. Tragic, pointless.

Vael ran at them, threw himself in their way. 'Hold back!' he shouted at the impassive golden masks, at the raised shields display-ing Sigmar's uncompromising heraldry. 'These are not your foes! Hold back!' Masked, faceless, but he knew them. His fellows of the forge, his comrades in their first incarnation as Sigmar's servants. Each one snatched from death by the god's own hand and remade into a paragon of justice and righteousness. But it was not just and it was not right.

'Friends, comrades!' he told them. Grasped for their names and found his mind empty of them. They had passed on, life to life, death to death, one suit of gilded mail to the next until the constant round had worn all their faces smooth in his mind, like stones. Until the last vestige of the men and women they had been was gone. They had marched to the Ruination chambers with all the other Storm-casts who had become… something other. Both more and less than the individual people they had been. Until, of all his peers, only Vael clung stubbornly to the last of his memories. Clung to *this*: this battle, this meaningless clash of mistaken allies. He could not let go of it, because it was his shame, the shadow on his soul. *The time we destroyed the temple of the sun.*

They pushed him aside. He felt the impact, armoured shoulders and shields just thrusting him away. All in his mind, of course. The spectral figures coursed through him as the lightning blazed, delivering more and more golden warriors to the bloody fray. Far below them on the bitter fields of Shyish, the vast bulk of Sigmar's army was engaging the Everchosen's legions, the armies of Order fighting the true fight, the necessary fight. But here, unknowing, ignorant, this consignment had gone astray. Intercepted by the flight of the Seraphon to the foundering of all.

Not again. He had just been holding on to the understanding that all this was just ghosts and shadows. The dust of another age raised up by the reverberations of ritual, forming briefly into remembered shapes. He felt his grasp on the situation slip, like a man in a torrent who loses his hold on the rock. Instantly he was carried into his own memories, clothing each spectre in flesh, feeling the ground beneath him tilt and fracture as the temple lurched in the sky.

He yelled a war cry and hurled himself forwards, bringing his hammer down on a golden shield. He would fight them, his comrades, his friends. He would stop them re-enacting the massacre.

Seraphon magic. I can change things. It will be different this time. A desperate, unreasoning belief.

The hammer struck, and a scaled shape reeled away from the blow. Vael felt the shock as though he'd taken the wound himself. Again he hurled himself at the golden line, wordless, screaming, striking at Sigmar's symbols and heraldry. Seraphon died beneath his assault, or the shields he beat on were stone and bronze, the faces behind them reptile-savage. Every action only recreated the pointless carnage. History would not be denied.

He cast his weapon away and rushed the Stormcast shield-wall. He closed his eyes against the sight, but the images flashed within his mind anyway, the unseaming of scaled hides, toothed clubs battering down gold shields. A dreadful waste of strength and courage like water poured into the sands.

There was armour beneath his hands, the familiar ridges of pauldron and breastplate. He opened his eyes. He had one of them in his grip, wrestling fiercely with a strength exactly equalling his own. Vael yelled curses into that perfect gilded face and then gripped it, digging his fingers into the eyeholes, prying with all his strength, tearing the helmet's mask free with a shearing of metal. The face within was mad with battle-joy, with righteousness. Its eyes blazed with divine fire. It was the face he saw in the mirror before he took a knife to it.

I said no! That was what he had clung to, thinking back on this moment. When Sigmar took him from his mortal death, when he had stood before the divine throne and been told of his fate to be a Stormcast, forever and forever, he had refused. He had pitted his minuscule mortal will against the god. *I am a kinslayer. I earned my death. Just let me go.* But Sigmar had chosen him, as he had chosen his pick of all mortal warriors. Sigmar had found in him the qualities necessary to wear the golden armour and wield the hammer against all the foes of the realms. Consent was not one of those virtues.

I said no. But he looked on his own face now, intoxicated with the knowledge of its own just cause, and knew that the *No* had not survived the forging. It had burned away in the flames and this creature of purpose was what had survived. His last defence against the knowledge of what they had done crisped and blew away like ash. Here he was, Vael of the First Forging, in the thick of a fight that should never have happened, and eager for battle.

The man he had been laughed into Vael's scarred face, cast off his later self and waded off into the fray. Unstoppable, undoubting, revelling in the strength and power that the forging had infused him with. Vael grasped for him, trying to haul him back, but he was just one more Stormcast amongst many, falling to the blows of the Seraphon and striking them down in turn.

For a moment it was all just ghosts and shadows again, and he was sane, or at least dancing on the knife edge of sanity. The past could be staved off, forced back into the gloom of memory. He could cope. He had a brief glimpse of Stanner staring at him, keeping well back. Of his hammer, head down, haft up, waiting for him. His gauntlet closed about it without thought, knowing its place. A weapon that knew no fear or doubt. That was what he was made to be.

The next instant it all flooded in on him again, the other sun, the walls. The great horned head of Dracothion worked in stone, louring down on him, judging him. He cowered from the dragon's spread stone wings, even as another flash of lightning drew a molten line down them.

Forgive me! Forgive all of us! But his fellows were gone beyond memory and beyond doubt, and without those things, how could they ever be forgiven for what they had done?

The battle around him swirled like smoke, Stormcasts and Seraphon blurring and flurrying as something forced its way through the memories to get to him. He saw a huge scaled form, crested head, gaping jaws. Gokumet, and he had no idea if it was the Gokumet of his mind or of the real.

Its toothed club was directed at him, though, calling him out, challenging him. Offering the only way out of the nightmare.

Vael bellowed out a despairing war cry and rushed forwards to join the fight.

CHAPTER TWENTY-THREE

GOKUMET

These things Gokumet understood. The warm sun on its hide. The orders of the mage-priests. War.

Oaxmal flashed urgent colours, saying, *No, no,* but while the scout was cunning, there were things it could not know. Some domains were Gokumet's alone.

Above was Sotek, font of all reptiles, hunter of rats in the dark places, youngest of the gods yet first amongst them while this age of war endured. Around Gokumet, the spectres of broodmates and kin glimmered and danced. A gift, from the past. Not a gift of sorrow, as it seemed to the Golden One. A gift of joy. Like one last mild autumn day at the very brink of winter. One final glimpse of First Home.

Gokumet felt as though it had never departed this place. As though some part of the champion had fallen with the *Wings of Serendipitous Fire,* even as Sek'atta commanded the retreat. Now that piece had been restored, for the saurus stood where it had been, and all around was the fight it had abandoned. A circle had been completed in its heart. When it had returned to First Home the stones had been dead and broken, but now First Home had returned to Gokumet.

The Golden One gave out dreadful lost noises, like a beast in a trap. It struck at phantoms, then dropped its own weapon, clawing at its mauled face. Gokumet was no seer. No human, to be consumed by inner tides like this. It understood ghosts, though. It had lived with its own on the *Celestial Eye of Tepok*. The ghost of First Home lost.

At peace now, it watched the Golden One devoured from the inside, a human haunting itself. Gokumet knew what action must be taken. The calm within, the acceptance of ruin, must be shared.

The saurus hefted its club. Oaxmal was still signalling *No* and the other human was shouting, but what did they know? This was warrior business. This was what Gokumet understood.

There were rituals – festivals, almost – when the Seraphon recounted their myths through acting them out, each participant exact in word and motion so that the paths of ritual power embodied in the stories could be reinforced. Stories that were magic, magic that was legend. Real histories idealised and corrected so that the future could be better, or future events re-envisioned so that the plan might be brought closer to fruition. It was skink work, mostly, the treading over of those stories. There was music, finery. Five of the little Seraphon might carry a cloth-covered jointed frame, dancing the steps of *The Great Dragon Rises In Flame*, or *The Banishing of the Daemon Lord*, or *Itzl Tames the Carnosaur*. Gokumet had never been a performer, but it stepped into the dance of ritual now, adopting the role of its own self, Gokumet of First Home, Champion of Sek'atta, Defender of the Fallen Temple, pacing through the remembered motions of *How the Golden Ones Were Fought*.

It passed through the steps of the challenge, simultaneously remembered and acted out anew, and the Golden One saw, and became calm, knowing his own role as the Lightning Bearer, the Bright Enemy.

Gokumet almost heard the crowd rustle in appreciation. *I am become a myth.*

The Golden One stepped forwards, hammer descending, just as it should be. Gokumet took the blow on its shield, letting the bright weapon slant away. The starmetal club slammed against the Stormcast's shoulder, resounding through the strong metal. Gokumet felt a deep satisfaction, stepping back as the hammer's next arc passed by, the Golden One letting its momentum carry itself under the saurus' following sweep. They parted, circled. Around them, the phantasmal melee wheeled, each fighting figure a star in its greater constellation.

The face of the Golden One was the one ill note in the precise steps of the dance. The Stormcast should have been masked, as it had been before. Or, if not masked, then serene, understanding its place in the cosmos. Instead, the human features stretched and twisted. As though it was real for it. As though it was fighting for its life.

Gokumet was not a creature of many understandings, but a revelation came then: how terrible it must be, to be human. To not know oneself part of a greater plan. Even the golden servants of their human god lived in such ignorance, it seemed. They must strive to *believe* when Gokumet *knew*.

Their weapons passed back and forth, each move perfect. The Golden One's mind might know doubt but its body and armour understood. Gokumet dealt and received a blow, knowing the pain was a step along the ritual path that the two of them had plotted out centuries before. They were coming to the conclusion. The saurus felt saliva well under its tongue at the thought. In the Golden One's face, a similar revelation came. The Stormcast remembered how this ended, and the knowledge at last brought it peace.

Gokumet stepped inside the Golden One's guard, letting the butt of the hammer bound from its shoulder. It grappled with the Stormcast, feeling the strength of lightning within the armour. Saurus jaws gaped, lunged.

Distantly there came one discordant note, the shocked cry of the other human.

Gokumet's fangs found their grooves, each fitting to a precise rut across the face of the Golden One. It held them there, biting slightly, feeling the resistance of the man's scars.

Around them, the last tatters of what-had-been blew away. The ghosts ebbed back into air. The distant clatter of battle faded,

Gokumet eased its jaws open and crouched back on its haunches. The ritual was done, the story was told. The Fall of First Home.

There were eyes on them. Oaxmal, the human scout.

The Stormcast spoke human words. *Thank you,* said its tone. If the madness was not gone from those lightning eyes, it had retreated. A wound unhealed but salved at least. These things Gokumet understood.

One more pair of eyes was on them. At the mouth of the ruined temple a single rat stood, frozen, staring in utter bewilderment at what had just taken place. Oaxmal hissed and brought up its blow-pipe, but the creature turned and fled, shrilling for reinforcements. It was time to move on.

CHAPTER TWENTY-FOUR

OAXMAL

The tail was dying. Written in its twisting and faded patterns were Oaxmal's final instructions from Irixi. One more shrine and its location before the work was done. *And be ready to act!* Irixi's coda. There were rites that bore no fruit for generations, whose workings would take a hundred years before their effect on the realms became manifest. This, Oaxmal divined, would not be one of those.

It flushed bright red across its crest and throat pouch to hook Gokumet's attention. The saurus was still crouching before the Golden One, lending the Stormcast strength to rise. The rats would be here soon, in strength.

Oaxmal weighed the oracular tail in its hands, seeing its final commands dying on its skin, then dropped it as the sympathetic link to the Starseer finally withered. The Chameleon's skin danced through a sequence of simple images, not the complex flicker it would use with its peers but ideas fit to communicate to a saurus.

Return. Gather force. Prepare. Seize opportunity. Assault. Then a second time and a third until Gokumet growled understanding. After which, between shoving, pulling and some brutal clubbing mime, it communicated the same to the Golden One. Soon enough, the pair of them were heading back to where the humans had their fire.

The other human, the useful human, watched all this, and Oaxmal eyed it thoughtfully. The path the tail had described in its last throes would take them to the very fringes of the Skaven camp, and the shrine was immediately below, perhaps swarming with the creatures. Mere force would not suffice, but subtlety? Perhaps.

The useful human nodded. It would follow Oaxmal's lead. Its dart-thrower was loaded, the little arms drawn back.

There were rats aplenty across the ruins, between them and their target. Oaxmal and the useful human ghosted past each pack, sometimes climbing high above across the jagged teeth of broken walls, sometimes slinking around fallen rubble, hiding in the shadows of truncated columns, crawling through the dried-up gutters of sacred water channels. The Skaven were making themselves at home, picking over the ruin, squabbling with one another, smearing their filthy sigils on the walls. Oaxmal saw the triangular rune of their rat god painted in blood and excrement over the ordered pictograms of the seers and knew a dull, patient loathing. All such sacrileges would be answered in the fullness of time, but Seraphon were creatures of patience. They had been created to enact a plan as wide as the realms and as deep as history. Not like humans with their swift, fierce lives.

They crept to the very edge of the Skaven's surface camp. Not the full, thronging host that was in the prophecy chamber deep below, surrounding Irixi's weakening shield, but still a festering mass of them. Oaxmal watched half a dozen separate fights amongst the creatures, the meanest of the mean fighting for lordship over the three or four others within reach of claws and teeth. Others had made themselves petty little thrones, sitting like deluded princelings as lesser rats brought them stinking delicacies or decked them in Seraphon-crafted anklets, rings and pectorals. A handful of rats were plainly supposed to be keeping watch, but their attention was mostly on the antics of their fellows. Oaxmal and the useful human drifted past them and they knew nothing of it.

There was a shaft with narrow, steep steps, burrowing crookedly into the earth at the very edge of the Skaven camp. Needless to say, the rats had found it already. A handful of them were clustered at the top, peering down with what Oaxmal identified as fear. Not just scurrying into the dark to scavenge, but certainly standing in the way.

Oaxmal tilted an eye at the human. It counted off the rats carefully: five. Was five too many, to kill them before word could spread? One squeak of alarm and the whole camp could be on them.

The Chameleon gestured for its companion to come close, then plucked the little javelin from the human's bolt-caster. A simple missile. Oaxmal drew the head along the slick skin of the frog at its belt, coating the metal with toxin, then handed it back. The human understood immediately, refitting the missile with great care and then handing over the rest of its ammunition. Oaxmal coated each in turn, knowing that this was, in some small way, forbidden. A Seraphon secret, a Chameleon secret, a venom sacred to Oaxmal's own patron, in the hands of a human.

The gods would have to understand.

They struck without needing a signal between them, Oaxmal's throat inflating to force the darts explosively from its pipe as the human's weapon spat out its own bolts, its fingers drawing back the string with deft motions. Three rats were down and spasming before the others understood they were under attack, and they had no chance to do anything about it.

The pair of them had the bodies down a pit in short order. Perhaps some rat taskmaster would miss them, but absent was less suspicious than dead. Then it was the dark, the human's half-closed lantern lending just enough light to see the precipitous steps.

Down below, they discovered why the rats had been leery of descending. They weren't the first to try, and the previous patrol hadn't come back out.

The near end of the small chamber was a scree slope of shattered stone. Beyond, the shrine itself was cramped, little space beyond that needed to kneel before the effigy itself. Oaxmal registered a square engraving in the far wall, crazed through with cracks but still mostly intact. Within that square was Huanchi. An older, more stylised representation than Oaxmal was used to, shown head down, teeth bared, head, limbs, body and tail tessellated so that there was not an inch of the design that was not Huanchi. The Hunter of the Night Forest, the Eyes in the Darkness, simultaneously the predator and the hunting grounds themselves. Oaxmal's own patron, who had blessed the waters of its birthing.

On the ground, before the icon and strewn halfway up the slope, were another half a dozen dead Skaven, killed as they tried to flee. And all around, the faint glimmers of motion, the very ghosts of ghosts, spectres of things that would have been hidden from sight even when they were alive. Oaxmal's kin. When the *Wings of Serendipitous Fire* had lived and flown, a brood of its own kind had dwelled and worshipped here. Now Irixi's ritual had roused them in spirit, and they had come to defend their sacred place. Oaxmal didn't know if the rats had died from some phantasmal venom or from fear.

It picked its way around them, approaching the effigy, feeling that fierce regard. Huanchi was like life: one could never be sure of it. Of all the Seraphon powers, Oaxmal felt, Huanchi was the wildest. Not cold and patient like the Serpent, Sotek, or the Sun-Lizard, Chotec. Huanchi was the Jaguar, swift and filled with passions. Hot-blooded, like a human.

If its broodmates had been at its side and living, Oaxmal would never have thought in such a way. Here before its god, with the desecrating Skaven making merry above, it felt their absence keenly. It had only the one ally able to walk where Huanchi's followers must go, though. A fellow hunter, despite everything that separated them.

Oaxmal crouched before Huanchi's stone likeness. One topaz eye had been prised out by the Skaven, but the shrine's defenders had manifested before the rats could blind the god entirely.

The useful human knelt beside it, watching intently. In a few heartbeats, Oaxmal would see if its blood would suffice to awaken its patron, but there was a necessary duty first. Huanchi must be told of those who had borne its blessing, and who would not be returning to its service.

Oaxmal drew their names with a finger – no blood, no lasting mark: those consecrated to Huanchi passed through the world and left not a ripple. As befitted a Chameleon, their names were writ invisibly, in silence. One after another, Oaxmal traced the sign of them, until every broodmate was accounted for save itself.

It hunched back on its haunches, feeling a weight taken from it. Feeling Huanchi devour the names of its adherents, to keep them safe and remembered. The useful human watched, and somehow the meaning of the rite communicated itself, because it also reached forwards and traced something, some piece of human writing on the stone.

'Arnulf,' it said softly, and Oaxmal understood. Arnulf: one more fallen hunter. For all it would never have known the god in life, Oaxmal felt Huanchi accept the dedication in death. Arnulf, a name to be held in the secret annals of the Stalker in the Shadows.

Keeping one eye on the effigy, Oaxmal turned the other on the human. The creature's blood had awoken Sotek when Oaxmal's had not sufficed, after the temple of the Serpent had been scarred by the power of human gods.

A great daring came to Oaxmal's mind. Something that others might decry as blasphemy but that seemed only natural here and now. There would be no more guidance from Irixi. Oaxmal had only its own judgement.

It wished it could know if the human felt the god speak to it, understood something of the meaning of the shrine. Human minds were stamped on human faces always, those rubbery features never still, yet it was a language Oaxmal could not interpret.

It drew out its flake of obsidian and indicated to the useful human to draw its own steel knife. Each of them drew blood, and then Oaxmal guided the human's hand. Not merely an enactment of Irixi's ritual to awake the shrines, and the temple. A consecration, an invitation to the spirit of the Jaguar god, to look kindly on this human creature, to find in it a kinship, a surrogate child to watch over.

Oaxmal reached up and smeared its own blood across the human's face, its own skin echoing the patterns it drew there. *Darkness. Fear. The unexpected strike.* Feeling through that touch a connection absent since the last of its siblings died. *Useful human, my brood-mate, we shall hunt together.*

It guided the human's hand one last time, and they daubed blood on Huanchi's remaining eye together. The topaz was just a faceted stone, now dulled with red, but inside itself, Oaxmal felt the god's regard.

Quetzl to ward the way, Chotec's warmth to give life and animation, Sotek to lend a predatory purpose, Huanchi to start the hunt. Gods. Philosophical concepts. Nodes in the disjointed network of arcane lines that had once stretched through the temple-ship *Wings of Serendipitous Fire.* Long severed in the sacred vessel's crash, and now rejoined.

Around them, a colossal grinding arose from every wall. The divine power of the Old Ones and their slann priests once more coursed through the ruin, even as the claws of Shyish rushed in greedily to take possession. Life and death met within the heart of the temple, not clashing as adversaries but growing together like roots.

STARSEER'S RUIN

CHAPTER TWENTY-FIVE

From the Scriptorium of Ferskine of the Eleventh Bell

Nownow slavescribe record faithfully these words of your better yes-yes?

Here in this ruin and rubble and wreckage comes the feeble workings of the scalepriest, seer thing, sad prisoner in its own bauble before us, that thinks itself so wise, yes-yes. Scrawny tail-gone lizard-thing, puppet of fat and senile toad beasts who look down on the blessed and ever-increasing progeny of the Rat, devourer of all things, gnawer beneath the foundations of the realms!

Scalepriest trapped-one knows life-strength exists yet in this living-dead place and seeks to separate it from dead-land root-clutch. Seeks to reclaim power lost careless and abandoned and forgotten in dark places. Set down this most ineffable truth, that all things left in the dark and the depths and the dimness are the true prey of the Rat. No lizard claws reaching for our rightful due!

Know that the most insidious Lord Ferskine, the sly, the subtle, the secret, has crept into these lizard riches and rites and rituals, plague seeping from every pore. Where life parts from death, there the plague shall begin. Where power calls to power, so it shall carry on the aetheric currents from lizard-creature to toad-thing, from ruin to temple. We shall poison them and their masters and their gods so their flying palaces fall like the leaves of the final autumn. We shall foster rat-brood in their decaying corpses. We shall paint the sigil of the Horned Rat in their holy places, yes-yes!

Set this down for the greater glory of the Horned Rat and of Ferskine, the most triumphant, the glorious, the victorious! For even now the lizard-working is complete, that shall be made to serve us. We see here the feeble hand of Death, that thinks itself master of souls but which, too, shall be made to kneel at the altar of the Rat! Watch it recede so that our feculent tide of corruption may roll in, and even as it does so, we bring our grasp to bear across the feeble shell-shield of the scalepriest and we crush and crack and crumble, we gnaw at the power of it until the thing and its pet are naked and helpless and screaming before the hungry children of the Rat. So says Ferskine the mighty, the magical, the mange-bringer, let the favour of the Horned Rat be upon him forever and forever!

Part 4

SET IN STONE

CHAPTER TWENTY-SIX

PERLO

Stuck in the bubble of force with Irixi, there hadn't been much for her to do save learn. Learning was what Perlo did, after all. She was no Azyrite born with a realmstone spoon in her mouth, a battle-mage for an uncle and a family with grand connections. Nobody had bought her an arcane tutor and a personal grimoire. She'd scraped lore together off the boots of the regular army and made herself the most piecemeal, shoddy sort of mage anyone ever saw. But she'd done it entirely through her own hard work and natural aptitude. The number of comfortable, complacent mages who'd dismissed her, then seen her on the front lines pulling together her patchwork magic to as much effect as any of their grand wizardry! She learned, from whatever was to hand, and right here and now she was getting the greatest lesson in ritual magic she ever would in her life. Also probably the last.

Irixi had been tracing sigils on the stone of the floating seat. Not even drawing *with* anything, just moving its finger in a sequence of angular glyphs that left a faint afterimage to Perlo's eyes. Past their shield, in the wider ruin, she could feel the counterpart workings being enacted by the Seraphon's underlings, like the teeth of a key meeting the levers of a lock. Turning, moving the greater elements of the whole, bringing all the notional tumblers into alignment. And obviously it wasn't that the actual stones of the place were grinding into new alignments – that would have been ridiculous. But that was how she *felt*, sensing the moving parts of the rite come together. Enough that she had to clutch at the throne to steady herself.

That was not the only lesson to be learned, unfortunately.

The Skaven had been at their own counter-ritual all this time, under the jurisdiction of their Plague Priest. The crowned rat had been chittering at its monk followers, abusing them, beating at them with its thurible-flail staff. They had cleared away rubble from a space before the shield and set out trails of filth, bones and rags there. Three bounding lines making a triangle with overlapping ends, and within them a series of other glyphs drawn in blood and worse fluids, punctuated by shards of glowing warpstone, the whole very definitely directed *at* the shield. Perlo didn't particularly wish to understand Skaven magic better, but the lesson was there to be learned. What looked crude to the mundane eye became a crawling, intricate tracery of power to a mage's sight, spreading towards them like infection through flesh. Where it approached the shield, she could see a dark bruise discolouring the violet energy, sapping at the strength of the throne's protections. There were cracks, at first imperceptible but steadily growing. She had the sense of an invisible rat hand closing about the sphere, adjusting its hold to exploit the areas of greatest weakness.

Every so often the priest had come to pontificate at them, and at first she'd been able to laugh it off as mere vainglory. By now she could appreciate that the creature really *did* know what it was doing. A ritual magician as potent, in its own twisted way, as Irixi. Because the Skaven working was not simply powered by monkish prayer and warpstone. It was feeding off the strength of Irixi's own rites. Irixi was working at the boundary where the latent Seraphon power of the ruin met the entanglements of Shyish that had grown in at every boundary. The sickly influence of the Skaven power crept in wherever there was a gap, gnawing at the foundations of everything it could reach. When it came to fruition then the shield would fail, yes, but worse than that, the rats would infest all the lines and channels of power in the ruin. They would make it *theirs*.

For a moment she bitterly envied her brother. If he were here, he'd know none of this, and surely better to be ignorant of it.

And now both workings, simultaneously, were reaching their apex. She felt, like a candle lit at the back of her mind, the final Seraphon node flare into life. The renewed shrines, pulling the reconnected strands of the temple's power taut, into a new shape. All around them the stones shuddered and dust sifted down from above. For a moment the Skaven monks, pacing over the lines of their triangular sigil, paused and looked up.

Nothing happened.

Or, rather, Irixi's working seemed to produce nothing. The Skaven's own rite redoubled its growth, festering through the newly opened channels of the ruin's arcane landscape like mould.

'This is where we get out, right?' she asked the Seraphon. 'Your "good purpose"?'

Irixi eyed her. 'The Good Purpose is achieved at the correct time.'

'Only, if this is one of those rituals that takes a year to come to pass, we may not be around that long. Or a day. Or an hour, even.'

'What indeed is time?' Irixi asked her. It was such a calm and abstruse question that Perlo just stared at it.

'What is… time? Time is what we don't have,' she got out.

'Time is the circuit of the stars and the realms, one around another. How can it be measured when every line becomes a circle? Above us now, the stars, a pattern, precise. Precise but not unique. A hundred years, a thousand, those stars in that pattern, understood? Time is all things and nothing. Time, a mere idea only.'

'I…' Perlo watched the cracks spread across the face of the shield. Faster and faster. Below them, the throne shuddered, and she could feel the strength being leached from it by the Skaven's hunger. 'I don't want a lesson, Irixi. I want to know we're going to live.' She was twenty-nine years old.

'What indeed is life?' Irixi said philosophically.

Perlo wanted to scream at it. 'Life is what we've got, Irixi! Life is all we have. I was born in Lethis. Life is what separates us from Shyish. Life is the treasure that this realm is constantly trying to take back from you. Life is the thing Nagash can't control or abide, the thing the Chaos powers want to twist to their image, the thing the orruks want to beat out of you. Life is that little part of the cosmos that isn't death and I really, *really* want to hold on to mine. And I thought that was what this was *for*, but now you've done your thing and you haven't even pushed the death away. It's still all around us. It's… Morrda help us.'

She felt the moment like a dam breaking. The ancient, damaged Seraphon wards that had been maintaining the ruin's fragile presence in Shyish suddenly collapsing inwards. The great hunger of Shyish coursing in through every point where the fallen stones touched the chill earth of the realm.

'You failed,' she told Irixi. 'All that work and you failed.'

The Seraphon regarded her with that maddening calm. 'What, indeed, is success?' it asked.

Perlo screamed at it. As though cued by her voice, the shield shattered into jagged shards of power that winked out like stars.

The Plague Priest's ogorish bearer took a single step closer. She waited for the self-aggrandising tirade that would surely preface the moment when she and Irixi were torn apart. And true to form, the team of monks bustled to drag forwards the bellows and the increasingly discoloured remains of Groslyn.

'Hear now the words of Lord Ferskine the magnanimous, the

all-generous, the open-handed,' droned the corpse. 'Such souls and brains as you are custodians of need not be devoured piece-meal by the least meagre servants of His Eminence, the grand and puissant Ferskine. You have proven yourselves delectable morsels whose meagre parts and powers may yet increase the beneficence and majesty of your most malignant and maleficent betters. Come down from that footstool and prostrate yourselves at the fragrantly foul feet of Ferskine, and admit that you are bested by his mightier magecraft.' Groslyn's lips quivered and he spat out two rotten teeth.

Irixi drew a little stone knife, which Perlo took for defiance.

'You'll have to come and take us,' she said, brandishing her cudgel.

Ferskine's green-lit gaze said, eloquently, *Which we obviously can do.* The only impediment would be the throne still being aloft, and it wasn't as though an energetic rat couldn't jump to them.

Irixi hoisted up its robes. For a moment Perlo had the mad image of the Seraphon presenting its abused rear to the rats as some final piece of out-of-character impudence, but instead it brandished its blade and then sliced at the stump of its tail, opening up the puck-ered wound and drawing blood. As though it didn't want to wait for the Skaven but was going to start its own personal death of a thousand cuts right there.

Ferskine's high voice rang out, and the monks stilled. Formed up, in fact, into a triangular formation, a wedge directed at the throne. Suddenly as disciplined as a battle-line of Stormcasts, they raised their staffs and brought the butts down in absolute unison, a single hollow impact that seemed to shake the entire chamber around them.

Her mage's eye saw the festering knot of Skaven power surge for-wards out of the near point of the triangle, and the throne dropped from the air and shattered on the ground, spilling the pair of them onto the jagged rubble.

She heard a shrilling chorus of Skaven voices exalting. Bells, staves beaten against the stone of the floor. She looked wildly around, seeing all the monks practically dancing with glee, as though it was rodent festival day. Past them, though, the priest was clutching the pulpit rail, snout in the air as though scenting. Its little scribe-rat was poised, bedraggled quill to page, but no proclamation came. Lord Ferskine the Magnificent was suddenly very still, sniffing, searching. Not, in fact, rejoicing at all. She saw it tap at its bell, the sound lost in the seething din. Then louder, and at last striking so hard with its staff that the bell sprang from its mount to jangle off into the gloom.

One by one the monks fell silent. Those who had been advancing on the two fallen mages stopped, looking back anxiously at their master.

Ferskine raised one paw in the air, a single digit crooked for attention. Its mouth opened to speak, and she saw the bellows team labour to fill up Groslyn's abused lungs for a new rant.

The air in the chamber was filled with the thought – shared by Perlo, Ferskine and all of the Skaven – of *Haven't we forgotten something?*

Because the magic had been all-consuming – the battle on the arcane plane for mastery of the ruin. But of course there were other battlefields, up to and including the mere physical.

The thunderclap resounded across the chamber, back and forth as it trampled its own echoes. The sudden incursion that surged in from the cracked walls was mostly composed of the big warriors of the Seraphon – not many but charging in with an unstoppable momentum. At their head was a golden-armoured figure with a ravaged face and eyes of lightning.

CHAPTER TWENTY-SEVEN

KENLO

Vael and the big lizardman had stormed back into camp double time, and without Stanner. Straight away the whole reptile contingent had been on their feet and getting their gear together.

'What is it?' Kenlo demanded, then remembered himself. 'My lord, what happened?'

'We…' Vael's eyes were unfocused. He didn't seem to quite see Kenlo. 'We march,' he said, and it could have meant anything.

By then Lofus and the rest were up with their hands on their shields because no guarantee the creatures weren't going to have a go at *them* for some reptile reason. Kenlo went to find the little one who acted as translator, and acted as though all the humans were something it wanted to scrape off its foot. Right then he'd take the abuse if he could get a word of sense out of it.

'Hey, Talker,' he said. 'What's happening. You're going to fetch your chief again?' That hadn't worked out so well the last time, but presumably all this carrying-on in the ruins had achieved *some* sort of magic that would make the attempt possible. 'A rescue, right? Yes?'

The lizard looked at him as though a dog had started talking to it. An impatient twitch ran down its spine.

'The correct alignment of powers has reached conjunction,' it said, as though talking to an idiot, yet not making any damn sense. 'This is the moment for action, that the message be preserved.'

'You mean a rescue, right?' Kenlo pressed urgently. 'Your mage, my sister, stuck down there? Only I thought that was what the whole business was *for*.'

Could a lizard look pained? This one looked pained. Pained at being spoken to by a human and having to speak back in the same way, no doubt. Kenlo could practically see it dragging itself down to his ape level. *I will beat you with a stick, you jumped-up snake.* But he kept his feelings to himself and larded on the patience.

'We go,' the interpreter said with exaggerated slowness, making little scuttling motions with its hands. 'Fight rats. Ensure it is safe, the Good Purpose.'

'Go fight rats,' Kenlo translated. 'Fight rats underground. Big chamber with flying chair.'

'Yes, yes, ape. The "big chamber", the "flying chair".' It turned out the translator could do a good enough Kenlo impression when it wanted. 'Fight rats. You grasp this meaning?'

'Yeah, yeah, I got it.' Talked down to by a lizard who barely came up to his waist. 'Lofus, sergeant, we're moving.'

And Lofus looked at him and said, 'Are we?'

We bloody are. It is not going to be just me and the lizards, Kenlo decided. But then Vael slammed down the head of his hammer, making a solid thud even on the earth of the forest floor, drawing all eyes.

'We march,' the Stormcast said. 'For Sigmar. To make amends for past errors.' As cryptic as the damn lizards.

Lofus opened his mouth to object, then shut it. He might back-chat Kenlo all day, but he wasn't going to go up against a Stormcast, one of Sigmar's chosen. Even a mad one.

The slowest Steelhelm was just doing up her last buckle when the lizards moved out en masse. Just a swift, almost silent rush of scaled flesh out of the trees and into the ruins, and woe betide any random rat scavengers they ran into. The human contingent hustled to catch up, a couple of them helping the Fusiliers with their pavises over the rough ground.

'Right, listen,' Kenlo said, shoving in beside Lofus as they ran.

'I reckon I've done enough listening to you,' the sergeant said sourly.

'No, we'll make this work,' Kenlo said. 'The lizards and my lord there take point, get all the attention. We hold the entrance and the flanks. So long as they do their job, that means just runners and rabble for us to deal with, right? And that place down where Perlo is, it's a damn *throne* room, sergeant. You and the lads fill your boots while the lizards are fighting, and I'll get Perlo out. Gravy, sergeant, enough for everyone to go back for seconds, only save some for me.'

'You reckon we're still coming out of this rich, do you?' Lofus asked sidelong.

'Richer than a Kharadron admiral,' Kenlo confirmed. 'Just hold out and let the lizards do the dying for us.'

'At last you've come up with a plan I can live with,' Lofus said grimly.

They found the same entryway as before, no rats guarding it now. Plenty below, though, and more on their camp on the surface, ready to surge down after them. But right then Kenlo wanted every pair of boots available to get down below, and not just so they could be filled with loot. *If I come out of this with nobody but Perlo beside me, well...* And Lofus wouldn't exactly be going back for Kenlo if their positions were reversed. Not how it was supposed to be, by Sigmar's creed. All shields together, the bastion of Order against the threats of the realms. But both family and personal enrichment tended to put the crowbar in, to pry some gaps between those shields.

They rushed in through the dark. Or at least clambered, climbed, dropped, splashed, stumbled, guided by the fickle light of a handful of lanterns. Ahead there was a brief, squabbling skirmish as Vael and the Seraphon surprised some less than diligent Skaven look-outs and practically trampled them down without slowing.

Kenlo checked his pistol: loaded and ready. He had his axe slanted over his shoulder. Around him the Steelhelms brought their shields up, seeing the greenish glow ahead. Moments later they were spilling out into the ruinous chamber on the tails of the Seraphon.

VAEL

Not really for Sigmar. Not really to make amends, or not in any way the Seraphon would understand or care about. But in another age of the realms, he had been sent to this place to fight the taint of Chaos, and it had been a pointless, tragic waste of life and fervour. Now he was here again, and here, infesting these ruins, was Chaos, in the form of the Skaven. He had fought through the battle that had clung on in his memory when almost everything else had been lost to him. He had come out of it, not forgiven but at least given another chance. He would complete that long-ago task.

Vael cried out the name of Sigmar and let the hammer fall. Bright Azyrite fire flashed as he struck the first wave of the rats, feeling their blades scrape against his armour, digging at the joins. To one side of him, Gokumet brought its club down to shatter a triangular shield, then lunged forwards to snatch up a rat in its jaws, shaking it as a dog might. On Vael's left, another Seraphon warrior thrust its jade-tipped spear into the mass of rodents, ramming its shield into theirs and scattering the line they were trying to hold. The attackers surged forwards, step after step, wringing every last drop out of their initial charge to turn the rats back on themselves, pack them in so that they became their own worst enemies, clambering over one another to reach the enemy or to get away.

Over the heads of the rat vanguard he saw their monks. Plenty had just thrown themselves towards the attackers, practically carving their way through their own kind, greenish froth foaming from their lips. Others had tattered scrolls and books, proclaiming from them in shrill voices. One of the big lizard warriors went down, scales blackening with rot, and then a Steelhelm, skin raised in red weals. Vael tried to shove forwards to get to them, but before he could wade waist-deep in rats to do it, the fusils were sounding like Sigmar's own thunder, monstrously loud in the closed chamber. One of the rat ritualists practically exploded, the ball finding its mark dead centre. Another was clipped, ducking away and dropping its rags of scripture.

The charge was slowing. The sheer mass of rats was dragging at them like a tide. Vael laid about him left and right, no shortage of targets, but every gap he made in them was filled by new foes, forced into place by the press of their fellows and fighting like rabid beasts because they had nowhere to flee to. Then a shadow fell over him and he saw one of their ogor-rats, trampling over the corpses of its lesser brethren, raising an arm that ended in the spiked head of a mace. Vael struck the thing full in its barrel chest without staggering it, and then its blow came down on his shoulder so hard he felt the agonising grind of bones as the mail gave. He snarled and let the hammer fly one-handed, landing a blow across the thing's jaw and closing up one eye. The other bulged with pain and rage, and it took him by the throat with its one hand, lifting the mace to smash in his skull.

At least I die fighting the true enemy this time. He smiled up at the weapon.

Gokumet took the creature's arm. The Seraphon was big, but

the Rat Ogor was easily twice the size. It swung the lizard warrior back and forth, trying to get rid of the weight. Gokumet's clawed feet and tail lashed out across the faces of the rat horde as he wheeled about.

Feeling that monstrous hand tighten, Vael reversed his hammer, gripping it tight behind the head, and slammed it down into the face of the Rat Ogor. Once, twice, again and again like – the image came to him, ludicrously inappropriate – a clerk furiously stamping some orders with a marshal's seal. Lightning flared with each impact, the fire of Sigmar, the fire of Vael's own frustrated existence.

The hand was gone from his throat. He dropped, landing on one knee, already punching forwards with the hammer. He took the beast in the gut, doubling it over so that Gokumet could club it across the back of the head. There was a metal plate there in place of the back of its skull, but the Seraphon's blow stove in the rusted steel and got to the life beneath. The Rat Ogor collapsed, and the lesser rodents eddied away from it.

Vael took stock. The advance had stilled and there were plenty of rats still thronging in. The Steelhelms had formed a solid line, the two fusils sounding sporadically, but they'd used up all the advantage of their surprise. Just as before, the rats were too numerous, already regrouping for a counter-charge that would scour the intruders from the chamber. What had all that skulking about and religion been *for*, if they were just stuck here again?

He saw fleeting movement around the edge of the scrum. Kenlo, the quartermaster, jumping from rubble to rubble as he skirted the melee. There, across the chamber, were his sister and the Seraphon magus. With all eyes on the battle-line, the man had a clear path to them. Was that enough? Would getting them out justify all the blood they were about to pay for the attack? Vael felt a new stab of doubt. Not for himself: live, die, he would only face another Reforging. Perhaps this time they'd hammer the last of the memory from him and he could finally be the immaculate servant Sigmar wanted from him. But Gokumet deserved better. The Seraphon and the humans both deserved better.

I will hold them, he told himself. Let the others retreat; he would hold the way to the surface. Alone, one-armed. It would be a redemption. It would be meaning. He hefted his hammer again, trying to track how far Kenlo had run.

GOKUMET

Gokumet understood that this was the end of it.

The humans, even the Golden One, were still pressing forwards. There was something in a human, Gokumet had learned, that did not see the world quite the way it was. Humans saw the world the way they wanted it to be. The champion understood it led them to strive beyond what was expected of them. Perhaps that was why humans were significant to the plans of the Old Ones, for those moments when what *was* stood too far from what *must be*. Sometimes you needed a human who didn't understand how great the gap was that they leapt across.

The gap here was too great. The rats were too many, Irixi Starseer too far. Gokumet and the Golden One and the others had pushed far into the cavern, but all that meant was that more rats could fight them.

It was *hope*. That was the human quality. Something that Gokumet couldn't have even conceived of before fighting alongside them. *Hope*, that let humans see the world they wanted, not the world they had. Seraphon did not hope, in that way. Seraphon understood that there was a plan, laid down in the earliest days of the realms, that would come to fruition in the far-distant future, and everything between was just links in a chain. Gokumet understood itself to be such a link. No room in that worldview for hope.

The saurus understood that the same part of being human, that unwillingness to accept the world as it *is*, also led them to folly. Overreaching, foolishness, vulnerability to the dark powers. You could not fall to the temptations of Chaos unless you could be led astray by the will-o'-the-wisp of a world where things were different.

They were going to die here. The other Seraphon were falling – slowly, and taking many rats with them, but with enough rats trying, the filthy, rusted blades found their way past shields. There were rats on either flank, rats attacking the knot of human shields at the crack they entered from. Enough blades for all of them, and the only uncertainty was how long it would be before the last of them fell. Gokumet did not feel bitter or angry at the prospect. Seraphon could not rail against their fate. They stood and fought and died, or won, as the alignment of the stars and the foreseen details of the plan required. That was all Gokumet needed to understand.

It was good, to have found the Golden One again. The loss of First Home had been like a thorn in the champion's skin all this time. Something that *might* have bred bitterness or anger, and thus a tool less fit to serve Sek'atta and the plan, the only important thing. Now Gokumet had walked through the Fall of First Home with the Stormcast, and all things were settled and easy in its mind. The peace it brought was an unlooked-for gift from the Old Ones' plan, and Sek'atta's champion accepted it humbly in the moments before the Skaven must surely overwhelm them all.

Beyond the mass of rats was Irixi Starseer, retreating from a pack of their grey monks. Gokumet could not reach its leader. It was not meant to be, therefore. Not something to be cursed, just the way things were. How terrible it would be, to be infected with human *hope* and be constantly trying to make the world other than it was.

Gokumet felt the blades scrape and stab at its scales. It crushed Skaven shields and skulls, felt their spines disarticulate within its jaws, the sour taste of rat blood on its tongue. Its heart was full of the contentment of knowing it was where it was supposed to be, and that was infinitely more important than the fact that it must die.

PERLO

The attack had claimed the Skaven's attention at first. In those first moments, with the Stormcast spearheading a wedge of Seraphon warriors, she'd thought nothing could stop them. Surely they'd trample every rat, drive clean across the chamber to rescue her and Irixi. Her heart leapt with the certainty that they were saved.

Only moments later she could see that they were doomed. Their furious charge had driven them right into the heart of the Skaven, and perhaps if this had just been some loose-knit raiding party then the rats would have fled. The shrilling of Ferskine was keeping them together, though, and now they were pressing back, a great tide of filthy, matted bodies choking the momentum of the advance. The most wretched, the rag-clad runts with their plank shields and dull blades, were thrown under the clawed feet of the lizard warriors to be beaten down and torn apart, so that the monks could form themselves up into a ragged battle order, chant their corrosive spells and work themselves up into a frenzy. She had a moment of cold appreciation, seeing how all the chittering, skittering chaos was bent to the will of their leader, channelled into holding the intruders still so they could be overwhelmed.

Then she realised the Skaven's appreciation of their superior odds meant they could spare some rats to go kill a couple of troublesome mages. A pack of the grey monks were picking their way over the rubble towards her and Irixi. Not charging like mad things, but plainly anticipating some sport after all that work cracking the shield.

'Irixi,' she said. 'We need to run. Come on.' Although the Skaven were surely faster and she couldn't see anywhere to go.

The Seraphon mage wasn't paying her any attention. Instead it had gone to the wall of the chamber where the great prophecy had once, apparently, been displayed. It was – she blinked – smearing blood from its tail stump on the stone there, almost dancing. She wondered if it had gone mad. Or if it had always been mad.

'Irixi!' She actually went and tugged at its thin arm. The Skaven had formed a loose semicircle now, closing in. Yellow-brown teeth bared in hungry, eager grins. She hefted her cudgel and reached for her magic, but there was nothing.

'What is going on with this place?' she whispered. There was magic all around her. Whatever ritual Irixi had performed had brought the whole ruin back to life. She should have been able to just reach and take hold of fistfuls of arcane might to sling at the Skaven. Even as poor a mage as she. And yet it slipped between her fingers like oil. Like plunging her hands into the fresh water of a spring and finding it only sand.

'Irixi, what have you done?'

'The Good Purpose,' said the Seraphon. 'The only way.'

'Irixi, they are going to kill us.' She snarled defiantly at the Skaven, and they snickered and sneered at her.

'Comecome, manling,' one said, a twisted approximation of human words. 'Kneel-quick before mighty Ferskine. Maybe keep one-leg. Maybe two-arm. Still serve Ferskine on one-one-leg.'

'Maybe one-arm,' another wheezed, licking its muzzle. Less than a delight, to discover they knew enough human speech to taunt her.

She pulled at Irixi's arm again, but the Seraphon dragged back with surprising strength, hissing, 'Of sole import, the prophecy must be known. It is the Good Purpose.'

'It's not going to happen.' Perlo heard her voice shake, tears coming to her eyes. The rats' eyes gleamed, and she saw that her sheer distress was the one thing staying their hands. They were enjoying seeing her break. They really were waiting for her to kneel.

I won't.

She wondered how much they would have to do to her before she did. Whether she would still be physically capable of kneeling by the time she begged to serve their master.

Irixi's cold fingers closed about her hand, drawing it behind her until her palm was flat against a glassy surface. One of the remaining ragged patches of obsidian mirror on the ravaged patch of wall. An island of prophecy left over from the cataclysm that had broken this temple. Rendered meaningless by catastrophe and time. Her own image, rendered in blocky Seraphon style. A human woman reaching up to offer… what? And was this something she had done in her past or some foreseen future? If the latter, it had better happen soon because she reckoned she didn't have much future left.

'You see?' the lizard said softly.

'No,' she told it sadly. 'I can't see. And I can't see that it matters now. We've failed.'

It dabbed another patch of blood on the stone. Just a random selection of red splotches across the riven surface. A pattern that could have been anything. A constellation.

The rats obviously felt that their victims had been given sufficient opportunity to bow the knee, then, or else Ferskine had given them a signal, for they were abruptly in motion, flurrying across the remaining distance. Perlo grasped for that vast rushing flood of power that was so strong, so rich all around them, and again it just fell away into the recesses of the ruin, all spoken for already, all serving some unknown purpose.

She brought up her club and swung the studded head at the lead rat, striking across its upraised staff and knocking it back. She screamed at them, as though sheer volume would turn them back.

The sound became thunder, and the rat that had been reaching for her spun away, a bloody hole punched in its grey robes. Abruptly Kenlo was at her side, hacking at them one-handed with his axe, thrusting his pistol at her, a sack of ball and powder dangling from its butt.

'Reload!' he yelled, and carved a slash across one rat's snout. A staff slammed into his side and rang against his mail.

She'd done this for him countless times in the battle-line, hands priming and charging the pistol without needing to see what she was doing. She shoved it back into his off hand and then lunged forwards to brain a rat that was trying to get its knife into Kenlo's armpit.

'We,' he said, 'are going!' He'd jumped down from the rubble mounded around the side of the chamber, and probably they could have climbed back up there, but not with rats dragging at their heels.

He made a break for that direction anyway, but a handful of the monks were already ahead of him, scrambling up the tumbled stones with horrible agility and then turning to threaten him with their blades and teeth. Kenlo fell back with a curse.

'Some spell would be a help!' he snapped.

'I can't,' she confessed. 'It's… all being used, everything around us, all…' And she couldn't understand *what* it was doing, because she'd thought Irixi had been severing the place from all the entanglements of Shyish, but the familiar shades of death magic were clouding her actual mundane vision now, they were so strong. Flooding into the metaphysical spaces of the temple that had been denied them for so long. The realm was reclaiming this holdout of Seraphon power, and had that been *it*? Had this whole charade just been Irixi burying the place with honours? Was *that* why they were going to die?

'Irixi!' she shouted. The Seraphon was still waiting patiently before the ruined prophecy. Before *her*, that stylised image of her. She felt a terrible hook in her heart, because even if she and Kenlo could just run away now, she'd never *know*. Irixi would die, and Perlo would live forever ignorant of whatever great purpose had been ordained for her.

Kenlo discharged his pistol into the rats, the sound more than the impact sending them scattering away.

'Move!' he yelled, but she looked back at Irixi and knew that she couldn't just *leave*.

She darted away from her brother, bringing her cudgel down on a monk that was clawing for Irixi. The prophecy was lost, surely, but if she could save the Seraphon then perhaps she could learn *something*.

'Come with us,' she shouted in the lizard's face.

'The Good Purpose.' Irixi seemed utterly unconcerned that they were about to be hacked apart by Skaven.

'Forget it! We've failed, but we can still get out,' she said, not even knowing if it was true.

'In the Great Plan, there is no failure,' Irixi told her. 'See.' Another gesture at the mute wall, a prophecy of nothing but broken pieces, as though the fall of the temple had transformed the oracular frieze into a vision of the realms with Chaos triumphant.

The three of them were backed against the wall now, rats all around them, testing the swiftness of Kenlo's axe. Over their head she saw Vael surge forwards suddenly, flinging Skaven out of the way, sounding Sigmar's name. Then Ferskine's Rat Ogor bearer trampled forwards through the throng, caught up the Stormcast and cast him down, pinning him to the ground with one foot as the Plague Priest squealed and swung its thurible about, drawing hideous sigils in the air with greasy smoke.

It came to her that she could *see* the detail of what was going on far too well. The sullen glow of the warpstone and the handful of lanterns should not have sufficed.

The walls of the chamber were limned in a cold light. A colour only a mage could truly see, that was simultaneously black and white and tinged with imperial purple, because Death was the emperor of the realms, who sought to bring all into his dominion.

The power of Shyish clung to the stones of the fallen temple, blazing like flames, blowing like tattered banners in a wind no flesh could feel.

'Irixi,' Perlo breathed. 'What did you do?'

From the Scriptorium of Ferskine of the Eleventh Bell

Yes-yes soon a feast a feast for all the children of the Rat. These foolish manlings are just appetiser for the greater gorging of lizard-flesh scale-savouring snake-morsels to be laid before the chosen of the Horned One served by none other than most generous Ferskine the might– Scribe, are you recording faithfully these the words of your magnificent master? Goodgood, all must be set down for posterity so that all to come may know the glory and the greatness and the grandeur of Ferskine the Festering!

Yes, slave, yes-yes, pound the armour of the Stormcast. Make its breastplate our bell and ring ring ring! Music to the ears of all the Rat's progeny! Slay the lizards! Flay their hides for our cloaks! Their teeth for our jewellery! We shall dine on scale-flesh and man-flesh, my feculent followers, yes-yes!

So good of the lizard priest to unseam the power of this place wide open. So obliging, yes, to play into the hands of great Ferskine, the cunning, the clever, the calculating. Let us reach our hands into the guts of this stony corpse and lift out its delicious organs! Let us…

Waitwaitwait, what is this creeping flood of death, that steals all the succulent wonders of this place from us? What is this mixing and mingling and merging of forces? We cannot find where the lizard magic starts and where the death realm ends. All muddied together like urine in wine. What is this entangling, this encroaching. Ferskine forbids it, he who is most beloved of all the brood of the Horned Rat! Ferskine has claimed this place for unreason and corruption. Ferskine will not be denied!

Where is it going, all the delicious power? What is it becoming? What transformations and ossifications and resurrections are these? Stop writing, scribe! This is not fit to be set down! What is this filthy lizard magic doing? I said stop writing!

CHAPTER TWENTY-EIGHT

STANNER

Escaping from the tunnels below the ruin felt like crawling from a monster's throat. Around them, stonework already disjointed from the original collapse was convulsing as though the whole edifice was in the throes of a seizure. Jagged edges twisted and writhed, each block seeming to fight its neighbours against its proper fit, those below seeking to overthrow those above. *Chaos*, thought Stanner. *The rats have rulership over it all.*

She and Oaxmal clawed their way out into the open air as, below them, the segments of the tunnel clashed like teeth. There was no sanity to be found up top. The mounded landscape rippled and shuddered. *Like rats are running beneath it. Thousands of them.* Nearby, a wave stirred twenty tons of fallen stone into spiralling coils. The air was mad with patterns of dust thrown up from every crack and joint.

Assuming Vael and Gokumet had made it back, they'd have been mustering while Oaxmal and Stanner daubed their conjoined blood onto the last shrine, and marching as the pair struggled to escape the suddenly unquiet depths. By now they'd be fighting.

Oaxmal darted forwards, then skittered sideways, cutting a crooked path that Stanner tried to match. Abruptly, the whole heaped landscape around them was tilted like the deck of a ship in a storm. Stanner skidded, rolled, came up on her feet and kicked off after the lizard scout. Oaxmal had stopped, though, crouched low, eyes swivelled upwards, in the shadow of…

Stanner let out a whimper. What had been the ground to their right was a slope, a cliff, a great massed tidal wave of crushing rubble poised above them. They were in its shadow, at its very base. When it dropped, there wouldn't even be a smear left of either of them. *Sigmar save me. Sigmar, hammer of Azyr, protect your faithful servant. Morrda, let not my death be here in this strange place…* The prayers she'd learned as a child, come unbidden to her head. And then, from nowhere she could have named: *Jaguar, show me the path.*

She saw the Jaguar. Just a flash. Not even a cat's shape so much as a suggestion of a spotted coat, the flash of feline eyes. A moment's hallucination before the end, surely, save that Oaxmal saw it too and was scrabbling on all fours in that direction, Stanner right on its heels. And above them, the monstrous weight of hanging stone…

Hung. Not only did it not fall, but it rose. Loose blocks crawled up its impossibly suspended face like spiders. The sheer, uncanny threat of it screamed in Stanner's mind, and she forced all that fear into her feet, catching up with Oaxmal and almost overtaking it.

Ahead, the loose sections of a fallen column leapt into the air like bludgeoning stone bees. A wall thrust up from the ruin as though it were a lower jaw in search of its counterpart. And bones. The ground before them was crawling with small bones. Delicate, long-snouted skulls, the fragile curves of ribs, spines slithering like serpents, and every piece in search of its fellows. She saw chips and powder clench together into recognisable limbs and digits, whole skeletons articulating piecemeal. The ground was giving up the dead of another age. Everywhere her feet came down there was a bony figure curled up in death. Oaxmal's people, the ancient casualties of the fallen temple, vomited forth to carpet the stones with their mute multitude. And here and there, the heavy, clublike remnants of warriors or vaster beasts still. Stanner, child of Lethis, was no stranger to necromancy. She'd played amongst graves as a child, and seen dead men walk wearing Sigmar's livery. The scale, though! A whole temple-city of Seraphon being exhumed and roughly thrust together as the earth around them heaved and bucked.

Ahead, again: the Jaguar. The god whose shrine she'd bled for, turning impatiently as its mismatched pair of votaries stumbled and tripped. *If you cannot keep up the pace of the hunt, I shall leave you.* Probably that was how the lizard gods felt about their worshippers, but then neither Sigmar nor Morrda nor any god Stanner knew spared their followers much. The realms were the battleground of greater forces than mere mortals. Gods had little time for kindness.

They burst out to the foothills of a great hill of stone even as it began to be hollowed away. The rubble beneath Stanner's feet was abruptly moving, and she had a terrified moment when she thought she would just drop into the hungry mouth of the ground. Oaxmal sprang aside as a swarm of tumbling blocks surged past like an outgoing tide, scouring the floor and revealing a grand spiralling mosaic, impossibly pristine. A scene of astrological bodies and constellations that was just a tangle of opaque symbolism to Stanner on the ground but perhaps would have been wisdom itself to some lizard sage looking down from on high. It boiled with more tiny bones, and now they weren't just assembling into the sad little memorials of where the lizard people had died. Now, when each skeleton had crawled itself back together, it shuddered and twisted, bony tail lashing, jaws gaping. Armlets and torcs and pectorals closed about wrists and throats, and she saw a phantom shimmer of scaled hide about them as they shuddered and twitched and began to clamber jerkily to their feet.

Towards the far side of the cleared square, the mosaic parted, and a great spine cut between the stones like the fin of a shark as some new titan was purged out of the ground. Stanner saw a skull as long as she was tall, bony jaws gaping wide as the spikes of teeth fitted themselves back into the sockets.

What have the rats done? What is this desecration? And then she could ask them direct because the rubble ahead rose up and clenched like a fist brandished against the heavens, and a whole pack of Skaven bolted out of it and practically ran right into them.

She could almost hear the Jaguar god snicker at her. *Oh, hunters, how are you caught so unprepared?*

There was a moment when she and Oaxmal might just have kept running one way, the Skaven the other, both just determined to get clear of whatever necromantic cataclysm was going on all around them. Then one rat struck out at her, the edge of its blade drawing a shallow line across her temple as she fell back. The rest took courage from this, and a second later, the pair of them were fighting for their lives.

Oaxmal had a fistful of darts between its knuckles and drove them into every piece of rat flesh it could reach, so that a handful of them were staggering away and collapsing almost instantly, shuddering and convulsing as the poison took hold. Stanner just had her axe, lopping at the arm of the rat who'd cut her, carving it up enough to send it skittering back. Then they were back to back, the Skaven circling them, darting in and out, chittering, jeering.

Oh. Seeing what was beyond them almost got her killed. She went still and one of the rats, anticipating her falling back, cannoned into her and knocked her down. Its blade was through the lining of her leather jerkin, the jagged edge worrying at her skin. Its dagger teeth were right in her face, snapping at her as she tried to hold it back.

Then the coil of Oaxmal's tail was about its throat, hauling it off her even as the lizard feinted at another couple of Skaven, needles in one hand and the actual dead frog in the other. *You know the fight's desperate when...* A hysterical cackle escaped Stanner's throat.

Not just at Oaxmal using a dead amphibian as a shield but at what was coming for them now. A threat to make the Skaven look like children.

The great bones hadn't just stopped when they breached the surface. They rose up and came together, forming not the dead length of the beast they had been but a mockery of its life. House-tall on two legs that withered musculature was growing up like vines. A lash of the tail began as a whip of vertebrae but was clad in scaled skin when it reached its apex. The gaping skull was still being papered over with false life when it lunged down at them.

It closed about a trio of Skaven who'd been hanging back out of axe reach and lifted high to gobble them down. She saw the mangled rats drop past an empty ribcage before dull scales scrolled up across its belly. When it roared, she heard the cry as though it echoed through hollow, lonely spaces. Echoed, she thought, across *time*, in a temple possessed by its own ghost.

That was more than enough for the Skaven, who fled in all directions. The monster's cadaverous head swung round to track one, and it stalked off.

Stanner got to her feet. Oaxmal's eyes pivoted and turned madly, trying to take in everything around them. All the dead lizard folk were rising up now. Drawing on their skins and likenesses, holed and imperfect so that the death showed through in every motion. At first they stood in swaying, half-substantial hosts, as though forgotten by the very power that had raised them. That was bad enough. Then, even as Stanner and Oaxmal dashed across the newly recreated square, they lurched into motion. Not clawing and moaning like the hostile dead she'd fought far too many times, but pacing about the spiral mosaic of the floor, kneeling before the restored shrines of the walls, performing a hundred incomprehensible votive acts drawn from another age. Trapped, Stanner thought, in what they had been doing when the end came. Following their natures just as the predatory beast had followed its own.

Ahead she saw another glimpse of mottled fur, the tail of the Jaguar slinking away. Oaxmal was already hurrying in that direction, and she followed as, all around, death finally took ownership of the ruin of the Seraphon.

CHAPTER TWENTY-NINE

IRIXI

Of all the great philosophical truths of the realms, only Death was singular. Beholden to a solitary lord who sought to place his chains on all creation. To bring a peace to the realms that would know only obedience and stillness, forever and forever. The powers of Chaos were many-headed, and the forces that opposed them expressed their Order in many ways. Irixi had even heard that the orruks worshipped some manner of twin god. But Death knew one master and sought a singular and uniform end to all the cosmos. The enemy of the Old Ones' plan as much as Chaos, therefore. Yet, that plan must in itself take account of the ambitions of Death. Death would play its part in restoring the realms to their perfected state, even as all things must: humans, aelves, orruks. Even the very powers of Chaos that were to be expunged from the world were accounted for in the plan, witlessly working towards their own extinction.

With a mind open to the complex interplay of forces all around, Irixi knew a distant, cerebral wonder. A terror too, or at least the intellectual apprehension of it, as close as its cold kind might ever come.

A Starseer was no mean thing, amongst the Seraphon, but Irixi was no slann. No great font of ancient power, as Sek'atta was, who could surely have waved a webbed hand and conjured a force to sweep the Skaven from the temple and learn the secrets of the Nine Orchid Path and probably a great many other worthy goals as well, all at once. Sek'atta had a thousand demands on his concentration, though, which a poor Starseer could not even comprehend. So it was that, in his great wisdom, he had sent this small servant to the grave of the *Wings of Serendipitous Fire*. A meagre ritualist, a scholar, one who would have been content to remain within a garden within the *Celestial Eye*. Irixi was not strong, as the Skaven Ferskine was strong, or Vael the Stormcast, or any of them.

But Irixi understood balance, and calm. It understood that if one balanced the scales of the cosmos very carefully then one did not *need* to be strong to effect great change. One needed only a deft and delicate touch to move them.

The shrines, the propitiation of the gods – simultaneously entities with desires, prohibitions and blessings, and also axioms expressing the essential nature of the cosmos – all that had been Irixi's precisely weighting the arms of the balance. On the one hand, the power of the Seraphon, the kernel of the *Wings of Serendipitous Fire* that had held out against the encroaching influence of its surroundings for uncounted ages since its calamitous fall from grace. On the other, the clutch of Shyish, Realm of Death, forever greedy to subsume and control all that varied from its cold uniformity. Every necromancer's first lesson, though, was how Death related to time – or that was how the Seraphon understood it. To bring animation to the dead was to recall the echo of a past living nature to ancient bones.

The Starseer wondered idly how a human would have gone about this task. If some human had, for unguessable reasons, desired to recreate the Nine Orchid Path and learn the details of that minuscule section of the Old Ones' plan. Perhaps there would be some great effort to locate every tiny fragment amongst the rubble of the temple-ship, to reassemble them painstakingly, puzzling and head-scratching, and even then to restore only fragments. A patchwork of broken revelation no more edifying than the shards and dust had been. But then humans were creatures of the here, the now, the moment. They were not capable of perceiving the grander picture and understanding how these things might be accomplished. There were simpler roads to enlightenment.

All around Irixi, Shyish flowed into the ruin like a flood when the dams break, hungry to claim what had been denied to it for so long. One did not raise walls against the flood, this the Seraphon knew. Instead, one channelled it, guided the waters to where they were most useful. In just such a way the Starseer had laid out the paths of least resistance for the eager tide of Shyish. The power of Death coursed through every corner of the ruin, just as it would into a necromancer's prepared cadaver. Simple, really. A novice's task, if only one could balance the scales just so.

Irixi watched as the entirety of the *Wings of Serendipitous Fire* resounded to the echo of its own past, recalling its people, its beasts, its architecture, the splendour of its shrines and statues. All around, the unquiet ghost of a whole temple-ship stirred and rose and rebuilt itself in its own memory, forgetting that it had been crashed and dead for whole ages of the realms.

CHAPTER THIRTY

KENLO

Perlo wouldn't leave the lizard mage and the lizard wouldn't leave off whatever it was so interested in, and *neither* of them was apparently going to do any great spell to scare the rats away. Which left Kenlo and his axe and pistol – hastily recharged – in front of a whole pack of the Skaven grey monks, just about the worst odds he'd ever run into. *Shouldn't have gone on this little expedition,* said the tiny part of his mind still concerned with duty to his city. Because there were a lot of downsides with being in the army – what with arrogant Azyrite marshals and forced marches, short supplies and discipline and having to fight every creature in the realms – but sometimes these were balanced out by the big advantage of having a few hundred other lads and lasses at your back when things kicked off.

Things were well and truly kicking off.

Past the monks there was the great mass of other Skaven. They were surrounding the lizard contingent entirely, because the reptiles had just charged in as far as their momentum would take them. At the back of the chamber there was Lofus and his people – about two-thirds of them still alive and on their feet – and they were surrounded too because as well as the rats in the chamber there were a whole bunch who'd come up behind them through that jagged crack of a passageway. And there was the Stormcast, Vael Scar-Helm, armour buckling as the chief rat's hulking bearer stomped on his breast-plate. All in all, not the proudest moment of the followers of Sigmar.

And now this. Because there were ripples going through the very structure of the chamber all around them like the skin of a fright-ened dog. He saw each and every individual stone move, from chips the size of his thumbnail to great chunks of masonry big as a horse. Any moment it'd all come down on the lot of them, crush lizard and rat and human beings flat. Except that wasn't what it was doing. The looming stone above their heads was seething and rear-ranging itself, actually shunting upwards and outwards as though an invisible giant had set shoulders against it. Weird flashes of colour bloomed and died across the rippling walls, picking out the figures in the shattered carvings. His breath caught as dozens of tiny dis-placed gems leapt up from their secret burials and flew upwards like a swarm of glittering bugs to lock into carved eye sockets or pattern themselves along the scales of stone serpents.

The dim chamber, previously lit only by the sickly green of the Skaven, then seething with phantom corpse-light, was pierced by the real day outside. One shaft, then a dozen more spearing in. A precise arrangement, maddeningly meaningful even to human eyes. There had been shafts in the collapsed walls, Kenlo under-stood, and now they were clearing, the rubble scurrying out of them so the light could get in. The light of Hysh, sun of the realms, filtered through the sapping air of Shyish. Where the light landed the Skaven shrilled and scattered. He waited for it to burn them up, but it was just light. The Skaven would get over their fear of whatever process was going on, and then they'd remember their guests, and their hungers.

He picked out his target, the one he'd get with his last pistol shot before they took him down. The biggest, ugliest rat he could spot amongst the ranks of the monks. He rested his axe across his shoulder, ready to whip it forwards the moment his gun was discharged. He didn't reckon he'd sell his life dearly, given the odds, but he sure as death wouldn't give it away for free.

At one wall of the chamber – surrounded by intricately carven sculptures that had been just dust a moment ago – he saw a crushed archway raise itself back into shape, capstone first and then each side of it busily pushing out until there was an exit there. His heart leapt. Not for him or Perlo, far too many rats in the way for them, but close enough to Lofus, and the man had obviously seen it. A determined push and they could be out!

They had even started to shove that way – not even hacking at the stunned Skaven but shunting them aside with shields – when it became apparent to all that the arch was not an exit after all. It was an entrance.

Into the chamber came the lizard dead.

If there was one thing you were far too familiar with, hailing from Lethis, it was the unquiet dead. Kenlo would have said he'd gone up against every possible flavour of undeath in his career, because Shyish's natural heirs were jealous of every foot of ground claimed by the Dawnbringers. These were something else.

These were bones, and he knew bones from clashes with the skeletal foot soldiers of the Blood-drinkers. These were withered flesh bound up in hide like the corpses that necromancers conjured, many of them still decked out in gold and precious stones like the immaculate mummified armies of the Ossiarchs. Yet around these physical relics swirled a phantom life, tattered and trailing. He saw, in flashes and rags, the hosts of the ancient Seraphon. Their painted scales and the geometric patterns of their shields, their living ferocity reduced to a phantasmal shimmer about their mortal remains. He had fought the spectral Nighthaunt, more than once, which fluttered and writhed in the eye just like that, but they were wholly insubstantial things, bad dreams given force and biting swords and scythes. The dead of the lizard ruin seemed like all these manifestations of undeath at once, and they marched into the chamber with the discipline of Stormcasts.

We are to be punished for our sacrilege, Kenlo understood. He'd always known it was sacrilege, right from the moment he'd first come up with the plan. You couldn't get rich in this realm without looting *someone's* tomb.

For a long moment they just stood there in their ranks, the bones beneath, the half-seen flesh and colour flaring about them. From outside and above came a cacophony of hollow roaring and snarling and the shrill cries of the Skaven left up there. But within this chamber, this throne room, the eldritch forces of the Seraphon merely waited.

Then the big lizard warrior, the one who had the problem with Vael, lifted its head and bellowed.

GOKUMET

Seraphon knew no grief as humans did, or were not supposed to. Every fallen warrior was a part of the plan. Each event, no matter how it might be subjectively unwanted, fell out how it must. They were taught fatalism out of the spawning pool.

What Gokumet felt, then, was not grief as a human might experience it. Was not anything the saurus had a word for, either. A tightness, within the great barrel of its chest and gut. A dryness to the tooth-barred cage of its mouth. Gokumet knew them. It knew them all.

Within its mind was a rain of dead names like stones. Hanuitzl, Tenimel, Amanzatzi, Istixen. Broodmates, fellows in devotion. Those left behind in First Home when Sek'atta had called for Gokumet to be his bodyguard and, thus, escape. Those killed by the Stormcasts, or else in the crushing impact of the stricken temple-ship.

In that moment the champion found it hard to breathe, and did not know why. Had no context for the unwelcome, unpleasant clench of sentiment within itself, at the sight of those abandoned long before. Not guilt, because it had been obeying Sek'atta, whose word was the law of the cosmos. Not loss, because these things had fallen out as the Old Ones decreed, and so how could a saurus wish them otherwise. But *something*. A discontinuity between the warrior it had been and the veteran it was now. *Is this how the Golden One feels?*

The dead waited. Gokumet waited. The Skaven stared, bristling shields and blades at the cadaverous newcomers but unwilling to shatter the moment. Their leader muttered and hissed to its scribe, a constant, monotonous torrent of infected thought.

Gokumet understood: they were waiting for their champion. Their leader, their broodmate. Even as the ghost of First Home returned its stones to their proper places, restored statues and set columns straight, here were its soldiers ready to be commanded one last time.

Sek'atta's chosen lifted its head and let out the word they were waiting for, and then struck forwards with its club, knowing a hundred kindred strikes would follow, dozens of deaths, the whole chamber ignited into fighting fury again. Knowing it was right.

FERSKINE

Hear now the words of yes-yes great Ferskine lord and master of life and death, not to be defeated by lizard magics no-no, always triumphant, favoured progeny of the Horned Rat write this down scribe write down Ferskine's majestic victory!

The Rat Ogor stomped down on the Stormcast again, but the metalclad creature still had some fight in it. At any other time Ferskine would have been enjoying the futile struggles, but right now he'd rather the creature just *died* and let him turn his full concentration on the necromantic battle going on aethyrically all around them. He was swiftly coming to an understanding of the sneaky little trick the lizard priest had played on poor abused Ferskine, the trusting, the innocent! Not separating *out* the living and the dead of this place but disentangling them like leashed pet rats, so that they could work together more smoothly.

Vile and tricksy little lizard priest whose entrails the all-consuming Ferskine, the ravenous, gourmand of all flesh, will take great pleasure in snacking upon! But cold-mind lizard-wiles shall not suffice to overcome the mighty Ferskine, unparalleled scholar of the nature of death and decay! These necromantic puppets shall be seized and shackled by his incontestable will and made to do the bidding of the Horned Rat! They shall be turned on their creator! The lizard dead of a hundred temples and cities shall rise and tear apart their living spawn at the word of none other than the all-potent Ferskine!

He knew the undead. He had brought his followers to Shyish, after all. Ferskine had defeated a dozen petty magnates who reckoned themselves lords of death. Necromancers and ghoul-barons, spectral knights and an over-ambitious neophyte vampire had all fallen to the great Ferskine's superior prowess. He would seize command of this host of lizard bones. *Offer them up in souls and bones to the Horned Rat, yes-yes!* Let him only grope within the rags and the tatters of them for the bindings that held them in the realms and he would…

I will, I will! Harken now to the word of Ferskine, scribe! Ferskine shall master these pitiful revenants, once he has found the, where is the, why can Ferskine not find the…

What has the filthy lizard-thing done?

Stop writing, scribe, stop writing, Ferskine needs to understand, needs to know, needs to...

They were not the ghosts of dead lizards. Ferskine – for he truly was a wise and potent magician, though perhaps short of his own estimation – finally appreciated the scale of the lizard priest's working. Echoes. Memories. Not spectres, nor souls bound to bones. They were the temple ruin's recollection of its inhabitants, given force and animation because it was the entire *ruin* brought back from the dead. A ghost of a million tons of stone, of carvings, of its own storied name and history, hailed forth from the dust-dry past and given a momentary lease of life. Ferskine felt the outward ripples of the magic as the entire ruin reconstituted itself, so that this new force of half-substantial lizard warriors was no more than a side effect, just as were the monsters even now savaging his forces up above. An unintended consequence of the resurrection of the entire fallen temple.

For just a moment even Ferskine, even he, the unequalled and superior, had to allow that it was a remarkably sublime piece of ritual-working.

The ground below shuddered, straining to lift the entire assemblage from the clutch of Shyish's earth and roots. To return, impossibly, to the sky.

The illustrious Ferskine has decided that at this moment of supreme import he is deeply and necessarily required in other places. Take this down, scribe, that the ever-stalwart Ferskine does not flee the enemy but yet must apply his munificent powers on other battlefields and possibly even other realms–

He beat at the Rat Ogor with his staff, distracting it from trying to pry the Stormcast's armour apart. *Yes-yes,* definitely time to be in some other place where the spaces around them were not about to collapse a second time when the lizard's feeble scale-magic ran out of strength. Ferskine could see exactly how it would go, and that the ruin of this place was due for a far more complete collapse the moment its motivating power left it. And whilst the Skaven were usually at home in narrow spaces underground, he had no intention of being within this fist when it clenched.

The Rat Ogor snarled and flinched as he struck it, then obediently lumbered away, kicking aside lesser Skaven that got in its path. *They*, after all, were not beloved of the Horned Rat like the great Ferskine was. They could look after themselves, and there would always be a new brood ready to do Ferskine's wise bidding if they got themselves crushed flat or killed by lizard ghosts.

The Rat Ogor stumbled and lurched sideways. Ferskine shrilled with rage and beat at the creature's head again for its clumsiness. A moment later he understood it was not just the shifting footing that was giving his mount trouble. Behind them, in the space they had left, the cursed Stormcast was on its feet and had just let fly with its lightning-bright hammer against the Rat Ogor's knee.

VAEL

His armour was as rugged with dents as hill country, the flesh beneath a mass of bruises. The metal had held, though, and so had the body. Sigmar had wrought well when he had Reforged Vael.

The head of his hammer crackled with fire as he drew it back again, and the monstrous rat-creature lumbered round to confront him. Its face, that rat head dwarfed by its massive shoulders, seemed aggrieved. *I was going. I was leaving you alone.* On its shoulders the rat priest railed and shrilled a curse at him. Vael felt the thing's noxious power seethe across his mail and through him, to burn and shrivel when it touched the core of lightning within him. The rage and the fury at the heart of every Stormcast.

He struck, hammerhead thundering square into the chest of the monster with a blaze of light. Its fist clenched about his waist, warping the metal, popping the clasps that held back and breastplate in place, so that he was crushed by the overlapping pieces of his own mail. It slammed him to the ground, trying to get its full weight bearing down on him. Vael snarled and powered his hammer into its elbow, shattering the joint.

The Rat Ogor howled, and another stinking wave of rat magic earthed through him. Then the beast's other hand had him by the throat, lifting him up high. He felt the strangling clasp of it, the links of his own mail pressed into his throat like a garotte. He struck at its face but its long arms held him too far. His breath was bottled in his lungs. Darkness danced across his eyes.

Something reared up, tall as the Rat Ogor. A thing of flayed skin and old bone, clothed in piecemeal memories of a predatory lizard-beast, saddled and caparisoned for riding. On its back was Gokumet, bringing a club down on the rat-monster's outstretched arm. The undead mount's bony jaws closed on its shoulder, and with a convulsive shudder of dead muscles it tore the creature's limb away.

Vael crashed down to the ground. The dying Rat Ogor was on its knees, keening out its pain. The pulpit, ropes severed and wood splintered, hung at a crazy angle from its ruined back.

He lurched to his feet, head spinning, for a moment losing touch with who he was and what he was doing. But he was used to that. When the thinning skin of *Vael* could not stretch to cover his existence, the purpose of Sigmar shone through.

The rat priest was disentangling itself from the pulpit, scrambling up. It hissed fury and spite at him. As he staggered over towards it, the creature tried to flee him, but its own followers were pressed in too close on every side as the necromantic tide of lizard warriors carved into them.

The rat priest turned, threatening him with its staff. The thurible was gone, just a slack length of chain at its tip. It bared its teeth at him, gaze seething with hate and rage.

He took its blast of green fire on the haft of his hammer, feeling it claw at the joints of his gauntlets, trying to find a way in. Then it struck him across the side, but he just let the mail take it, bracing against the force. More than he'd expected. Perhaps more than the rat had expected because its staff snapped halfway, the chain-bearing end whickering away to lash across its followers.

With a final, convulsive effort, Vael brought the hammer down in a blaze of light and brought an end to Ferskine, the mighty, the doomed.

CHAPTER THIRTY-ONE

IRIXI

Somewhere behind the Starseer, there was fighting. Its bodyguard and the human mage's retinue, clashing with the Skaven. And perhaps one would win and perhaps the other. Matters would fall out as decreed in the plan of the Old Ones. Perhaps, even, Irixi would see the result of the fight on the wall before it, part of the great stone tapestry of fate that was the Nine Orchid Path.

Irixi's golden eyes might see its own likeness depicted with a Skaven blade entering its back, even as the event happened. Or the ghosts of the *Wings of Serendipitous Fire* driving the rats from their home. Or the Realm of Death triumph over all and lock all their souls in its skeletal fist.

Beneath the Starseer, the bones of the temple shrugged and twisted, trying to pry themselves from the earth in a mindless attempt to resume their proper position. And it wouldn't work. There was not enough magic in all Shyish to maintain this fragile dream-life of the dead temple. Just enough, though. Just enough.

It had not been to save one Starseer's scaled hide, of course. It had not been to drive the Skaven from these halls. Sacred they had been, but an age ago, and all the true relics of the Old Ones rescued when Sek'atta departed. All save this, that could not be moved.

Irixi had been given one task. Such a small one. Sek'atta, who had sat in this throne chamber whole ages of the realms ago, could not recall the details of the prophecy. The mage-priest was ancient, the particulars many. Hence, he had one trivial task for his servant. *Go, remind me of how things shall be.* As though the timeworn slann had misplaced some bauble. But, sent, Irixi had gone.

All around, within the chamber and across the face of the ruin, the *Wings of Serendipitous Fire* lived again in this brief flare of excess. Its people, its beasts, its monuments, its desire to return to the skies. A momentary, innocent joy in its own tenuous existence.

Before Irixi, the walls shifted and groaned, cracks closing up, defaced sculpture washed over with whole features. Somewhere across the meditation chamber, there was a chorus of shrill screams as the crack the humans had come in through, now crammed with Skaven, closed like jaws.

Dust began to sift upwards. Sharp-edged fragments of obsidian, sharp-edged fragments of prophecy, spun and danced in the air.

Beside the Starseer, Perlo the human gasped and clutched at Irixi's shoulder. An unwelcome familiarity, under other circumstances, but here it was welcome. They were, in a strange way, comrades. They had endured together; Irixi had taught and Perlo had learned. Now, when the fragments of the Nine Orchid Path began to fall into place, the human *understood.* Knew the importance of what was happening, would not let its fellow human drag it away.

Irixi's eyes feasted on each section of the obsidian frieze that fell into place. Such wisdom! Such foresight. Whole future ages revealed in meticulous detail. Every figure and pictogram to be perfectly recalled. Along with a score of other Starseers, Irixi was the memory of ancient Sek'atta, whose mind was so crammed with his years that he must rely on others to be his stray thoughts. The details stacked up in Irixi's mind, the vast majority of them impenetrable to a mere Starseer, meaningful only to a mind as great as Sek'atta's.

The boom of thunder and the howling of beasts and the clash of weapons meant nothing. Irixi's task was accomplished at last. The anxiety of failure fell away like a barbed cloak, to be replaced by contentment.

The Starseer stepped back, almost stumbling over a robed Skaven corpse, almost stepping through a half-substantial saurus warrior. Before Irixi's gaze, the last pieces of black glass clicked into place and the mirrored finish of the frieze was whole, a vast and complex history of battles and rituals, figures, landscapes, astronomical conjunctions, comets and the dance of the realms.

And there, insignificant really, tucked into one corner of the great and complex whole, was the image of the human, hands up in offering. Perlo, immortalised, of cosmic significance to the future as poor, humble Irixi would never be.

Hmm.

A great honour, of course, to be included in the plans of the Old Ones. No creature could wish for more. But somehow Irixi felt that Perlo – with that fleeting, human viewpoint – was going to be less than delighted.

In the image, Perlo's stylised likeness was proffering up a heart, before a grotesque, beaked monster of horns and wings and eyes, crowned with the fiery symbols of Chaos.

Part 5

RETURNED TO RUIN

CHAPTER THIRTY-TWO

PERLO

'No,' she said, staring.

'I wouldn't,' she said.

'Irixi...' *You know me,* but it didn't, and couldn't. The distance between them, not physical but of body and mind, precluded it.

She tried to see the thing, the recipient of the offering, as some Seraphon god. They were hideous and grotesque, were they not, the lizard people? They had monstrous beasts and terrible ways. But the intent of the carver was very clear, in depicting the beaked, winged entity. Every line of it spoke, *Enemy, Other.* She had just enough Seraphon understanding to appreciate the artist's meaning.

She tried to see the offering as something other than a bloody heart, but again the significance spoke to her through the blocky style of the depiction. She tried to see the votive figure as someone other than *her,* Perlo Marinta, self-made mage. And surely it could be anyone, limitations of the art form being what they were. Any human at all. Any creature.

A mage's sight didn't lie. However anonymous the image might have been to another, it spoke to her. *I am you, this is your fate.*

'Take it back,' she stammered. 'I've always marched under Sigmar's banner. I've never even been *tempted*. I've faced the forces of Chaos again and again. A dozen different battlefields I've fought them on.' Kenlo was plucking at her sleeve, baffled, not understanding.

She'd heard the accusations more than once. Everyone knew the stories, about incautious mages. More than one true battlemage she'd approached for tuition had looked at her with a mixture of disdain and fear, seeing her unguided studies as a threat by which Chaos could enter into the heart of the Dawnbringers. But she'd always been steadfast in her adherence to the right cause. She'd *known* the threat, and not taken it lightly. And more than one true battlemage had fallen from grace, in thinking themselves beyond question, while she had soldiered on in faith and duty.

'You can't believe it of me,' she said to Irixi. The Seraphon met her gaze, and she saw that *of course* Irixi did. She, Perlo, was just a human. A fallible, corruptible human. Of course she would fall to Chaos. A wonder she wasn't growing the hideous marks of it even now as she stood here. A sob escaped her. 'It's wrong,' she insisted. Somehow the regard of this reptile meant more to her than that of any haughty battlemage. 'It's false. It won't happen.'

A reaction at last, a slight widening of Irixi's yellow eyes. 'The plan of the Old Ones, this,' the Seraphon said. 'These things, they must come to pass. That is the Good Purpose.'

'You're dooming me,' Perlo got out, 'to fall to corruption. And you're calling it *good*?'

Irixi tilted its head almost quizzically. 'What will be is set. The plan *is*. Your path *is*. Be content.'

'Content?' Perlo shouted. All eyes on her now, Seraphon, human, even the battered Stormcast. 'You can't just tell me I'm – I'm going to become – a *monster*, and say, "Be content"! I mean–' And she wanted to yell, *You're the monster,* into the creature's lizard face, but it wasn't true, and what would that achieve?

Irixi looked from her to the great panel of carved obsidian. Puzzled, Perlo thought, by the outburst.

'It is how things shall be,' the lizard said, running reverent fingers across the glassy surface. 'The Good Purpose, so in the end the realms become healed.'

A shudder went through Perlo. *No.* Not this, not her. She was a good servant of Sigmar. There was no vileness in her. She would not be thrown away like this, all her life of staunch service ground into the dirt. No better than the ranting rat mage with the crown. An enemy of all that was good. That wasn't *her*. Other mages, certainly. Cultists and mad tribes and the irredeemably foul. Not Perlo Marinta, who had only ever tried to better herself and do good.

Her cudgel was in her hand still. Irixi was right there, no bigger than one of the rats. A smug little lizard-thing who saw her as just one more ape to fall from the tree into wickedness. Just one more fallible human, despite all they'd gone through together. Her knuckles whitened on the grip. She could dash the brains out of the creature here and now. Who then would ever report on this terrible future? And if it wasn't known to Irixi's masters, then perhaps it wouldn't happen.

And she knew she couldn't. Not Irixi, who she'd shared so much with. And in that moment Perlo *knew* she was not the thing in the obsidian frieze, because she would not strike at her friend. Instead, she whirled and brought her club down against the black glass carving itself. Striking right at her own carven image, dashing it to pieces. Shattering the votive figure and the heart and the dread beast of Chaos. *Changing the future!* she thought, desperately. *Altering my fate.* She let out a harsh cry of triumph, that she, with no more than a studded cudgel, could rewrite all the ancient Seraphon visions of what was to be.

She stepped back, panting, laughing. Irixi would be outraged, but Irixi would live, and would have to report only nineteen-twentieths of the future. And she, Perlo, would be saved.

The fragments of glass shifted at her feet, as though stirred by an invisible stick. Before her gaze they swirled upwards, each one finding its exact place and merging seamlessly with the rest. The image, reproduced perfectly: Perlo making her offering to the vile powers. Immutable. Set in stone.

'No,' she got out. 'It's not me. I wouldn't. I won't.'

Irixi just regarded her calmly. 'These things are known now,' it said.

Perlo stared at it wildly. 'Then why not just… have your warriors kill me? If you believe that I'll become *this*?'

She knew the lizard well enough to see she'd genuinely surprised it. 'Because these things must be,' it told her blankly. 'This is the plan. Coming to pass, one detail and then the next. The proper path to the good future.'

She backed away from the Seraphon, shaking. Bounced off Kenlo and flinched back from his hand, looking into his face for the disgust that must surely be there.

CHAPTER THIRTY-THREE

KENLO

After the Stormcast killed their leader, the remaining fight went out of the Skaven and they bolted every which way. Mostly trying to force their way through – even over – the whole new host of dead lizards who'd come in. And Kenlo had been braced for those cloudy reptile eyes to end up turned on the humans who were just as much intruders in this lizard place. The reptile host had mostly flowed outside on the tails of the rats, though, and even as they did, they'd seemed to Kenlo's eyes to be less substantial. More just dry skin and bones already starting to go to dust.

Let them hunt the remaining rats through the ruins out there – if it was even still ruins! What he could see through the resurrected archway showed him whole buildings, statues, a complete and pristine temple complex. He felt like he was going mad.

Perlo was shouting, though. Something was up with her. She was standing before some big slab of black glass with what looked like a million tiny carvings on it. Her and the lizard mage she'd been trapped with. The one she'd been trying to talk to before the Skaven arrived and all this kicked off.

'What?' he asked her. 'What is it?' But she barely seemed to hear him, yelling at the lizard about… something about the carvings. She was scared. On her it came out as pugnacious, spoiling for a fight, but she was his sister. He knew what she looked like when she got scared.

She smashed the glass. So sudden that he wondered if she'd gone mad. She'd been about to clout the lizard, and if she'd done that, it would have been out with the axe and back to back with her, ready for all hell to break loose.

The carvings broke under her swing, and Kenlo put a hand up to ward off the shards. He needn't have worried. They were all just swarming back into place like wasps to a nest. The lizard mage, who obviously felt this wall was so important, didn't bat an eye at the vandalism. None of them did. Someone beating up their sacred icons didn't even register, apparently, because the things could just piece themselves back together.

And at least Lofus and the others were coming closer now the rats were gone. A shield-wall to shelter behind if it all went bad with the lizards. Like it surely would. The sergeant and a few of his people were already surreptitiously prying gems out of the wall carvings and peeling off the gold. Not like one of the lizard lads wasn't going to spot their little larcenous desecrations, and Kenlo only hoped Lofus saved some of it for him. Once he'd sorted out what had Perlo so rattled–

She backed into him, and he put a hand to her shoulder and turned her round. She recoiled from him, in that moment as frightened of her brother as she had been of the lizards or the stone.

'What?' Kenlo asked her. 'What is it?' Because, absent the rats and with the lizards just standing around, he couldn't see the threat. But Perlo had a mage's eyes. More than once she'd spotted a problem the mundane Steelhelms couldn't.

'Look.' She had a trembling finger out towards the restored carving,

He squinted at it. A nondescript figure doing something towards a nastier figure. Making a sacrifice, the way these lizards surely did, to one of their lizard gods.

'What?' he asked, holding her by the arms, desperately trying to understand. Because Perlo was steady. She was a solid presence in the second rank, always ready with countermagic or a shielding ward no matter how monstrous the opposition. You did *not* rattle Perlo, not like this.

'It's me,' she told him. 'It's their prophecy. It's the future they've set for me. Look.'

He looked, and couldn't see it. 'It's not… How is that you?' Honestly, the way the lizards did their pictures it didn't even look human to him. Just some flat-faced lizard without a tail. 'It could be an orruk, even. It's not you.' He looked round, caught Lofus' eye as the man shoved a fistful of valuables into his pouch with so little stealth Kenlo was amazed the Seraphon hadn't killed him on general principles. Lofus raised his eyebrows pointedly. *Don't you think it's time to go?*

Kenlo did, indeed, think it was time to go. 'Look,' he told his sister. 'Forget it. It's lizard nonsense. What do they even know? Just forget it. You're good. You're one of us. You're not… whatever that nonsense is.' He tried to pull her away, and she twisted out of his grip. Not, he thought, because she wanted to resist his grip but in case touching her transferred some corruption over to him. Trying to protect *him* from *her*.

'Perlo–' he said helplessly, but she shook her head, eyes wide, and turned back to the lizard mage.

'You have to tell me,' she said, 'how I stop this. What do I do that doesn't lead to this? You *can't* want this for me, Irixi. Please, help me. Show me how this doesn't happen.'

The lizard cocked its head. Was it sad or angry or contemptuous? Kenlo could have read anything in its inhuman features, and perhaps lizards couldn't *be* any of those emotional states. Perhaps those were just human things.

The first crack shot vertically up one wall of the chamber, branching upwards like lightning in reverse. Perhaps it was where the original seams had been, between the fallen shelves of stone, or perhaps ruin would follow new patterns when this place came down.

'Kenlo…' Lofus breathed. All around them the Seraphon stood like statues themselves.

'I know, I know,' he growled, but then the lizard mage spoke.

'These things are,' it said to Perlo. 'They must be. The plan, that must come about. It is not the wanting. It is that this is the Good Purpose, that none must go against. So – you are doomed, and that is good.'

Something kicked in Kenlo, at the sheer casual brutality of the pronouncement. Vicious enough to say about anybody, but about Perlo, about his *sister*. Just throwing her away, everything she was and everything she could be. Just spitting on her with its damned lizard words.

His pistol was still in his hand, still charged and ready for that final shot into a Skaven skull. Now he thrust it forwards, almost into the lizard's lying mouth.

'Unsay it,' he hissed. 'Take it back.'

'Kenlo, no!' Perlo managed, and then the big lizard warrior hit him.

CHAPTER THIRTY-FOUR

VAEL

Vael had been watching all this blankly. Some of the humans were upset. The substance of the matter washed over him. It couldn't touch the quiet triumph he felt within him. Redemption. Who'd have thought a Stormcast would ever feel the need of it? To Kenlo, to those other mortal servants of Sigmar, probably he was some untouchable colossus. They couldn't know the scars he'd carried with him since his death in the gold armour. Not the ones he painstakingly recreated on his face. The wounds inside that hadn't healed. Even when time and the hammer had erased almost every other marker of what it was to be Vael Scar-Helm. His memory of that first battle, the pointless, needless struggle with the Seraphon. The wrong he and his fellows had done, in their eagerness to bring Sigmar's wrath to the followers of Chaos.

And was this not the quitting of all accounts, that he and this ragged band of Dawnbringers had stood alongside the Seraphon, in this very place, to smite Chaos together? As though he had been silently begging Sigmar for a chance to put things right, and at last he had been heard. Some echo of hammer on soul had come to the god, and he had spared poor Vael a second's grace. *You shall have the balm you seek.*

Vael was happy, in those few brief moments between the fleeing of the last Skaven and Gokumet cannoning into Kenlo, knocking the man to the ground, snapping furiously at his face.

'No!' Vael shouted. He'd not followed any of the talk. It hadn't seemed important. But now they were fighting again, just as they'd been fighting before the rats came. Just the same senseless, idiot round.

He rushed forwards, even as Seraphon and humans squared off against one another, shield to shield. He forced himself between the lines, got a gauntleted hand on Gokumet's crest, another on Kenlo's collar, hauled them apart with all his Stormcast strength. 'You have to stop!' he was yelling, but even to his ears his voice just came out as a despairing howl. He cast Kenlo from him, sending the man skidding away across a floor that was rapidly becoming jagged with fresh cracks. Gokumet weighed twice as much, and he saw a brute determination in the Seraphon warrior's eyes. Kenlo had threatened its ward, its leader. Of course it couldn't just stand idly by.

Gokumet thrust Vael away. Somewhere behind, Kenlo was picking himself up, probably waving that pistol around again. Gokumet's eyes were only on Vael now. The Stormcast had a dreadful sense of the inevitable. *We were here before. We have walked through the steps of this, over and over. And now, one last time.*

'I do not want,' he managed, 'to fight you.'

Gokumet's gaze seemed to say that what any of them *wanted* was not important. Only what must be.

There had been no explosion of violence between the two sides, he realised. No sound of sword on shield, screaming and fighting and dying. A glance round told him why. They were watching him and Gokumet. They all were, Seraphon and human alike. *Trapped. I'm trapped in this same mistake, over and over.*

'Please,' he said. Stormcast did not beg, though he had begged once – Vael the man, before Sigmar the god. Begged to be allowed to just pass on. Tried to turn away the gilded chalice of divine blessing.

Gokumet shook itself, scales rattling. It was still bloody from the teeth of the rats, and Vael's armour was buckled and rent in a dozen places, leaking blue-white fire. They were neither of them the pristine exemplars of their role and station.

The Seraphon whirled its toothed club high and sprang forwards, and what could Vael do but rush to meet it? Swinging his hammer one-handed, feeling bones grate in the other shoulder, each wound like a hook in him, slowing him down. Seeing fresh red across the Seraphon's hide from the warrior's own reopened gashes.

They crashed together, shoulder to shoulder, inside one another's reach. The club drew fresh scratches on his backplate. Stray lightning from his hammer clawed black lines down Gokumet's flank. The Seraphon's jaws snapped at his face and he ducked aside, losing a hank of hair but no more. He butted the Seraphon in the eye socket, feeling the jagged edges of Gokumet's scales gouge his face. Then they were staggering apart, and he brought the hammer up and caught the Seraphon a glancing blow across the ribs.

'An end!' he roared. 'An end to this! There must be!' He brought the hammer down, but Gokumet caught his wrist and twisted aside from the blow. His club slammed into Vael's side, springing the abused plates of his armour apart, leaving them hanging from half their straps. Vael got his injured arm about the Seraphon's neck, the pain of his mangled shoulder transformed into righteous fire. *Sigmar, Sigmar!* The way all their imperfections were beaten out of them. No love in the forging, no pity for what was lost, only anger, only driving purpose. He bellowed into the Seraphon's jaws and cast the warrior down with an effort that felt as though it tore every muscle and tendon in him. Swaying, his body screaming at him and being shouted down by the fire within it, he raised his hammer. There was only one way he could put an end to this cycle, even as he was trapped forever within the greater cycle of Sigmar's blessing. The ever-turning roil of the divine storm.

Gokumet's tail swept his legs out from under him even as he brought down the final hammer stroke. He crashed to the ground, feeling the stones shudder and shift. Seeing the carven ceiling above riven with fresh fissures, the carvings defaced anew, everything about to come down. Returning to the meaningless ruin that he and his comrades had made of the place.

The Seraphon grabbed him by the throat, pinned his good arm. The jaws gaped. Of course they did. Why else had he readied his face for them over and over, each time Sigmar brought him back. Somehow he had known the inevitability of this moment.

'This pointless ruin,' he said, hearing his voice, cracked and coming apart just like the temple. 'Meaningless. What we did here. Can there not be an end?' A pitiful plea, from a Stormcast.

'No events are meaningless.' It was Irixi, the seer, crouching close by, staring at him. 'That you brought down the temple? It was meant. That you fought us here? Meant also. This is the plan. If not this ruin before, then no more could be this restoration now. In this way prophecy is preserved and plan furthered.'

Vael stared at the creature. All the fight had left him. Gokumet's jaws waited before his eyes like a hawk about to stoop. 'I... don't understand.'

'Know peace, Stormcast. You have played your part, both then and now. All is as it should be.' There was a terrible, pitying understanding in Irixi's eyes.

He felt something, then. Cool in his fiery heart. A still centre in the violent storm of him. *Peace? Is this what peace is like?* It seemed to him he'd never known it before now.

He looked up at Gokumet, met the warrior's eyes. There would be the hammer, once again. Another Reforging. Perhaps, when he opened his eyes anew, the wounds of that long-ago battle would be beaten out of him at last, and he would have no remembered scars to carve on his face. He would be Sigmar's instrument at last, and know no doubt or grief.

A terrible fate, forever and forever, but he found that he was ready for it. He let go of the man he had been. He accepted the will of Sigmar the god.

'Do it,' he told Gokumet, and those jaws came for him.

CHAPTER THIRTY-FIVE

KENLO

The lizard monster killed him. Kenlo hadn't thought it possible. Just took the Stormcast's face right off, but that was what happened when you went around without that golden mask, he guessed. Not exactly Kenlo's preferred outcome. He'd hoped for the lizard warrior to end up laid out on the ground, but apparently it wasn't the day for Sigmar to triumph over all the odds.

Thankfully, Kenlo also wasn't the man to just go starry-eyed over prayers to the gods. He was someone used to making his own luck. That was why he'd been sneaking closer to where the lizard mage – Irixi? He thought that was the name – had been crouching near the combatants. The moment the lizard warrior's jaws closed on Vael, he'd known it was time for his backup plan. He knew how Storm-casts died. There was a bright blaze of power as Vael's body was consumed, the divine substance of him flashing upwards, funnel-ling out through one of the shafts to seek brighter skies and Sigmar's court. In that moment, Kenlo had Irixi up by the back of the neck, hoisting the creature into the air with his pistol pressed right up against the base of its skull.

'You all stay right still!' he shouted. The big warrior made a move for him, but he wasn't going to get blindsided twice in one day by the same reptile. 'Tell it to get back!' he snarled at Irixi. 'Because I've got a gun right to your head, and whatever you just learned from all that scribble-scrabble's getting spattered right back across the wall.'

The warrior watched. Irixi hadn't given it any orders, but maybe it understood about pistols and skulls.

'Kenlo,' Perlo said. She had a hand out, as though it was *her* he was threatening. As though he'd *ever* do that. 'Kenlo, put it down.' Meaning maybe the gun, maybe the lizard mage. Kenlo shook his head furiously.

'I'm doing this for you,' he spat. 'For all of us. Look at the bastards. You reckon they'd not just eat the lot of us if we gave them a chance?'

'Kenlo,' she said again. 'Don't do this. There are other ways.'

'They just murdered one of Sigmar's champions!' Kenlo spat. And honestly, he hadn't liked Vael much, but it was a good flag to wave right then. 'Get with Lofus and the others.' Because if one of the lizards thought of it, they could grab Perlo and put some teeth to *her* throat, and then they'd have a right and proper stand-off.

She tried to object again, and he snapped, 'Do it! I'm in control here. I've got it.' The lizard mage weighed as much as a child and wasn't even fighting him, just hanging in his grip like a dog held by the scruff. He'd thought it would try to bite him, but it was just looking back at him. And normally when he had his gun to the back of someone's head they weren't in a position to do that, but between the creature's flexible neck and the way its eyes were set, there wasn't any escaping that calm, snake-eyed stare.

'What you are going to do,' Kenlo growled at it, 'is take that curse back off my sister, right? Unmagic her. Unsay it.'

No human expression to be read in that lizard face. 'There is no curse. Nothing of mine to be taken back,' it said, still so damnably calm.

'You said my sister goes bad, goes to the enemy.' The true enemy, of all Sigmar's foes, the most despised.

'No,' Irixi said, and for a moment Kenlo wondered if he and Perlo and all of them had just misunderstood. The picture didn't mean that, the lizard hadn't meant that, it was all some stupid mistake. But then it added, 'I say nothing. The cosmos says. It must happen.'

'Must?' Kenlo demanded.

'It is within the prophecy. To further the plan, it shall come to pass. Before, these things were clouded and unclear. Now the intent of the Old Ones is revealed.' And then, spoken as though he was being very dense, 'Rejoice, so.'

He heard Perlo make a hurt sound, back where Lofus and the other Steelhelms had her safe.

'*Rejoice?*' he hissed. 'This is what you want, is it?'

'No, again,' it said, just hanging serenely in his grip as though he didn't have the barrel of a gun about to rob it of its brains. 'The desire is not mine, it is of the cosmos. The plan shall be moved forwards. It is only important that these signs and instructions be known, so that it might happen.'

'All this,' Kenlo said. 'Just for that. Just to know what some damn piece of old writing said?' And there was a crack across it now, and the ceiling above was looking less steady than it had been. Lofus and the others were shifting, foot to foot, looking nervous. But they weren't leaving without him, and he wasn't leaving until he'd made this lizard do… what? Whatever it could. Something that would stop Perlo living under that shadow. Wasn't just being a citizen of Lethis hard *enough* without lizards turning up and telling you that you were doomed?

'You take it off her, bless her, protect her from it,' he told Irixi. 'Or what you learned, it dies with you.'

At last some shift of expression. A widening of the pupils, a red flush to its blue-grey skin. 'The realms, your home. You care nothing for them?'

'I care for my sister,' Kenlo said. 'You don't report back, what happens to your plan then? If it's all so inevitable, then what does it matter? Only it can't just have been about to happen anyway, can it? Or you'd not have done all this mad necromancy to find it all out.'

'You cannot conceive of time,' the creature said. Sadly, he thought, as though he'd failed some basic lizard test.

'You're born, you live, you die. That's time.' Kenlo shook it, then had to snarl around at the other lizards as they twitched towards him. 'I mean it! One more step from any of you, you'll be choosing a new leader.'

'Your understanding lacks. The Stormcast understood. There are many births. The same constellations reign again, that we see now. The realms have held this station before, and will again. The plan follows the cycles of all things,' the lizard mage said. 'With the instructions of the Nine Orchid Path, the Good Purpose can be advanced in ten years, a hundred, rather than a thousand, or a hundred thousand. These things have been foreseen. They must come to pass. How many must know agony or corruption because your actions force Sek'atta to await another turn of the cosmos? By this means, all things are improved.' Earnest, if he could judge a lizard's sincerity. Earnest and patient and utterly insane.

'You're mad,' Kenlo told it. 'You're all mad. The whole breed of you.'

Lofus called his name. They'd all backed off towards that archway. A steady rain of dust and stone fragments was sifting down all around. Webworks of cracks crept up the walls, and pale roots were pushing up underfoot.

'Right.' Kenlo felt his breath and heart both coming too fast. The great mass of warriors followed his every move with their lizard eyes. 'This is how we're going to do it. We are going out of here, all of us. All of us humans. And we're taking your mage with us. I've got the gun, right here.' Jamming it into the hollow under Irixi's jaw. 'Any one of you so much as twitches a claw, it's dead, head clean off, right?'

'Kenlo, no,' Perlo told him again, but they'd gone beyond *No*. The lizard was the only security they had to stop its bodyguard tearing every one of them apart, chewing them up like it had the Stormcast. He'd keep Irixi close as a shield, and then when they were outside he would – do *something*, make it change this *plan*, this *prophecy*. Just have it say the words, unblight his sister's future. Because he desperately wanted it to all be some ridiculous lizard superstition, no more than carvings on a wall. But Perlo didn't believe that. Perlo *knew* it was real, and of the two of them, who was going to understand that sort of thing best?

He backed off, and the warriors all lurched forwards. He could see the bloody murder in every reptile visage. 'I have a *pistol*,' he shouted, 'to its *head*! You understand me, you devils? *Bang!* Dead! One more move!'

'Why do you so hate the cosmos, that you would delay the furthering of the Good Purpose?' Irixi asked him.

Kenlo choked. Right then it wasn't even the curse, or prophecy or whatever it was that was going on, that only a mage would be qualified to pronounce on. It was the sheer *calm* of the creature. The utter, maddening peace to it. Its refusal to understand that one twitch of his finger would put a hole in its head for all that tranquil wisdom to rush out from. It wasn't even *scared*.

He was going to kill it, he realised. That calmness had pushed him past some innate limit. He was going to kill it, and maybe start a war, and maybe bring some worse curse down on him and Perlo, and maybe set the entire bloody realms back a thousand years on some impossible oracular clock. But right then it was more than he could do to stop himself. He rammed Irixi up against the prophecy wall and jammed the gun against its eye.

Something hit him, not even hard but very precisely. Went in right over the collar of his mail, into the hollow alongside his neck and deep within his ribs. In the corner of his eye he could just see dull blue fletchings. There was a quite extraordinary amount of pain, but only for a moment. His pistol dropped from fingers that suddenly had no strength in them, not even to pull a trigger.

CHAPTER THIRTY-SIX

STANNER

All eyes were on her, crouched at the mouth of one of the light shafts, the crossbow in her hands. Lofus and the other Steelhelms, the Seraphon, all of them. A harsh and many-pronged regard. She heard Perlo start to wail.

She'd not seen the death of Vael, though the charred husk of his armour told the tale. Instead, she'd arrived at the underground chamber in time to see it start to come apart. And there, centre stage, she'd found Kenlo, threatening the Seraphon leader, shouting, carrying on like a madman. Some doom pronounced on Perlo, threats, babbling. And the lizard mage talking philosophy in reply, just the way you'd do if you really wanted to wind Kenlo up.

Beside her, Oaxmal had lifted its blowpipe up, eyes twitching as it gauged the range. But Stanner had seen how those poison darts worked. There was a lot of spasming and flailing before the scout's victims died. Good against enemies armed with a bow, maybe, or a spear. With a finger on the trigger of a pistol, maybe not so much. She'd put a hand up. *Hold.*

Oaxmal had eyed her. And it was the one whose leader was

under threat – who was she to give it orders? But after a considering moment, it had lowered the pipe.

Stanner had given herself the space of a breath to weigh the state of her soul. She liked Perlo, or liked her enough. Or liked her as much as Stanner liked any other human being. Kenlo she liked less. Able enough quartermaster, perhaps, but a man who *wanted* too much. Stanner, who wanted very little, didn't trust people who let their desires lead them around. And Lofus was even more so, as were the rest. Who, after all, would go on a venture such as this who wasn't putting their own future above any grander belonging: city, faith, realm?

She'd belonged once. There had been those who could walk where she walked, and she'd fought for them, taken wounds for them, grieved them when they'd fallen. Her comrades of the Wildercorps. Arnulf, her dog. She'd felt a keener loss over Arnulf than she had for any human being. But Arnulf had died, as they'd all died, and when there had been new recruits into the corps, she'd declined to become attached to any of them. Every one of them was going to die, after all, or she was. That was how you wrote the history of the corps and of the Dawnbringer Crusades. In blood and corpses, scrawled like Morrda's signature on every stretch of taken ground.

Something had stirred in her, though, when they'd made her shed blood on that first shrine. The one the Stormcast had sworn was Dracothion, the dragon ally of Sigmar, the celestial serpent. Where the worlds of human and Seraphon met, perhaps. And it had been *her* blood that woke it, in that ruined shrine scarred and seared with antique lightning.

Something more had moved within her at that other shrine, the buried one. She'd mourned her dead there and she'd shed her blood. Back in the army she'd bowed her head to Sigmar while the priests prayed, sure enough. She'd made her little offerings to Morrda, asking the death raven to pass over her without alighting. They'd never touched her, though. Sigmar was too bright and distant, Morrda too dark and brooding. It had all just been mumming over the words. But when she'd touched her blood to the Jaguar shrine, she'd felt a distant force stir and notice her. She'd been recognised. Not by a storm-bright bringer of battle, nor a dusk-winged bird of death. By a hunter, as she was a hunter. A god of stalking and shadows that had looked upon Stanner and known her for its own.

It was strange, to *belong*, after so long.

Perlo was screaming, fighting against the Steelhelms, who were struggling to keep her behind the shields. The lizard seer, Irixi, picked itself up and brushed off its robes almost absently, no acknowledgement that there was a dead human at its feet, certainly not a human who'd been about to end the seer's life. Stanner slipped down from the mouth of the shaft and stood there, apart from all of them. She could still feel the sacred patterns on her face, drawn in Oaxmal's dried blood. The Seraphon, whose ranks had closed about Irixi, stared at her, uncertain. Then Oaxmal was beside her, unfading from stone colours to make itself visible.

'What,' Lofus got out, 'did you just do?'

Stanner looked on him, the old, venal sergeant. The man of a hundred vices. And yet a good servant of Sigmar? A good battlefield officer? A man who cared about his troops? Yes, all of these, and also a thief, a bully, a thug. Humans had so many cracks and edges to them, each one a ruin of the thing they might have been. Small wonder Sigmar chose so carefully when selecting new Stormcasts.

'You'd better go,' she said. Her voice sounded strange, unnecessary. A rough and wasteful way of making her thoughts known, compared to the silent hunters' communion she'd shared with Oaxmal.

'What?' Lofus choked. 'Go?'

'Back to the troops. If they've survived the Skaven,' Stanner said.

Each word like a lead weight, tiresome to force out. Perlo was still fighting to get clear of them, threatening them with magic, screaming for her brother. But it was too late for her brother. Because Stanner had made her choice.

'But you…?' And Lofus had just seen her put a lethal bolt into Kenlo, but he still couldn't get his head around it. 'You can't want to…'

And if she'd had the sheer human energy, she could have sat and explained it to him. The Jaguar, the hunt, the way the cold and distant shape of her *fit* for the first time, when with him and the army she'd always just been this odd appendix. How too many dead comrades had carved the humanity away from her, because holding on to it would have hurt too much. She had made herself, all unknowing, proper company for lizards, and other cold and unfeeling creatures. But what a waste of sound and effort it would have been, to unseam her mind for Lofus and the others, when she could just shake her head and tell him, 'Go.'

CHAPTER THIRTY-SEVEN

PERLO

She could hear herself keening in grief, her wail the loudest thing in the chamber, as though it was her voice driving the fresh cracks through the stonework and the clenching roots up through the widening gaps in the floor. But beneath it, some childish part of her kept expecting him to get up. He was Kenlo, her brother. He was always making fun. He was pretending. He'd leap up with a laugh, and the Seraphon would laugh too. It would all be a great jest at her expense, and then Irixi would reveal the *real* prophecy.

Or else he was dead, but this was a time of resurrection, wasn't it? The whole temple ruin had been dead when they came to it, and now it had been returned to its former grandeur. There would be just enough magic left to give her brother back to her. She would explain it to him and he'd understand. They could all be friends again.

But beneath her cry of anguish was the groaning of stones that were coming apart, not together. The ruin's brief moment of rec-reation was done, and every piece of it was beginning to part company with the rest. And she was still within it, beneath the tottering weight of tons of ancient stone.

And Kenlo lay there, the fletchings of Stanner's bolt just visible at his neck, like some ornament he had decided to affect that didn't suit him.

She fought against Lofus again, trying to twist out of his grip. He was stronger, though. He wouldn't let her go. Enough of a good man hiding in all that self-interested lump of flesh that he would do his best to bring her alive out of this, for old times' sake. She screamed at him and struck at him but he just held on, kept her penned behind the shields, her proper place in any clash.

She looked across the buckling ground to Irixi.

'I won't be what you want!' she yelled.

The Seraphon mage tilted its head, peering between two of its guard. 'It is not I that wants,' its voice came to her. 'The cosmos–'

'Damn the cosmos!' Perlo yelled at it. 'It's my *life*! It's my *future*!'

'You do not have a future,' Irixi said, and for a moment Perlo thought it was pronouncing an even worse doom on her, but then it went on. 'There is just the future of *everything*, in which all play a part. You are revealed by prophecy, a great part to play. A role of significance. I could envy.' And the creature was being so *sincere*, genuinely trying to make her see things its way. 'Know joy, therefore,' it said, 'that you must fall. Embrace it.'

Perlo barked out a furious sound and the magic came to her, Shyish rising from between the blocks below her like a pale stench. She gripped it and twisted it into a spear, casting it at Irixi. Willing the Seraphon to wither and parch and be a dead thing beside her dead brother. Irixi's hands moved in small, careful passes, and the killing power earthed between them, unwoven effortlessly. And though probably the lizard didn't feel contempt like a human did, Perlo could read it there. The same disdain she'd received from almost every battlemage, with their vaunted training and ivory towers, when they looked on her, the self-taught, the gutter mage. What was *she* to challenge the scion of a tradition that stretched back to the dawn of the realms? How could her meagre stock of tricks prevail against a creature like Irixi?

'Give it up,' Lofus was shouting, dragging at her. 'There's too many of them. Come on, woman!'

'Stanner!' Perlo yelled. 'How could you?' But the scout just looked back at her, inscrutable as any lizard. And with her arcane sight, Perlo could see the change in her. The new power that had claimed the scout, its spotted mark on her brow, its cat eyes blazing from behind her own. Stanner was lost to the cause of Sigmar, which had brought her nothing but grief.

A chunk of masonry dropped between the humans and the Seraphon, smashing the flags of the floor. At one wall of the chamber, a statue tilted precariously. Jagged lines ran across the face of the prophecy.

'Come on!' Lofus was still saying. 'Let it come down on them! Let it crush them flat, but let's *go!*'

Behind the Seraphon she could see a light. A warm golden radiance quite alien to the realm of Shyish, slowly spreading behind them like… like a new sun. It came to Perlo that she and her fellows could call themselves Dawnbringers all they wanted, march across every realm, stand in opposition to every dark force that pitched itself against them. All they'd be doing would be bringing one new day after the next. Each morning they'd win themselves another sunrise, and the sunset would follow just as surely, the cycle of time on its endless round, as Irixi had spoken of. But the Seraphon would march in darkness for a thousand years so that their descendants could bring the dawn of a whole new age of Order.

Know joy, therefore. Embrace it.

Never. She would be true to Sigmar and Morrda and her people. She *wouldn't* become that figure in the glass.

When Lofus dragged her outside, she felt like she'd left a piece of herself behind. The good piece. The piece that wouldn't.

CHAPTER THIRTY-EIGHT

IRIXI

Irixi knew that it should feel only content. The divine task entrusted to it had been accomplished. The details of the Nine Orchid Path were stored in its mind, not understood but recorded by a memory specially trained to hold such details. Sek'atta would – well, not be *pleased*, because that would be an excess of emotion the old mage-priest probably hadn't displayed in a thousand years. Sek'atta would withhold his distant disappointment. That was a grand reward that Irixi would take and treasure for many years.

At its back, it could feel the way opening. Not Irixi's own power – a poor Starseer could not pierce the fabric of the realms in such a way. Sek'atta was creating a path so that he could receive the bounty of recovered knowledge. Not even with a conscious effort, as Irixi or the human might wrestle with the forces of the arcane, but almost in a dream. Knowing innately the proper time and place for such a working and, through that slumbering thought, making it happen.

One day, a hundred or a thousand revolutions of the realms from now, he would wake fully, Irixi thought. All the slann would, for the time would come to bring about the final passes of the Old Ones' plan and repair the realms. Banish the taint of Chaos and put all things in their proper, ordered place. Tame the orruks and ensure that death was merely a thing that happened at the end of life, and that it was final. No more unquiet souls, no more shambling bones, even Sigmar's Stormcasts banished to their final rest. Every part of creation fitting together like perfectly measured blocks. And perhaps the knowledge that Irixi had restored here meant that the blessed day would arrive ten revolutions sooner, sparing the realms that much more misery and loss.

That was important, the Starseer knew. Its own life, the human man's life, the human mage's corruption, these things were dust between the stones of history. If Irixi or Perlo or any of them could act as a speck of mortar, to bind the greater whole together, then what an honour it was! How devoutly to be wished!

It gestured, and its bodyguard formed up at the croaking order of Gokumet. The champion was gashed and bloody and triumphant, a creature that embraced its lack of understanding of any grander vision, surely. Understanding only obedience and duty, and perhaps that was why it had understood the Stormcast, which had been forged in so similar a mould. Forged awry, Irixi thought, but perhaps perfected now, as all things must seek to move towards the cosmos' final perfection.

Oaxmal slunk in at the Starseer's other side, one eye swivelling to stare. The Chameleon had served well as a conduit for the ritual workings. An able pair of hands, and perhaps its destiny would see it given more responsibility, a greater role in Sek'atta's future machinations. Its new protégé was beside it. The human, about to step across the realms to the *Celestial Eye of Tepok*, where no human had ever stood before. But Huanchi, that mercurial force, had blessed it. Had judged it and found it worthy of the hunt. Who was Irixi to say no?

Another load of broken masonry thundered down. The air was

thick with dust. Shyish would reclaim the *Wings of Serendipitous Fire* now. Not just its former ruined state but interred within the earth and the grim forest of anonymous graves grown over it. One more nameless memorial. The power that had held off death for so very long was spent. The doors that had kept out dissolution had been thrown open. It had been necessary, and perhaps the ancient place deserved its final rest as much as any old warrior.

As Irixi took a final glance about the disintegrating chamber, its eyes lit on the fallen throne. Sek'atta's place of privilege from when he had sat and meditated here. The Starseer had taken his place there, a moderate sacrilege. Possibly that presumption would earn a swift death after Sek'atta had received the details of the prophecy.

If so, then so. Who was Irixi to rail against fate? Leave such foolishness for humans.

The warm radiance of home was on the Starseer's back. The clear, pure stars of High Azyr and the *Celestial Eye* cast the collapse of the chamber into stark relief. Irixi turned and led the way into a bright future.

EPILOGUE

OAXMAL

Another realm, another relic. A lost trinket of the Old Ones, or simply some mundane object that had received their power after the sundering of its proper container. It was not Oaxmal's role to know the details of such things. It just knew its instructions and its task.

And the others. The new brood. A dozen Chameleon Skinks, crawled from the pools so recently Oaxmal felt they were still wet. And though by the measure of most other creatures they were already capable of moving through the forest, stealthy and camouflaged as the wind, to Oaxmal their every motion was clumsy, the shift of their skins jarring. They seemed to cry out their presence with each step, when they should whisper. Oaxmal's skin – the flank turned towards them – instructed them in stark colours. Its stern eye chastised them. They flushed with shame and would do better. The realms were harsh, and the Old Ones' plan could spare no time for them to learn their trade in safety.

At Oaxmal's side, its human – the useful one – crouched, looking ahead. The forest here was thick, twisted together, the ground underfoot stagnant and marshy. They were within the realm of

Ghur, the place of beasts. Oaxmal could feel Huanchi's breath on its neck; this was one of the god's favourite hunting grounds. The human moved well through this ground. It lacked the advantages of a Chameleon, but because of that, it had learned many other tricks. It, too, was a good teacher for the young ones. When Oaxmal had named Stanner as one of Huanchi's own, not one of them had even questioned it.

Ahead was a section of cleared ground. The chopped trees had been bound together into a crude palisade. There was an encampment of lean, gangling orruks within, along with some of their lesser kin and a few prisoners they had been amusing themselves with. They had no idea that caught amidst the roots beneath their feet was some fragment of the Old Ones' power Sek'atta had decreed must be recovered. To further the plan, always to further the plan. A thousand small moves, towards one great end.

Gokumet would be leading the main force of warriors, to come rattle spears at the palisade. Probably the saurus would end up charging the orruks' rough gates, beating them down with the Kroxigor's clubs and then charging in to massacre every one of the creatures, but Oaxmal knew that wasn't even necessary. The plan of the Old Ones was silent on living or dead for this pack of miscreants. It only required that Gokumet made enough of a spectacle that Oaxmal and the scouts could creep over the wall and recover the relic. One more piece of the Great Plan achieved. Another step towards the perfection of the realms. Playing their part, as everything did. The trees, which had grown in a certain way, the relic, the orruks even. If they had not camped here, perhaps some worse power would have claimed the artefact already. So all things could be made to serve the Old Ones' purpose. Perhaps, one day, Oaxmal or its descendants would stalk alongside the orruks themselves, or some ogor from the cold places, or a cadaverous huntsman bearing the grisly writ of a ghoul monarch. All things were good if they furthered the plan.

Oaxmal heard Gokumet's contingent approaching, making no attempt to be subtle. Orruk horns blew warning and the creatures within the palisade scrabbled for their spears. The Chameleon stalked forwards, the colours of light and shadow passing across its hide.

VAEL

He drew breath. For a moment the fire that infused him was pain, the agony of a hundred deaths. Blade, poison, bludgeoning clubs, jaws, fire, foul magic. Deaths, and then the thunderous hammer of Reforging, forever dragged back into awareness of the realms. Vael opened his eyes. Sat up, feeling the familiar armour encasing him, plates sliding smooth over plates, unmarked, pristine, a second skin.

He stood, feeling a curious hollowness within him. Reaching back through time for what it had been, the thing inside. The knot, which he could only recognise from the contours of its absence.

'Brother,' said a metallic voice. 'Welcome back.'

He looked up. Found a face. Familiar, one that he should know. A comrade, a friend. No name came to his mind. No names at all, save *Sigmar*.

'Sister,' he replied steadily. That much he knew. She smiled, clasped his arm, metal to metal. One perfect champion to another.

'It's good to have you with us again. Are you ready to march? The realms have need of us.'

'Always,' he said. The truth. His feet were restless to carry him into battle. His hands reached for the hammer. Lance him down on the lightning road into the thick of a melee and he would smite Sigmar's foes without a moment's thought or hesitation.

In the shine of her breastplate he saw a face. Long-jawed, pale, unmarked. For a moment he felt it was missing something. It was too perfect, when it deserved to be marred, gouged, cut jagged into the shapes of memory. The instant passed and was consumed in the fire within. It was just a face, and though he was intellectually aware it must be his own, it stirred no particular memories.

'What are our orders?' he asked her. Not that it mattered overmuch, save he must know whom to smite and whom to spare.

'The Gnawing Blight has made gains across Chamon,' she told him. 'The Kharadron have sent to us for aid, and it suits Sigmar's plan that we defend the bastions of our allies. Are you ready to bring the hammer down on more rats, brother?'

He waited for the moment when he would know doubt, guilt, shame, any kind of uncertainty, feeling out the edges of that absence within him. Wasn't it always that way? That some remnant part of the man he'd been railed against the ceaseless cycle of life and war, death and Reforging? Nothing came, barely even a hollow echo. The knowledge that he was a soldier in Sigmar's cause, blessed to return forever and forever until the god's work was done. Should that day ever come.

'Sister, I'm ready.' Though, just as they set off, a strange flicker of memory came to him, enough to interrupt his stride. His sister glanced back at him, one eyebrow raised.

'I thought...' He found a strange smile coming to his face, disconnected from anything he could consciously understand. 'For a moment I felt I had a brother with a lizard's face, who taught me duty and meaning.'

The other Stormcast – her name would come to him soon, surely – actually laughed at that. The woman she was, not the champion she was being beaten into, death after death. Younger than he was, still with the rags of her old life trailing from her.

'I had a brother once,' she said. 'He...' And then she frowned, and her voice trailed off, finding that she could not remember, that the family she had been born mortal to had been hammered from her in her most recent forging. 'He...' And Vael recognised the sudden conflict on her face. Recognised it from the shape of that emptiness within him, the doubt he had been finally rid of.

'It's all right,' he told her. 'Be well. Sigmar's gifts are great, and so they must make room in us, so that we can hold them. What is lost is little, compared to what is given.' Words that he remembered being spoken to him, though not who the speaker might have been.

She smiled, uncertainly at first, then with renewed purpose, and the pair of them strode off to the muster, and to battle.

IRIXI

The garden had not been properly tended. Those lesser seers to whom the task had been left had lacked a thorough understanding, and some plants had grown beyond their assigned boundaries while others had dwindled. A sorry state of affairs, but it brought with it the minor benefit of being able to show mild disapproval to underlings, and watch them being properly penitent at their failings.

Looking over the sadly imperfect chamber, the tiers of plants rising up and hanging down, Irixi had a moment's impious thought: *Is it like this for Sek'atta? Was it like this for the Old Ones themselves?* Reprehensible, of course, to compare one's meagre self to such greatness, but still. A garden, overgrown and badly tended. Was this how so mighty an intellect as Sek'atta saw all the realms? Sending forth an army of saurus to do bloody battle, raze towns, take fortresses, all the equivalent of Irixi clipping one sprig of a herb. A precise and carefully weighed action taken because of the long-term benefits it would bring, both to the individual plant and to the garden as a whole. Well, Irixi plainly thought too highly of itself, in making the comparison, but nonetheless it felt humbled. Perhaps that had been the purpose of thinking it. Imagining the magnitude of the task the Old Ones had devolved to the slann and grasping that it did not matter whether one skink understood the instructions it was given any more than the trowel or the knife understood why the wielder dug or cut. And sometimes a plant must be pulled up, removed from the garden entire. Doubtless, if it could, it would plead for its continued existence. It would tell Irixi it had only the one life, the centre of its own little world. And Irixi could feel sad that it must pass, but that would not stay the diligent gardener's hand. One could not let the garden sicken, just so one bloom could have its brief moment of beauty.

Kenlo had been such a bloom, Irixi understood. Perlo was such another. Each must ripen in their time, be cut at the correct hour and be replaced by new growth. Each generation of plants healthier and more diverse and wondrous than the last.

The Starseer found itself not actually taking up its tools, for all the remedial work those inadequate underlings had left undone. Instead, it sat within its slightly unruly garden and entertained new thoughts. Unprofitable thoughts unlikely to progress the greater plans of better minds, yet Irixi had experienced a great deal of new and often trying events in the last few days, and must process them so that they could be disposed of.

What must it be like to be human? What a curious speculation! And yet the Starseer had spent some time with Perlo, and developed a fondness and respect for the mage's understanding and adaptability. If it had been Irixi having to grasp a human schema of magic, would that even have been possible? Starseers were taught only a fraction of a slann mage-priest's learning, but they were taught to a perfect and ideal system. Hard to pierce through to the truth of the cluttered and superstition-heavy methods of a human or an orruk or the festering Skaven. And yet Perlo had made some advances in grasping Seraphon perfection. A shame. A waste.

Not a waste, Irixi told itself sternly. Not even a shame. Those gifts were worthless unless they served the furtherance of the plan. The *Good Purpose*, the phrase to which it had reduced thousands of years of complex calculation, so the human might understand it. Perlo would further the plan. The mage would do so by becoming corrupt and serving the powers of Disorder. How did that further the plan? Irixi would not presume to know, but one might speculate that perhaps Perlo would seize power that some worse votary of Chaos might have laid claim to, or defeat some greater threat in the constant squabbles of the ruinous champions. Or some other, far more tangential business, just some decision randomly taken, to lead a warband *here* instead of *there*, so that some other key individual might be saved, or killed, or given motivation for another great deed. Perlo might doom a hundred thousand, but if, out of that wrack, came one single individual whose actions achieved some key element of the plan, so it must be.

Irixi had disgorged the precious information to Sek'atta. Worked with skink artisans to recreate a rendering of the entire prophetic wall that tied exactly to its trained memories. Talked through each image and panel as the mage-priest listened with closed eyes, head low on his chest. Absorbing, Irixi was sure, every detail. And there was no thanks, of course. No honours or parade or promotion, such as a human might have demanded and received. The Starseer was exactly where the greater scheme of the cosmos required. Seraphon craved no reward, and such craving was what led other beings to fall to temptation.

Irixi stood, brushing away idle and unsuitable thoughts. The garden needed a Starseer's touch, just as the garden of the realms needed the Seraphon. One day, both would be perfect.

PERLO

I will not. Her daily mantra. Not even from fear of corruption but in defiance of prophecy. She would not fall. She would not be the thing in the carving. She would *not*.

They'd returned to the army to find it fortifying after repulsing a Skaven attack. Lofus, career sergeant that he was, somehow managed to talk their absence into a daring strike against a rat flanking force. Perlo suspected some of the loot had gone into fancier purses than a mere Steelhelm's, but it had served.

They'd fought three skirmishes with the Skaven since, neither side ready to get properly stuck in. Reinforcements were on their way from Lethis, but maybe the rats had a whole new generation of vermin clawing their way up from wherever it was they bred. And Perlo had stood behind the shields, countered enemy magic and raised shielding wards, and not been tempted to fall to Chaos even slightly. In the heat of the fight she was professionalism personified. Not even a full battlemage could have found anything to criticise, about her conduct or her technique.

It was after the fight that she felt it. An absence. Kenlo. It had always been the two of them against everything the realms could throw at them, after all. And now he was dead. Stanner, the traitor, had murdered him.

It didn't have to be this way, she told herself at night. *There was another way. I could have got through to him. He'd have listened. Nothing* had *to happen.* That creeping idea of predestination, every seemingly random action fulfilling a part of some grander plan. The weird way that Irixi – intelligent, learned, powerful – somehow just *accepted* such things. The terrible fatalism of the Seraphon. What would they not do, the lizards and their masters, to bring about their supposed better world? How many good men would they sacrifice without a thought – with *joy*, even? She'd lived her whole life believing that the worst threat to her way of life came from the legions of the dead, or the mad followers of dark gods. What if that had always been a lie? What if it wasn't Chaos that was the great threat but the rigid shackles of Order, which didn't care if you died or suffered so long as it served some greater scheme? The Seraphon, Sigmar, even the marshals of the army, hadn't they all thrown away count-less lives, and demanded that you trust their judgement?

She fully understood where thoughts like that could lead. She fought them off, filled her mind with prayers, with recitations of the names of saints, with the stories her brother used to tell. She lay awake long into the dark, holding out against the blandishments of Chaos that were just words inside her head. And when she slept, she knew that the argument raged on in her sleeping mind. In her dreams she met Kenlo again, pierced by Stanner's bolt but still talking, reminding her bitterly of all those times the officers had got it wrong. In her dreams her world expanded from just this army on just this crusade to the whole struggle against the dark powers, a view surely only Sigmar could appreciate. And when she looked down on the circling realms crawling with clashing forces, she saw only pointless loss and waste. An endless road that fed the brave and the cowardly alike into the chewing teeth of the mill. And every figure of autho-rity she'd ever known, telling the witless soldiers how it was a right and proper thing to march straight towards the crushing gears. She woke feeling sick and weak, and then had to march right alongside Lofus and the others as the army pushed towards the next battlefield.

There must be another way. She told it to herself every night, feeling the iron bands of Irixi's destiny forcing her forwards. *I have free will. I can choose.*

And, at last, one night, another voice answered her that had an echo of Kenlo to it, stretched over something far older and more cunning and wicked, and it said, *My child, of course you can, let me show you how,* and she knew that she was lost.

THE SCRIBE

The forest had wasted no time encroaching into the shattered stone, the new ruin made out of the brief resurrection of the *Wings of*

Serendipitous Fire. Roots had clutched the stones and pulled them apart, and new crooked saplings were already thrusting their way towards the gloomy sky. Watch long enough and it was possible to *see* the woods closing their hold on the ancient stones. Soon, any remaining secrets of the Seraphon would be locked away in the grasp of Shyish, as jealously as any of the deathly realm's treasures.

The hunched figure wasn't trying to unearth some last piece of lizard treasure or learning. It just dug with grim determination, scrabbling at the rubble with filthy nails, hissing and chittering to itself, sniffing desperately for a faint hint of a familiar scent, then digging once again.

A white-furred Skaven, dressed in tatters. The one survivor of the force that had been led here by none other than Ferskine the majestic, the mighty, the master. Greatest of all the Plague Priests of the Clans Pestilens, surely. Or at least he'd always claimed to be, and who was this minion rat to gainsay so grand a personage? Not this slave, who had crouched so long at the Plague Priest's side and recorded every word that escaped his constantly chattering mouth.

Ferskine's ragged scribe burrowed desperately around the massive blocks of stone, as it had day after day, knowing only that to return to its people with nothing would see it become just material for some experiment, meat for some greater rat's table.

Its claws scraped against familiar metal. A brass cornerpiece. It paused, filled with desperate, wretched hope, then redoubled its efforts. *Yes-yes! The book!* It had found the book. The great metal-bound volume it had been shackled to for so long, writing out the capacious thoughts and musings of Lord Ferskine the erudite, the wise, the profound!

The pages were tattered, but much of that long labour of transcription remained legible, at least to Skaven eyes. The rat scribe hugged the book to itself. Here were the teachings of Ferskine. Here in these pages was a path to power. By emulating its late master, the scribe would become a priest itself, and serve the Horned Rat, and have its own scribe and servants and menials. It would wield the sacrificial blade and unleash rot and ruin upon the realms for the greater glory of the gnawing tide!

Something else caught its eye in the dust. With a little whimper of joy it reached down and pried forth a crooked crown of horns. Chipped, and some of the points broken, but it was Ferskine's own adornment sure enough. The sign the great lord had ordered, to show the favour of the Horned Rat.

With trembling hands, the white rat placed the crown upon its head, feeling itself grow in majesty and stature already. It had left the halls of the Clans Pestilens a slave; it would return a *lord*. They would bow down before it, respect its divine favour, give it gifts and offerings, *yes-yes*. It would lead incursions into the lands under the light of Hysh, unleash fresh plagues upon the humans and the lizards and all the other inhabitants of the realms. It would be great, the mighty, the majestic!

Already babbling to itself of the great destiny that awaited, it took the book and scurried away into the trees.

ABOUT THE AUTHOR

Adrian Tchaikovsky is the author of the acclaimed ten-book Shadows of the Apt series, and many other novels, novellas and short stories including *Children of Time* (which won the Arthur C. Clarke award in 2016) and its sequel, *Children of Ruin* (which won the British Science Fiction Award in 2020). He lives in Leeds in the UK and his hobbies include entomology and board and role-playing games. His work for Black Library includes *Day of Ascension*, the novella *On the Shoulders of Giants* and several short stories.

MORE FROM
BLACK LIBRARY

SKAVENTIDE
by Gary Kloster

Beyond the mountain range of the Adamantine Chain, Aqshy lies destroyed. Noxious fires light up the horizon, death skitters in the smoke, and a wasteland of horror threatens the entire realm. Humanity has but a single hope: the Reclusians of the Ruination Chamber.

MORE FROM
BLACK LIBRARY

THE HOLLOW KING
by John French

Cado Ezechiar, a cursed Soulblight vampire, seeks salvation for those he failed at the fall of his kingdom. His quest for vengeance leads him to Aventhis, a city caught in a tangled web of war and deceit that Cado must successfully navigate, or lose everything.